T3-BPD-619

VAMPIRESS

She was draped in deep-purple cloaks with her arms out to the sides. Around her swirled pink energies that must have been spirits. She seemed to bend and fold them with just a flicker of her fingers. Her resonant voice filled the hallway, lifting the temperature even more.

And now the cloaked figures of her cronies joined the chanting, lifting their arms and moving in time to her sways.

Then the chanting abruptly stopped.

And Arvella spoke.

"The time, at last, is at hand," she said. She turned to an attendant flanking her on the right. "Bring him to me."

Quicker than I would have expected, the attendant nudged a small boy forward.

Jack.

He looked scared.

Cancel that, he looked absolutely terrified. And if I'd been scared about taking this place down a few seconds ago, that fear was immediately replaced with a burning rage and a need to get Jack the hell out of here.

I might have killed his father by mistake, but I wasn't about to let Arvella exploit this poor kid.

I felt Wirek and Saano looking at me.

I nodded my head.

It was time to hit them with everything we had. . . .

Books by Jon F. Merz in the Lawson Vampire series

THE FIXER

THE INVOKER

THE DESTRUCTOR*

*coming soon

Published by Pinnacle Books
(Please visit http://www.lawsonvampire.com for more information.)

THE INVOKER

Jon F. Merz

PINNACLE BOOKS
Kensington Publishing Corp.
http://www.kensingtonbooks.com

PINNACLE BOOKS are published by

Kensington Publishing Corp.
850 Third Avenue
New York, NY 10022

Copyright © 2002 by Jon F. Merz

All rights reserved. No part of this book may be reproduced in any form or by any means without the prior written consent of the Publisher, excepting brief quotes used in reviews.

If you purchased this book without a cover, you should be aware that this book is stolen property. It was reported as "unsold and destroyed" to the Publisher and neither the Author nor the Publisher has received any payment for this "stripped book."

All Kensington Titles, Imprints, and Distributed Lines are available at special quantity discounts for bulk purchases for sales promotions, premiums, fund-raising, and educational or institutional use. Special book excerpts or customized printings can also be created to fit specific needs. For details, write or phone the office of the Kensington special sales manager: Kensington Publishing Corp., 850 Third Avenue, New York, NY 10022, attn: Special Sales Department, Phone: 1-800-221-2647.

Pinnacle and the P logo Reg. U.S. Pat. & TM Off.

First Printing: October 2002
10 9 8 7 6 5 4 3 2 1

Printed in the United States of America

For the real Jack,
An inspiration even before . . .

Chapter One

Killing is never easy.

Between the preparation time, tracking your target, and making sure things go like they're supposed to—it gets complicated.

In the end, pulling the trigger is actually the easiest part.

For some.

Lying underneath the battered, rusting hulk of an abandoned Buick sedan set on top of crumbling cinder blocks wasn't the kind of activity I normally prefer for a Saturday night. Especially since the freezing rain made the ground underneath me soggy and home to all sorts of creepy crawlies that enjoyed the warmth bleeding out of my body and into the ground.

But a job's a job.

My name's Lawson.

I'm a Fixer by trade. I serve and protect the community. But mostly I help maintain the Balance. It's a noble profession and those of us born into it would never really feel at ease doing anything else. But there were days when I'd give anything to know the monotony of an accountant who stared at numbers all day long.

Right now was one of those times.

Lightning flashed overheard, briefly illuminating my surroundings. Damn. I could be seen if the lightning lit up the area at the wrong time.

And I definitely did not want to be seen.

Otherwise, I wouldn't have been under that damned car.

But cover and concealment in this deserted auto-wreckage yard was scarce. I could either hide inside a compacted car or under one. And since trying to get out of a car is harder than rolling out from under it, I chose the latter.

But I didn't like it.

I shifted and instantly regretted the move. My crotch lay in a fresh pool of water that quickly soaked through the tough denim of my jeans. The cold helped shrink my balls further into my tight scrotal sac, making me feel more like a castrato gunslinger than the professional killer I am. It would take a generous serving of Bombay Sapphire and tonic, as well as a hot bath, to help me relax after this escapade.

The air shifted, blowing in sideways from the east, and I caught a scent I hadn't detected before. Cologne. Cheap. Like the million department store samples that flutter out of my credit card bill envelopes every month.

I heard the squishing sound of water and mud under shoes.

The footsteps sounded like rotten tomatoes being mashed together. But they seemed hesitant. They didn't sound purposeful.

But it didn't really matter how they sounded.

My job remained the same.

And it wouldn't be long before I finished it.

That was good. I didn't like soaking in fetid rainwater and melting ice any longer than absolutely necessary.

The footsteps approached just as another thunderclap exploded in the night air. I held my breath and waited for the next round of lightning.

But nothing happened.

I exhaled just as the shoes drew abreast of the car. I could see the soles and what looked like handmade brown leather uppers. Even in the dark, I could see loose threads dangling from the cuffs on his suit pants. The hemline needed adjusting, too.

Strange.

I wondered briefly if maybe this wasn't my target. But I shrugged that off. According to my information, there were only two people in this junkyard tonight: my target and his executioner.

The smell of the cheap cologne was killing me. I tried to mentally analyze it—to break down its individual components so it wouldn't bother me as much. I got as far as the ethyl alcohol before I realized I was going to sneeze.

There are a few techniques you can normally employ when sneezing isn't appropriate. The first involves sticking your tongue to the roof of your mouth right behind your front teeth. I did that.

It didn't work.

The next best option is to rub the spot under your nose and press in with a finger. It's an old pressure point a Japanese martial arts master once showed me.

I'm sure that would have worked fine, if both my hands had been free. They weren't. In one hand, I held my modified pistol. In the other hand, I had my small black bag that contained some other items I might have needed tonight.

Hands unavailable, I steeled myself for the sudden expulsion of air. I tried to stifle it and did a good job. But as the air rushed out, I tensed my body, which then caused me to jerk upward suddenly and hit the steel, aluminum, and plastic undercarriage of the Buick with the back of my head.

And since bone and metals do not make fond friends or even remote acquaintances, I saw stars.

Shit, that hurt.

My eyes clouded briefly with tears before I realized the shoes had shifted.

Double shit.

I'd been heard.

Calmly, I thumbed the safety off the pistol and waited. Most folks don't think to look above or below their line of sight, so if I stayed cool, he might not see me.

The shoes moved around the car. I could visualize him checking the area, searching the heaps of rusted mufflers and hubcaps, looking for the source of the sound. I watched as the shoes started to take a few steps away. Seemingly satisfied, he turned and came walking back toward me and the car.

Which, of course, was the exact moment Mr. Lightning decided to put in his overdue appearance and illuminate the entire area—including the Buick, the cinder blocks, and yours truly.

The shoes stopped.

Past experience has taught me it's better to go on the offensive at times like this than wait. I've debated that idea in the past and usually come away with some bad scars because of it.

Not tonight.

I rolled out and got a bead on him center mass even as the shocked expression began to register on his face and he started to back away.

I squeezed off a single round—watched as it caught him square in the chest, lifting him off his feet and pitching him back over. He crashed to the ground, kicking up mud, icy water, and sludge before rolling a short distance away.

I got up—my gun at low ready—and walked over, squishing all the way like I was slogging through chest-high mounds of wet pasta noodles.

He was breathing, but just barely. Dark blood soaked his shirt; diluted by the icy rain pelting him from above, it turned a softer shade of frothy pink. The shocked expression still clouded his face, almost as if he couldn't believe what was happening.

I knelt down. "The Council sent me."

He tried to speak. It came out as a stutter of gurgling consonants. "F-f-fixer?"

I nodded. His eyes grew wider. I'd seen the look before. Technically, most of my kind don't think Fixers exist. They think we're just legends told by parents to get their kids to behave.

But we're real enough. We work in the shadows. Our accomplishments go unnoticed by all but a select few.

Unfortunately for this guy, tonight was the time he found out we really did exist.

I frisked him, looking for his gun. I came up empty. "Narcotics trafficking is bad business for humans to be in. It's even worse for a vampire."

He grimaced, feeling the agony of the wooden splinters in his heart, courtesy of the wood-tipped rounds my pistol packed. In the night air, he drew his head back, trying to inhale a raspy breath. His canines lengthened, fully exposed. That happened only during feeding or when a vampire is close to death.

"You could have exposed the community. You threatened the Balance." I leaned closer. "You know the penalty for any of those violations is death."

He frowned, but it looked more like an upside-down grin. "They . . . they told you that?"

"The drugs? Yeah. I wouldn't be here otherwise." He only had a few minutes left.

"Lies . . . all of it . . . lies. . . ."

I'd heard that before. Claims of innocence come with the job. Even when you've put them down, some of the most hardened criminals will deny they did anything wrong. They go off to the afterlife convinced of their own innocence.

"Whatever you say, pal." Time to end the repartee. I started to stand.

But he grabbed my hand, clutched it and squeezed. Hard.

I started to pull away, started to try to break his grasp. He wouldn't let go. He still had some strength in him.

He pulled me closer, until his mouth was just a few inches away from my ear. I could hear the rasping of fluid in his lungs as he breathed in short gasps of dwindling air. And then he managed to cough out two words.

"My son."

I frowned. "What about him?"

He closed his eyes; tears were running out of them now and dripping off his wet face to the ground beneath him, where his blood ran crimson tinged with silt and grime. "You . . . must . . . protect him."

His head lolled back and to the side then as his hand went limp in mine. As his palm opened, a small photograph rolled out and fluttered toward the rain-slicked ground.

I scooped it up, wiping the bloody mud off it. Lightning flashed again and I peered closer. The picture showed a small boy. His son, no doubt.

But protection? What the hell was that about? The mission had been a simple termination order. Punishment for crimes committed. There had been no mention of protection.

None whatsoever.

And that's precisely what worried me even as the rain increased and pounded against my back. I looked up, feeling the cold rain pour down my face, coat my lips, and bleed into my mouth.

I swished around a mouthful and spat it back toward the ground.

Why was nothing ever as easy as I wanted it to be?

Chapter Two

It actually took more hot bathwater than Bombay Sapphire to help elevate my mood after my nocturnal jaunt. For some reason, I didn't feel much like taking a drink.

My muscles ached after lying prone in cold rainwater for so long, but the steamy vapors seeped into every pore and gradually wound me down to almost total relaxation.

I love hot baths.

I picked up the affection for them while I was in Japan some years back. It's a cultural necessity over there. The super hot *ofuro* baths can scald you if you don't treat the water with the respect it deserves. I suppose it's got something to do with the Shinto religion. Respect nature and it will respect you back.

Following one of my Japan trips, I had a hot tub installed at my house. Actually, it looked more like a really deep bathtub than a hot tub. It was built for one. Or two people planning on getting very, very intimate with each other.

Time was, I would have been pretty mellow after a quick shower and a few hours of sack time. Nowadays I preferred the luxury of a good soak followed by a generous dollop of rapid eye movement.

So I sat neck deep in the bubbling water as steam rose in misty swirls around my head, opening pores, unclogging sinuses, and generally making things very . . . wow.

But as I approached that delightful Nirvana state of total relaxation, something barred my way. Something stood out in my mind as strange. And it wouldn't leave me alone.

Moderately annoyed, I replayed the events of the evening in my mind, looking for the culprit.

Henry Watterson dealt drugs.

Specifically, he imported them from China via Amsterdam and then sold them to the local gangs here in Boston. Cocaine used to be the drug of choice, and for the Mexican and Jamaican cartels, it still was. But a newer crop of addicts wanted opium and heroin. Injectable, sniffable, smokable, they'd take it any way they could. Add to the more hard-line narcotics a heaping pile of special designer drugs like ecstasy and something new called saber, and Watterson's business must have been booming.

Nowadays the addicts could afford whatever prices he charged as well. Following the dot-com explosion of the late 1990s, a lot of young millionaires were born. Those who didn't suffer the financial equivalent of a nuclear melt-down when the dot-com world imploded, around the new millennium, found themselves with even more power and money than before.

With all that disposable income and a lot of stress, they craved release the same way I crave Tia Carrere.

The Communist Chinese government in Beijing kept them supplied. Slave labor camps outside of Manchuria, worked by imprisoned Falun Gong members, churned out the designer drugs, while other camps closer to Qinghai in Center-West China harvested opium and derivative narcotics.

In exchange, the money Beijing earned from drug sales went to fund their nuclear weapons research. Current speculation was that the Chinese would have a new and improved intercontinental ballistic missile able to reach out and touch the U.S. by 2005. At least, that was the intelligence coming at me off the rumor mill.

Normally, that information would have been supplied by my Control. Currently, I didn't have a Control.

Poor guy had suffered an accident of sorts a few months back.

Some folks just don't have a lot of good luck.

Damned shame, that.

The Council, the governing body for whom I worked, hadn't found me a replacement. Which meant I was working without a net. That was okay with me. I'd been out in the cold before. Alone. Strung out. With only myself to rely on.

Or blame if I failed.

I had my own networks to some extent. I called an old friend of mine who worked down in Washington at some office building that ostensibly doubles as one of the major clearinghouses of raw intelligence for the U.S. He tuned me in to the Chinese connection.

The Council had turned me on to Henry.

Explanations never came with the dossier. Just a name and a face. That was it. That was the Council. If I'd had a Control—a decent one—I could have asked what the deal was. I liked knowing why I was being dispatched to dispatch someone.

It takes a lot to get a call from me.

There are rules, though. Laws, if you will. Our community survives because it obeys those rules. There's not a lot of wiggle room. A delicate Balance exists that ensures the safety of my society.

Individuals who compromise the Balance put all of us at risk.

It's not allowed.

I take my work seriously.

Time was, I didn't much like it. Time was, I didn't know what I wanted out of life.

Time was.

Nowadays I've mellowed a lot. I've got other interests aside from my work, but more on that later.

My mind revolved back to Henry Watterson and his dying plea. So he had a son. So what? A lot of my targets in the past came from big families. That fact hadn't stopped them from breaking the law. And it didn't lessen the sentence.

It never did.

What made Watterson's son so special that he needed protecting?

And then I thought about how vehemently Watterson denied his crimes. Sure, I get that sometimes, but the tone in his voice seemed so . . . genuine?

Maybe that's what disturbed me.

Coupled with more than a polite request to make sure some tyke stayed safe, something definitely felt odd.

Watterson's request to look after his kid echoed in my mind—a real plea for help.

Strange.

I sank deeper into the hot water, letting it come up to the edge of my nostrils, closing my eyes and trying to allow anything to pop into my head. Sometimes the positive ions help me think.

But right now, they weren't doing shit.

I left the bath reluctantly, quickly dried myself off and wrapped a towel around my waist. I paused before the mirror and appraised the results of my recent resurgence of interest in lifting weights. My pectorals were rounding out nicely and my arms seemed a little denser than a few weeks back. Good.

There was something instinctively primal about heaving iron plates. I loved the rush of blood into my muscle bellies. I loved the effort it took to push past my thresholds into higher ground. And damned if I didn't like cranking up some old AC/DC tunes and feeling the walls reverberate as Angus Young cranked out his riffs and solos.

Go figure.

I stepped into a pair of loose black cotton pants that were fitted around my ankles, then padded up to the third floor, where I keep my television set. I slumped onto the faded blue couch covered with tufts of cat hair, courtesy of Mimi and Phoebe, and flipped on the TV, searching for something decent. I passed the History Channel's documentary on the Allied advance across the Pacific during World War Two (seen it twice) and settled on the local news.

No mention of Watterson.

Good.

There shouldn't have been. If his body had been found, it would have spelled disaster. I took care not to leave any evidence behind. My presence—the entire community's presence—had to leave no trace in our passing.

Vampires have existed alongside humans since the dawn of mankind. We're parallel lines of evolution, not the undead your silly myths and legends make us out to be. And all those horror novels might put a spike of adrenaline into your daily dull life, but truth be told, we're out there walking right beside you. We're in your offices. We're in line at the registry of motor vehicles. And we're in the car behind you at the McDonald's drive-through.

We eat food. We walk in the sunlight. We live. We even die.

Eventually.

Along the path of our evolution, we began hunting other humans. Our ancestors decided that the blood of other humans would give us more power. They were right. Human blood contains the life force that helps sustain us. It makes us more powerful. It slows our metabolic process and we age very slowly. We live for hundreds of years.

Do some research. You'll find mention of us in every every annal of time. Long-lost legends in pre-colonial America, the Caucasus Mountains, Central Asia, Japan, China, Europe, everywhere. We're there.

Bram Stoker did a lot to resurrect the old tales. But he added a lot. He made us undead. Insulted us by forcing my kind to sleep in coffins during the daytime. Weakened us with silly holy water, garlic, and crucifixes.

It's rubbish.

But there *is* something about wood that kills us once it enters our bloodstream. I'm not a scientist, so I can't explain it fully. But the ammunition I carry in my gun has wooden tips for just that purpose.

Killing vampires.

It might seem a little strange for a vampire to be killing other vampires, but it's my job.

Watterson should have been just another easy assignment. Should have been. Lately, it seemed that life had it in for me. Every time I thought something was going to be cake, I ended up getting food poisoning licking batter out of the damned bowl.

Chapter Three

Snow in Boston is one of those bizarre things no one ever seems to be able to figure out. Meteorologists always draw a line that cuts the city in half, call one side as a blizzard and the other as rain. Then, of course, the opposite happens. Or, as was the case tonight, both happens.

Which, naturally, was the reason why my black Volvo S60 was currently engaged in negotiating the winding and decidedly treacherous Jamaicaway down toward the Fenway. Time was, the J-way used to be the most dangerous road in America. I'd hate to see what street stole the title away.

With the lane markers blurred under a half inch of slush and ice, and Boston's snow removal plows doing their usually shoddy job, it was a wonder I made it down to the intersection of Longwood Avenue in one piece. But I did. I turned left at the lights, taking the street into Brookline, past the Longwood Towers and the elegant Veronique Restaurant, where I've taken a few dates in the past.

The address I had for Henry Watterson put his house behind the Longwood Towers, in a part of Brookline that's nice, but not too nice. Old Henry was smart—to a point. He wasn't flashy with his cash, at least not where his house was concerned. Or his cologne, either.

It was a single family in white with black shutters and no aluminum siding. In this area of town, most of the houses still used wooden clapboards.

I slowed the Volvo to the side of the road between a snow emergency tow-away zone and a resident-permit parking sign. Then I waited.

Rain tainted the snow tonight, making the thick flakes fall with water weight, almost dripping on their way to the ground. Like bloated leeches, they clung to everything before their sheer weight caused them to drop off in chunks. I had to flick the wipers every few seconds to keep the house in sight.

Honestly, I wasn't quite sure what I was doing there. A simple request to keep a kid safe wasn't so simple anymore. The prospect of baby-sitting didn't wow me. I'm not comfortable around kids. Never have been. It's not an easy thing to con a kid. Adults are easier, but kids are sharp. They know when you're lying.

They make me nervous.

So here was Henry Watterson's house. His wife and kid were probably safe inside. And here I was, waiting in my car with the heater on full blast, listening to a bit of Delerium on the CD player and watching a dark house, a dark night, and white flakes coat everything in sight.

Just as I was chalking this up as one of my more thrilling nights, the shit hit the fan.

Albeit subtly.

I'd parked three houses away, but even the presence of my car engine's obvious life didn't seem to make much of an impact on the three goons in black who were maneuvering their way up toward the house from three angles.

Maybe they couldn't hear the engine over the roaring wind.

Maybe.

I watched them for a few seconds and came to my professional opinion pretty soon thereafter. They weren't good.

I shifted in my seat, feeling a rush of blood spike into my legs like so many needles, and frowned. I should have been home asleep. I should have been anywhere but here.

I should have been.

Instead, I jacked a round into the chamber of my pistol and got ready to leave the obvious comfort and warmth of my car to go protect the kid of someone I'd killed earlier in the evening.

Ain't life grand?

I double-checked to make sure my interior lights wouldn't come on as I exited the car. The three goons in black had closed on the house now and still seemed largely oblivious of me.

I pulled back on the door latch and cracked the door; instantly, the cold and flakes stung my skin. I eased out, crouched down, staying next to the car's profile, then closed the door very carefully.

Black is a preferred color for me. I'm not into depressing gothic nightclubs or any of that crap. I just happen to like the color and it allows me to get work done that wearing white corduroys might not.

Tonight I was glad to be wearing it. Even with the whiteness of the snow, there were still plenty of dark shadows I could use as concealment while I worked my way toward the house.

I moved ahead to the nearest tree and knelt down, chancing a look around the trunk. One of the goons was working the front-door lock. The other two were crouched beside him.

I smiled in spite of the situation.

As a rule, I don't tolerate fools gladly, and I tolerate obvious amateurs even less. These guys ranked about as skilled as a bunch of blind nuns at a firing range.

Check that, I'd probably put my money on the nuns.

At the very least, one of them should have been on the lookout for anything that could have threatened their security. Namely, they should have been looking out for a roving police car on patrol. Or even a vampire stupid enough to wander out in that godforsaken weather.

But as I've noted more than a few times before, *should have*'s don't figure into my line of work very often.

Which is why my appearance on the scene a minute later, precipitated by coldcocking one of them upside the head and then pointing my very persuasive-looking pistol at the other two, shocked the hell out of them.

I love a captive audience.

My stage domination didn't last very long. The goon on the left decided he could move faster than one of my bullets and tried to tackle me on the steps.

Bad move.

I sidestepped and he slipped on the ice-covered bricks, falling down about six feet—ass over teakettle—and slamming his head against the iron railing with a dull but audible crack.

Unfortunately, his lack of balance kept me occupied long enough for his buddy to knock my pistol out of my hand and try to punch me in the head.

I ducked out of the way and brought my hands up for cover while simultaneously counterattacking with a palm-heel strike to the underside of his chin. His head snapped back. I followed up with a sharp knee to his groin, doubling him over, and then brought my elbow down on the back of his neck. Judging from the series of creaks and cracks, he wasn't going to be doing any yoga for a while.

I dragged both of them down next to their third friend and frisked them. Aside from three pistols, they carried nothing else. No identification. No papers. Nothing.

I turned my attention back to the guns. Three SIG Sauers. I popped the magazine out on one and frowned.

The rounds had wooden tips.

The guns were Fixer pieces.

Like mine, they'd been designed to kill vampires.

But these guys weren't Fixers. I was sure of that. They moved like amateurs. Offhandedly, I tugged down the base of one goon's turtleneck, searching for the birthmark that marks every member of my race. We've all got them, and even the latest in cosmetic surgery and laser erasure can't wipe it off.

Nothing.

That accounted for the relative ease with which I'd been able to knock them out. Usually, vampires are stronger than normal humans. These guys were pretty easy to take down.

So, the equation, thus far, on this shitty night was three humans armed with vampire assassin guns targeting a vampire household during a blizzard.

I chewed my lip and nodded. Math always was my worst subject in school, but even a dolt like me could see this was going nowhere good and fast.

And even though I still had no clue as to why anyone would want to knock off a vampire house, I wasn't at all comfortable with leaving the inhabitants alone, either.

I ripped the magazines out of the three guns and tossed them into a nearby snowbank before retrieving my own piece.

It felt weird ringing the bell, considering that it was going on one-thirty in the morning. Still, as soon as the mother came to the door, I could explain everything; she would then call the authorities; I'd be on my way.

The door clicked open and once again I found my plans being tossed in the air with reckless abandon.

The boy in front of me looked like a twelve-year-old human who had just been woken up from a nice sleep. Poor kid had no idea three bad guys were just on their way to whack him.

He had scraggly brown hair jutting out of his head at strange angles and a pair of glasses that hung heavy on the bridge of his nose. Freckles tickled his cheeks and wound their way down his neck. The frown on his face counterbalanced his decidedly apple-pie looks.

"Yeah?"

"Hi, is your mother around?" I glanced off the stairs and saw that the raiding party was still fast asleep.

"She's dead."

Okay, I wasn't expecting that. No problem. Adapt and overcome is my middle name. "I'm Lawson," I said, extending my right hand.

"I'm tired." He rubbed his eyes underneath the glasses. "What do you want?"

I made a decision. "You've got to come with me; your life's in danger."

He grinned. "Funny. My dad's coming home soon, mister, so you'd better get outta here." He started to shut the door.

I put my foot on the inside so he couldn't close it. "Listen to me—"

But at that precise instant, the kid opened the door and then slammed it back—right on my foot.

I must have hollered, because his face took on a scared

look. But even though the pain was intense, I kept my foot there. I couldn't risk him locking the door.

I took a breath. "Your dad's not coming home tonight. There's been an accident."

"Huh? What do you mean? What happened?" His eyes got that wide-eyed stare that kids reserve for genuine surprise. I could sense the tears starting to form somewhere back in the depths of his emotions. I swallowed and took another breath. I couldn't very well tell him I'd wasted his father for breaking the law. That wouldn't do any good.

"He was in a car accident, son. I'm sorry."

"He's . . . dead?"

It looked like the Hoover Dam might burst open, but then I saw his eyes go from mine to focusing on something behind me. "Hey, who's—"

But I'd already begun diving inside the house, wrapping my arms around him, tucking him into a ball and rolling toward the first room doorway. I felt the air break hard around my head as the bullets went past—smacking into the wood trim of the doorway.

Damn. I'd hoped the bad guys would be out of commission a little while longer. Should have figured from the way Lady Luck was teeing off on me tonight they'd come back around quicker.

I unfolded the two of us and pushed him down to the floor. "Stay down!"

Another bullet whizzed into the room, biting through the drapes. I yanked my pistol out, clicked off the safety, and stuck the muzzle around the corner, squeezing off two rounds. Inside the house, the shots sounded like explosion, making me wince. Beside me, the kid stayed quiet with his hands clamped over his ears.

Another two rounds came zinging in. Then there was a break.

This was bad.

Gunshots in Brookline usually herald the unleashing of the town's entire police force. We needed to move, and move fast. Questions were something we couldn't afford.

I leaned down next to the kid and broke one of his hands away from his ear. "We're getting out of here, you understand?"

He nodded and looked up at me. He actually looked okay.

I poked the muzzle of my gun around and squeezed two more rounds off. A dull thud and a clunk followed along with a low groan. Good. Maybe I'd nailed one of them.

Two doorways led off this room and I chose the one that looked like it led toward the back of the house. Hopefully, a back door. I just hoped all three members of the hit team were at the front—otherwise, we might be walking into an ambush.

But I didn't have a choice, and I've often found a lack of choice always makes decisions easier. I grabbed the kid under one arm, kept the pistol pointing behind me at the first place the bad guys would come around the corner, and hustled.

Inside the kitchen, I went to the back door, opened it, and pushed our way outside, plowing through the snowdrift piled up against the back door.

We dropped off the steps into the snow. Within the space of just a few minutes, it had gotten deep. The kid didn't have any shoes on. He'd survive. For right now, we just had to get out of here.

The backyard sloped down toward the street. If we could reach the Volvo, we'd be all set.

Right then I tripped over an unseen tree root jutting out of the ground and masked by the snowfall. The kid and I went sprawling—my gun flipped over into a snowdrift the size of a garden shed.

Shit.

The back door banged open.

Double shit.

The bad guys, two of them now, eased out of the house and fanned out to either side when they spotted us. I got to my feet, but things weren't good. Both of them carried the pistols I'd tossed away earlier.

If they'd had regular guns, it would have been one thing. But Fixer guns can kill me. As a general rule, I'm not a big fan of things that can kill me.

Seeing I was unarmed, one of them looked at the other and smiled. Great.

Almost in unison, they raised their guns and aimed at me.

That's when I heard the moaning. I glance over quickly and saw the kid writhing in the snow—of all the weird things, sweating. He was groaning loudly and making a pea-pod-shaped impression in the snow. His eyes were closed tight and he'd wrapped his arms around himself.

But what was he . . . saying? Chanting?

It sounded a little bit like the old language. But I couldn't make out a single word of it. It flowed out of the kid like an endless litany of harsh consonants and flowing singsong rhyme.

Unfortunately, I didn't have much of a chance to consider what it might have been. The two goons approached and heard the moaning, too.

They both looked at each other and then at the kid.

The chanting grew louder, as if a chorus of other voices had joined in suddenly. The wind started kicking up snow around us like some freakish hailstorm. I ducked down and covered my face from the snow, rain, and hail. It was like standing in the middle of a whirlpool—or a cyclone.

I felt twin blasts of intense heat—like someone had opened a forge or belched fire—go rushing past my body.

Then I heard screams.

I tried to open my eyes, but the heat surrounding me forced me to squint to make anything out. What I could see didn't comfort me one bit.

The two bad guys grabbed at their faces, clutching folds of sweaty skin, almost gouging their eyeballs out, ripping tufts of hair out in big, bloody chunks. And all around their heads swirled this funnel of pinkish haze that screeched as if a thousand voices were echoing up from the depths of hell.

A wide swath of snow melted around me and blossomed out, hungrily devouring any ice and snow and reducing it to grimy water. In seconds, the kid and I were on wet, muddy ground.

And still the kid lay where he was, writhing and chanting.

Both goons dropped to their knees, screaming; blood gushed out of their faces in a torrent. I saw an eyeball plop to the blood-soaked ground; I grimaced.

My gun lay a few feet away and I scrambled for it.

Then the screams stopped.

Abruptly, the inferno of heat vanished, replaced by winter. Snow rushed into cover the ground once again.

The kid stopped moving.

And so did the bad guys.

But the kid was alive.

I didn't think the bad guys were. Something about watching two guys tear their own faces off has a way of convincing you that death can't be far behind.

I grabbed their guns, slippery with gore, and then poked the kid.

"You okay?"

His eyes fluttered once, then opened. He exhaled in a long stream, but then nodded.

Jesus.

In the distance, the first of several sirens began to pierce the night. I hustled the kid down to the Volvo, buckled him in, and then jumped into the driver's seat, gunning the engine.

As I sped back up Longwood Avenue toward the Jamaicaway and out of Brookline jurisdiction, I kept stealing glances at the kid. He was curled up on the seat, looking out the window.

Suddenly, he didn't seem very much like just another kid anymore.

Chapter Four

I still didn't have a replacement Control.

One thing I've noticed is that bureaucracies, whether they're human or vampire, all function at about the same two speeds—slow and stop. The odds of me getting a Control I could bounce my current situation off were about as great as my chances of winning a trip to the Moon.

And going to the Council was out as well.

Call it paranoid insecurity if you want, but nagging doubts have kept me alive in the past. Plus, recent experience has taught me that despite appearances to the contrary, the Council wasn't the most secure organization around.

Still, I needed to bounce some ideas off someone. I needed answers about the kid. About what had happened last night.

We were at my place.

Considering I couldn't really stash him anywhere else, and since he'd be safest with me, I'd put him in one of the guest rooms last night when we got home. He'd fallen asleep almost immediately.

My two cats, Mimi and Phoebe, set about making him feel welcome by falling asleep on his head and stomach. Well, that's how they make guests feel welcome. The few times I actually have them.

Morning dawned and nothing seemed clearer than it had when I finally fell asleep last night. I ducked out quickly and scored some jeans and shirts from a clothing store in West Roxbury, a short five minutes or so from my house. I didn't like leaving him alone, but the kid couldn't walk around in his pajamas.

When I got home, he was still asleep.

I went downstairs to the cellar and spent forty-five minutes trying to pound reason out of my 150-pound leather heavy bag. Not having much success, I slapped a few weight plates on the bar and ground out a solid twenty minutes of bench presses, pyramiding up and down until my chest could take no more abuse.

Finally, at eleven o'clock, I rousted the little guy, told him to wash up and come down for breakfast.

He stumbled into the kitchen twenty minutes later, already showered and dressed in some of the clothes I'd bought him.

"Clothes fit okay?"

He nodded.

"You like eggs?" I pointed to the frying pan, where I had a few yolks cracked.

He nodded, then sat down at the heavy wooden table and looked at me. "I'm hungry."

"Yeah, I'm working on it, slick. Hold tight, okay? The eggs'll be up in a sec."

"No. Not the eggs," he said. Then he leaned forward, as if unsure how to exactly say it. "I'm hungry."

He meant juice. Blood. I call it "juice." I hate calling it "blood." The idea that I've got to drink human blood still freaks me out. But the growing boy needed his nutrients. I opened the fridge. "You like it cold?"

"Yeah."

"Right." Who wouldn't? Drinking warm blood is like sucking on a penny. I took out a bottle of what would have looked like chilled red wine to the uninitiated, uncorked it, and poured a tall glass. I poured myself a smaller glass and then passed the taller one to the kid.

He looked at it, sniffed at it, and then drank it down in six big gulps. Then he belched.

"Ugh," I said. "Watch the burps, okay, sport? They stink."

He grinned for the first time, and I scooped some scrambled eggs onto his plate. "Here. Get these down, too. You need more than just juice to go on."

He tore into the plate, asked for another glass of juice, and polished off two white powdered doughnuts. Helluva appetite, this kid.

I watched him eat while I finished my own meal, juice, and then a tall glass of orange juice. "Listen, I don't even know your name." I wiped my mouth. "You do have one, right?"

"Yeah."

I smiled. "Well, I can either keep calling you sport, slick, dude, buddy, and governor . . . or you can tell me your name."

He frowned. " 'Governor'?"

"Maybe not governor."

He sat there another minute. "Jack."

I held out my hand. "Jack, my name's Lawson. Nice to meet you."

He shook it tentatively. "Are you sure about my father?"

I looked away. "Yeah. Yeah, I am. I'm sorry."

"Damn."

I cocked an eyebrow. He blushed. "Sorry."

"Forget it." I poured myself another glass of orange juice. "Listen, Jack, you know anything about those men at your house last night? Anything at all?"

"Like what?"

"Like why they were there?"

"They had guns."

"Yeah, they did."

"Guess they weren't very nice."

"No. Did you ever hear your father mention anything about some bad people? He ever tell you to be careful of certain people he knew?"

"No."

"You sure?"

"Yeah."

"All right." I sighed.

"Did they kill my father?"

I ran my hand over the orange juice glass, feeling the slight condensation on the outside. "No. No, they didn't kill your dad."

"Were they going to kill me?"

"Yeah, Jack. I reached for a doughnut. "Yeah, I'm pretty sure they wanted to kill you."

"You stopped them, huh?"

I grinned. "Actually, Jack, I think you stopped 'em, buddy. Doing that thing you did—"

"My gift."

"Your gift?" I bit into the doughnut.

"That's what my father called it. What we called it." He looked away.

"Yeah, well, that works for me. We'll call it your gift, too, then, okay?"

"Okay."

"Why don't you tell me about your gift, Jack."

"Can I have some orange juice?"

I got him some and then sat back down. He took a couple of sips, then wiped his mouth on the back of his hand. "It only started a few months ago."

"When, exactly? Do you remember?"

"When I turned twelve."

He was older than that, but most of us convert our vampire age into human years. It keeps things less confusing. "On your birthday?"

"Uh-huh. The night of my birthday. I thought it was a nightmare."

"I can see how you might think that. Pretty scary, huh?"

"Yeah. But I don't really remember much when it happens. All I know is I get really hot and sweaty and then stuff kind of comes out of my mouth. I don't know what it is—the words, I mean."

"You don't?"

"Nope. I've never heard that language before. Dad said it sounded kind of like the old language, but I haven't studied that yet at school, so I don't know about that. I don't even know how I can speak it. But I do."

"What else happens when you do your gift?"

"Nothing happened before last night. It would just get hot, that swirly stuff would come and then the room would get real hot. After a few minutes, it would go away." He looked around the kitchen. "Last night was different."

That was an understatement. "Did your father tell anybody about your gift?"

"I think so. He wanted to try to figure out what it was. I think he was kinda scared of it."

"He probably just wanted to make sure you were okay."

"Yeah."

"Who do you think he told, Jack?"

"I dunno. I never met many of my dad's friends."

"Did your dad's work keep him out late?"

"Sometimes. I got used to it since Mom died."

"I guess you would."

"She died when I was real young. Dad said she was pretty old."

"My mom died when I was pretty young, too, Jack."

"But now my dad's dead, too." He looked at me. "Does that make me an orphan, Lawson?"

"Maybe."

He frowned. "I don't want to be an orphan."

"Hey, pal, listen to me." I laid a hand on his shoulder. "I know this isn't going to be an easy time for you. But I'm here, okay? And I'm not going to let anything happen to you, understand? I made a promise to your father that I'd look after you."

He looked at me, eyes bright and moist. "You knew my dad?"

"Only for a short time. But I know he loved you very much. And I know he was worried about you. That's why he sent me to look after you, okay?"

"Yeah."

"So, we're buddies, okay? And maybe we can make some sense out of what's going on here and get you back to an almost normal life. Does that sound okay?"

"Sounds okay."

"Good. Finish your orange juice. We're going to see a friend of mine and maybe see if he can help us get some answers."

"Does he know about my gift?"

"We'll find out," I said. "He knows a lot of interesting stuff about some pretty strange things."

"I guess my gift is pretty strange."

''More likely, it's pretty special, Jack. Try to remember that.''

He looked at me for a minute, nodded, and then finished his orange juice.

Chapter Five

I didn't actually consider Wirek a friend.

Truth was, he was a drunk who lived on the underside of Beacon Hill, close to where the Council was headquartered. Whereas the Council owned a beautiful brownstone mansion as its headquarters, Wirek lived in a rickety triple-decker above a convenience store whose staples were lottery tickets and booze. Lots of it.

Good thing, too, because a prerequisite to visiting Wirek was to first make a stop downstairs and pick up a gift of the fermented type.

Inside the convenience store, it stank like old milk. The floor was littered with kernels of corn from where a bag made for popping had spilled open and no one ever bothered to sweep it up. An inch of dust caked every shelf.

I kept a close watch on Jack, but he seemed pretty okay. For someone without any parents, he was handling it like a trouper. He wandered around the store, hefting cans of beans that looked like they belonged in a nuclear fallout shelter rather than in that place. I picked out a bottle of tequila from among the musty bottles of gin and brought it to the counter.

The twentysomething behind the counter gave me a frown. "Buying that shit in front of your kid, man? Get some class."

I slid a ten onto the counter. "Shut up. Put the bottle in the bag. Don't say another word until we are gone. I don't need life advice from a burnout gutterball."

Smart kid that he was, he decided not to debate the issue.

Outside I pressed Wirek's doorbell and waited. After four minutes and three more buzzes, the intercom speaker finally clicked on. "What?"

"It's Lawson. Let me up."

"—the hell for?"

"Open the door, Wirek. I need your help."

More profanity followed, but the door finally buzzed open. I looked at Jack. "This isn't going to be pretty. Just let me do the talking, okay?"

"Okay."

It still smelled as bad inside the hallway as it had the last time I'd been here a few months back. Stale booze and piss has a way of clinging to walls and woodwork like no other smell I've ever known.

Above us, Wirek's door opened. I led Jack up the stairs and we climbed, listening to them creak under our weight the entire time. I seriously wondered if the whole building wasn't due to come crashing down around us.

At the top of the stairs, Wirek stood waiting. He didn't look happy to see us.

But he still looked about the same. Flaps of old, useless skin hung off him like handbags, while he seemed to have lost some of the precious little hair he'd had the last time. The remaining tufts sprouted at weird angles. He was dressed in gray blotchy-stained sweatpants and a T-shirt that had KISS MY JAMAICAN ASS ON IT.

"Nice shirt," I said by way of hello. "Never figured you for a Rastafarian."

"I got lots of shirts like this. Maybe I'll let you have a few."

"Great, I'm sure my wardrobe would appreciate the infusion."

He noticed the bag. "You bring me a gift?"

" 'Course." I handed it to him and watched him unwrap it like it was Christmas again and I'd just delivered the baby Jesus to him.

"Lawson, you shouldn't have."

"You're damned straight; that stuff'll kill you. Just do me a favor: I need you sober, so hold off on the party until after we leave."

" 'We'?"

I looked down. Jack had managed to hide himself behind my right leg. I nudged him out. "This is Jack."

Wirek frowned. "What'd ya bring a kid here for, fer crying out loud. This ain't no day care, Lawson."

"Jack's got himself a gift, Wirek. Jack's also got himself quite a fan club."

"Everybody should be so lucky," said Wirek. "I'm not interested." He started back inside his apartment.

I stopped him. *"Unfortunately,* these fans are humans."

Wirek stopped. "Humans?"

I nodded. "And interestingly enough, they happen to carry Fixer guns."

"Popular kid, huh?"

"Seems that way."

Wirek gestured toward the open door. "Better come inside."

We walked in and I blanched. Wirek must have cooked

something earlier that smelled like roadkill that had been left in the sun too long. "Jesus, what the hell did you incinerate in here?"

"Got some leftovers, if you're interested."

"Not even remotely."

"Hmph, should have figured you wouldn't be the type to appreciate fine cuisine."

"I'm not even going to dignify that with a response."

Wirek plopped himself down in his orange plaid recliner and pointed us to the couch. I cleared off the old newspapers and booze bottles, then sat us down across from him.

"So. Tell me about it."

I filled him in the best I could, which in truth wasn't all that much. After all, I'd come to him for answers, not the other way around. I looked at Jack from time to time to make sure I was getting it all correct. When I was finished, both of us looked at Wirek expectantly.

Wirek looked like he'd passed out.

I poked him. "So?"

He opened his eyes. "I listen with my eyes closed lately. Don't mistake it for sleep, Lawson."

"Fair enough. What's your take on this thing?"

"It sounds," said Wirek, stretching his arms over his head slowly, "as though your young comrade there has the Gift of Bilau."

"Okay, and that would be what exactly?"

"He's an Invoker, Lawson. He can summon spirits forth from their existential plane. It's a latent ability that crops up in only a very few of our race." He glanced at Jack. "How old did you say you were, boy?"

"I'm twelve in human years."

Wirek nodded. "And right on schedule, too, by the looks of it. The ability usually surfaces about that age. But it's so rare that it isn't even discussed in the course of normal vampire society."

I knew that feeling. Fixers weren't discussed, either. "It doesn't explain the hit team, though."

"Doesn't it? Evidently, someone knows about the boy's gift. And someone obviously wants to possess it." He took another glance at Jack and lowered his voice a bit. "Or else, do away with it altogether."

"Who? Who would know about it?"

"You mentioned his father told some people about it, right? So I'd assume some of them told some other people, maybe."

"Can you think of anyone who'd be interested?"

Wirek shrugged. "That's your department, Fixer. Not mine. I think I've given you some decent information. Certainly fair trade for the small gift you brought, hmm?"

"Yeah." We were being dismissed. I nodded to Jack. "Let's get going."

We headed for the door. I stopped and looked at Wirek, who was already taking a swig of the tequila. "Do me a favor?"

"Another one?" Wirek sighed. "What?"

"If you ever manage to drag yourself out of this dump, keep an ear to the ground. Call me if you find anything out, all right?"

Wirek waved me off. "I'm a retired Elder, Lawson. You always seem to forget that fact."

"You're retired because you want to be, Wirek."

"I'm retired because I *have* to be, Lawson."

"Yeah, well, we both know you miss the old days."

Wirek didn't say anything but took another long drag on the bottle.

I steered Jack out of the door and then looked back one last time. "I'm giving you a chance to stay in the loop, Wirek. Help me out."

But he'd already closed his eyes and drifted away again.

Chapter Six

So the little guy was an Invoker.

His ability to summon forth spirits certainly helped explain what he'd done to those two goons over at his house. I shuddered thinking about death by spirit summoning. Not something I ever wanted to go through, that's for sure.

For the bottle of tequila, I'd gotten a fair trade from Wirek, I suppose. Part of me wished he'd given me more to go on. But then again, my job is to figure this shit out.

Difficult as it was bound to be.

Outside Wirek's apartment, I steered Jack toward the Volvo and watched him strap himself into the front seat. Twelve seemed plenty old enough for the guy to be riding up front, anyway. But then again, my experience with kids is about as much as my experience with driving a nuclear submarine. I felt sure there were probably a million child safety advocates who would have been only too glad to jump down my throat and tell me I was doing something wrong.

Some people seem to live for doing that.

We got as far as Exeter Street before Jack turned to me and dropped his bombshell.

"What's a Fixer?"

I'd cringed when Wirek had used the term at his place, knowing that Jack seemed smart enough to pick up on it. I hoped he hadn't heard. Apparently, he had.

"You've heard of the Council, haven't you—in your government and history class?"

"Yeah."

"I work for them."

"Doing what? Fixing stuff?"

"Kind of." I pointed at a couple walking a black Labrador outside a brownstone on Beacon Street. "Humans. They don't know we exist. They don't know people like you and I are always around them."

"Yeah . . ."

"The reason they don't know that we exist is because of something called the Balance. You might call it the biggest secret you can think of. You know what that's like? When you've got something so special that no one else can know? You might be dying to tell them, but you just can't. You know what that's like?"

"Yep."

"Well, I help keep that kind of secret. There are rules in our society. Laws that our people have to obey so that our secret remains safe. If humans found out about us, they'd probably hunt us down. They don't know the truth about what we are, how we came to be, and what we can do. If humans heard there were vampires living in the same neighborhoods with them, they'd all freak out. We wouldn't be safe. Anywhere. You wouldn't want that, would you?"

"No."

"So, then, people like me—Fixers—we help make sure our people don't break the laws. We make sure the humans never find out about us."

"You're like the human police?"

"Sort of, but we're also a lot more than just police. You see, we sometimes have to punish the people who break the laws, too. And sometimes we have to do other things. Sneaky things. We don't like to have any attention. We fulfill a special job in our society and we're almost a secret, too. Do you understand?"

"I guess."

That was good enough for me. "I know it's all a little confusing, but this is a part of our world."

After we passed a few more streets down close to the optometry college, he spoke up again. "Lawson?"

"Yeah?"

"Have you ever punished someone for breaking the law?"

The car felt warm then. "Yeah. Yeah, I have."

"What did they do?"

"Different things. Bad things. Always bad things. It's tough to explain sometimes, Jack. You have to understand that our people need to survive. And if some of our people put our existence in danger, they have to be punished. It sounds complicated and sometimes it is. But what I do is very necessary."

"How did you get to be a Fixer?"

I smiled. As if choice had had anything to do with it. "When I was a young boy I took a test of sorts. The answers I gave told some people that I was supposed to be a Fixer."

"You couldn't choose?"

"No. Apparently, it was something I was born with."

"So it was kinda like my . . . gift?"

"Kind of, yeah."

"Do you think I'll have to take some sort of test, too, Lawson? Will I have to meet with the Council? What kind of job do you think I'll have?"

Kenmore Square blossomed in front of us and I wheeled the car farther down Beacon Street. "I don't know, slick. But let's take it one step at a time, though, okay?"

"Okay."

"You like Chinese food?"

"Yeah."

"Well, we're going to have the best Chinese food in town for lunch, okay? And then maybe afterward we'll go see a friend of mine and see if we can't make some more sense out of what's going on."

"That sounds good."

I grinned again. "I'm glad."

Chef Chang's House sat just outside Kenmore Square and served the best Peking Duck in the Boston area. They had some pretty great luncheon specials as well. Complete with a steaming bowl of hot and sour soup, a plate piled high with Chef Chang's food could pretty much keep you fortified for the rest of the day. I knew because I ate there at least once every damned week.

We sat in the inner dining room, away from the windows, even though it wasn't crowded. Precautions like that were drummed into my head with such thoroughness that, even years after graduating from the Fixer Academy, they still instinctively guided me in my daily life. Thank God because they'd saved my life more times than I usually cared to recall.

Jack ordered the orange-flavored chicken and I stuck to the spicy beef with vegetables, extra sauce on the side for dipping the dry noodles. I like a lot of sauce with my meals. And the wait staff here knew me well enough by now to bring the sauce automatically, which cut down on explanations.

The waitress brought our soup first and I smiled as Jack poked at the steaming broth with the ladle spoon.

"What is this?"

"Hot and sour soup. It's good. Give it a whirl."

He frowned, bent his head lower and took a quick sniff. His eyebrows perked and he took a spoonful into his mouth.

"It's good," he said around chews.

Smart kid.

We finished the soup and I checked my watch. We had plenty of time. Our main dishes arrived and Jack's eyes exploded at the sight of so much food.

"Wow!"

I watched him while he ate the egg roll that came with his meal. Kid was taking this all pretty well. After all, according to Wirek, he'd been born with a pretty special gift. Add to that fact he no longer had any parents, one of them courtesy of yours truly, and the guy was quite the trouper.

Most of my experience with kids at that point was limited to thinking they were the only innocents on the planet. That their time was far too short before they realized that most of society sucked the big one.

And vampire kids had it rougher than normal. Striking up friendships with human kids meant trouble. So vampire kids tended to stick together—which was okay, provided you had a good neighborhood. Trouble was, most of the time, they only saw each other at school. It was tougher nowadays, especially in the cities, to have a secluded enclave of vampire families.

Families.

Occasionally, I'd see a couple with a baby carriage and think about what a peaceful life they must have been living. I don't actually think it was envy that made me wish on those rare times for a child; more likely, it was for the tranquillity and domesticity they seemed to represent.

Because being a Fixer, the last thing in your world you ever get to appreciate is tranquillity.

I sucked down another Coke to finish up the meal and glanced again at Jack. Good table manners on the kid, too. I chalked it up to his mother since he'd said himself his father wasn't home most of the time.

"You like?"

He nodded. "Really good."

He was laconic the way most of the kids his age seemed to be. The way I remembered being at that time.

"You missing much at school?"

He shrugged. "Some. I'm not really interested in it."

"What's your least favorite subject?"

"Math."

"Join the club. I was awful at it in school. You into algebra yet?"

"Yeah."

"Learn about FOIL yet?"

"What's that?"

"First, outers, inners, and lasts. Ring a bell?"

"Oh. That." He nodded. "Yeah."

I could tell the topic was about as popular as it was for me. "How you feeling? You need any juice?"

"I'm okay."

That was good because I didn't want to head home until I'd had a chance to check out a few other things. I motioned for the bill, paid it up, and got us back to the car. Once we were inside, I turned sideways to face him some. "Okay, we're going to see another friend of mine. He's a cop."

"Human?" He seemed shocked.

"Yeah."

"Is that allowed?"

"Our society doesn't say friendships with humans are illegal, Jack, just that they can cause problems. Getting too close can be dangerous is all. So we have to be careful. In my line of work, however, I need to have what are called 'contacts.' "

"Not eyeglasses."

"No, different. A contact is someone who gives me information about something. And a lot of my contacts happen to be human."

"Do they know about you? About what you are, I mean?"

I thought about my old friend Simbik. He'd suspected something but respected me enough to never ask. He died at the hands of my oldest enemy before he could figure it out. "No."

"So, why do they give you information?"

"Depends. Sometimes it's a favor; sometimes I pay them; sometimes I have to persuade them in other ways."

"You beat them up?"

"Not usually." I cleared my throat, wanting to change the subject. "See up there?"

The Brookline police headquarters straddled Route 9 in the old Brookline junior high school building. Cruisers and prisoner transport vans lined the street on either side of the divider. I pulled the Volvo into a space behind an unmarked patrol car and turned my cell phone on.

"Now what?" asked Jack.

"I'll call my buddy." I punched the number in and waited. Three rings later, it was picked up.

"Larazo."

"It's Lawson."

"Hey, hey. What're you up to?"

"I'm outside. You got a minute?"

"Not especially. But since you went through all the trouble to drive on over and park—probably in an illegal police parking space—I suppose I could scare up a cigarette break for ya.''

''Thanks.'' I hung up and looked at Jack. ''Do me a favor. Don't say much when this guy comes out, okay?''

''Okay.''

Larazo sidled out of the station a minute later, hoisted his gun belt over his hips, and ambled down the steps toward the street. He turned away from the wind and lit his cigarette, but I knew he'd just been verifying where we were parked. For a cop, Larazo was still pretty sharp.

But at forty-two years old and fifty pounds heavier than he should have been, he'd been sidetracked to a desk job in the station. Larazo missed the fieldwork and never stopped telling me that, as if I had some magic wand I could wave and get him back on the street. I'd known him for seven years, since I'd helped him break up a convenience store robbery.

He made it to the car and slid into the backseat, deftly tossing his cigarette into the gutter as he did so. That was good. I hate cigarette smoke.

''Long time, Lawson.'' He looked at Jack. ''Who's this?''

''My nephew.''

''Nephew? I never knew you even had a family, Lawson. You're full of surprises, huh?''

''Something like that.'' I leaned back over the seat. ''I need some information.''

''I didn't think this was a social call.'' He grinned. ''Now, what can a humble Brookline civil servant score for you that your buddies at the Bureau can't?''

Despite my never confirming or denying anything, Larazo assumed I worked for the government. As long as he kept feeding me solid intelligence when I needed it, he could assume anything he wanted.

''Home invasion last night over on Longwood.''

Larazo frowned. "We were supposed to be keeping that one hushed. How'd you hear about it?"

I raised an eyebrow and he grinned. "Yeah, yeah. Okay. What do you want to know?"

"The three stiffs that were brought in—"

"Three?"

I stopped. Shit. "How many were there?"

Larazo frowned. "Two dead on the scene. No sign of anyone else." He eyed me. "You know something I don't?"

I shrugged. "Probably just a grapevine error is all. I heard there were three dead."

Larazo's frown eased. "Nah, just two. Strange thing about their deaths, though."

"What's that?"

"Well, they had plenty of external injuries. One of them raked his own eyeballs out. Pretty grim." He glanced at Jack. "Sorry, son."

Jack just nodded.

"Anyway," said Larazo, "autopsy report says they both died of massive heart attacks. ME said that there was a huge dump of adrenaline into their system right beforehand. Like something scared them to death."

"You got any sort of make on who they are?"

"They weren't carrying anything. We took them to be pro hitters. Possibly gang-related. We think the guy who owned the house might have been involved with drugs, but we're still checking. We haven't been able to find him anywhere."

Next to me, Jack's body stiffened. I nodded at Larazo. "Okay. I appreciate the info."

He started to move toward the door. "Lawson, you hear anything, let me know, okay?"

"You know I always do."

"Try *never,* you ungrateful bastard." But he smiled anyway and got out of the car.

Next to me, Jack's eyes shed a single tear, which rolled slowly down his cheek and ended somewhere down his neck.

I put my hand on his shoulder and gave it a squeeze, even though I didn't think it would do much good.

Chapter Seven

Hard-charging, chain-smoking, waistline-expanding Officer Larazo of the Brookline Police Department had given me something to go on—whether he knew it or not. And naturally, it seemed preferable that he not know.

There had only been two stiffs.

Not three.

And there'd been three goons at Jack's house.

I thought I'd nailed one of them with a shot before Jack took over with his gift, but I must have only winged the guy. And since they were humans, the wooden bullets wouldn't have necessarily killed them like they would a vampire.

That meant there was someone alive, hopefully, who might know who was behind sending a hit team to either kidnap or kill Jack.

Now I had to find that guy.

I still had reservations about dropping Jack off at Wirek's

place. While the old drunk might have supplied me with some vague information, the fact remained he was still an unkempt mess.

Maybe it was some long, silent parental instinct coming to the surface that made me want to leave the little dude with someone a bit more responsible. I couldn't fathom it, but I sure wasn't going to ditch him at Wirek's pad.

Still, I did know someone who might fit the bill nicely. If only he could be convinced . . .

The Council headquarters sat in a beautiful, old brownstone on Beacon Hill just a quick spit from the State House with its gold-domed top. Iron fencing closed off the front courtyard proper, small though it seemed.

Once inside, however, the place exploded in size. The Council had purchased the surrounding brownstones almost one hundred years before and knocked down the interior walls, thereby connecting them all with an intricate series of long, winding hallways, dark sublevels, and antechambers.

The Council decided to use Boston as the seat of worldwide power just over a century ago. Boston, with its unique location, layout, and history, appealed to the more traditional inclinations of several of the older Council members. Historically speaking, the Council vampires were a bunch of addicts.

But finding your way around the inside of the Council building took a lot of time if you didn't know where you were headed. I should know. I'd broken into the Council building a few months back with my friend and mentor, Zero.

But Zero was dead now, too.

I forget which well-known poet said something about being judged by the friends you keep. If that's true, I was headed for a long downhill slide since few of mine seemed to be alive still.

In the process of breaking into the building, however, we'd met up with one of Zero's old friends, a former Fixer named Arthur. Arthur now spent his days acting as a butler and caretaker for the Council building and lived there year-round.

Part of me thought it kind of sad that after faithfully serving the Council for years as a Fixer, Arthur was now relegated to that boring existence. After all, he'd risked his life more times than most other vampires in our society.

But Zero assured me that peace and quiet was a wonderful reward following years of active Fixer duty. It seemed a foreign thought back then, but lately I had to admit the idea did have some appeal.

Boring existence or not, Arthur was my only choice as a suitable guardian for Jack. He could look after him while I went hunting.

The question was how to get in touch with him.

Simply showing up at the Council building unannounced wasn't a good idea. I wasn't normally well liked around those bureaucratic parts. Even though my record was almost immaculate, my bedside manner apparently left a lot to be desired. Go figure.

Fortunately, vampire society functions a lot like human society. Bureaucracies rule the day with their mounds of unending paperwork and banker's hours.

The Council might rule the building between the hours of nine-thirty in the morning and five o'clock in the evening, but Arthur ruled the night.

We made it back to Beacon Hill by four-thirty, just in time to avoid the rush of fleeing city workers who scampered home to their suburban three-bedroom homes to live a few short hours before returning to their indentured servitude the next morning.

I parked in the Boston Common Garage, underneath the

Boston Common itself, the oldest tract of public land in the city. Over the years, the Common had served as a gallows, a place for troop encampments, and a place to graze livestock.

Nowadays, during the winter months, they had an ice-skating rink, Christmas lights, and a fair assortment of homeless folks out searching for liquid warmth and a few coins.

And vampires parking their cars underground in the garage.

Jack's energy level seemed okay, although I could tell the strain of the day was probably getting to be a bit much for him. Running back and forth all over town can get exhausting even for me. And I'm not twelve years old.

We crested the stairs leading up from the garage. I don't normally use elevators if I can avoid them, preferring the exercise of stair climbing where I can find it.

Outside felt like a frigid wind tunnel as the icy gusts ripped around our coats, poking into open gaps and robbing us of precious warmth.

I wished it were darker, but evenings in February don't grow black until well after five. I checked my watch, saw it was only a few minutes past, and steered us over to a gray bench.

"Why are we stopping?" asked Jack. "It's freezing out here."

I nodded. "Think you can hold tight for about ten minutes? I need to see someone and he may not be available yet."

Jack frowned but hunched down farther into his collar and plopped beside me. We sat there on the hard wood, feeling the cold seep into our backsides and up our spines. People rushed past us, intent on catching a bus or a train, virtually ignoring two vampires on the bench. We might have been homeless, but for our clothing. We might have been just another father and son spending time together, but for the bad weather. We might even have been humans. . . .

We might have been.

Ten minutes sped by mercifully fast and I hustled us across Beacon Street, dodging a Boston Transportation Department van that carried the meter maids on their rounds of plastering orange tickets on windshields all over town.

I paused outside the brownstone and whispered a silent prayer that everyone would have gone home by now. Late workers were a rarity in vampire society, except for those of us always on the clock.

Jack tugged on my arm. "What is this place?"

I looked down at him. "This is where the Council works."

His eyes grew wider. I remembered the same feeling when I'd come here so many years ago for my first meeting with them. Every vampire comes here around their centennial birthday. That's when you find out what your job is going to be in our society. For some, it's a fairly simple matter of having a normal job. They go to school, graduate, and enter the swim of society.

Then for the people like me, it gets weird.

I opened the iron gate and nudged Jack up to the heavy oak door that had been lacquered black years ago. A small buzzer to the left beckoned and I pushed it once.

It took Arthur just over five minutes to find his way to the front door from wherever in the huge building he'd been. Still, when the door opened, he didn't ppear out of breath, even though he must have been pushing five hundred easy.

He squinted at me, making the crow's feet at the edges wrinkle deeper. "Yeah?"

"Good to see you again, Arthur."

His eyes opened a little bit more and then he cracked a smile. "Lawson. Good to see ya, lad." His thick British accent still clung to him despite years of work abroad. Arthur, it always seemed to me, was at once the stereotypical butler and also one helluva deadly guy.

He looked down at Jack. "Who've you got with ya?"

"This is Jack."

Arthur nodded and stood back, opening the door. "Come inside before ye catch your cold. It's freezing out tonight, eh?"

"Sure is."

The reception hall looked much the same as the last time I'd been here. Big and spacious walls with mahogany paneling sprouted from the floors of thick carpeting. Framed portraits of old vampire leaders hung from the walls, while a few plants in antique chamber pots marked time in the corners. A vague smell that seemed part musty and part exotic spice—like myrrh—lingered in the air.

I shrugged out of my coat and saw Arthur hadn't answered the door alone. In his left hand was the same shotgun he'd cornered Zero and me with a few months ago before realizing we weren't a threat.

"Still taking precautions I see."

Arthur smiled. "Zero tell ya I was once one of you?"

"He did."

Arthur chuckled. "Old habits, they die hard, you know?"

"Fortunately."

Jack was still standing in the hall, just looking around. Arthur clucked, lowered the shotgun, and put a hand on his right shoulder. "Impressive, ain't she?"

Jack nodded.

"Never been here before, lad, have ya?"

"No, sir."

Arthur clucked once more and led Jack toward a doorway set back off the hall. I followed behind. We pushed into the kitchen and a wave of warmth swept over us. A raging fire in the woodstove kept the whole room toasty.

I leaned against a gray granite countertop while Arthur steered Jack to a chair by the woodstove.

"You warm up some here, son. I'll be back in a flash."

He came back to me. "Wanna tell me what's up, then?"

I filled him in quickly. Arthur might have been getting on in years, but he was still a professional. He didn't stop me once during my rundown of the events of the past few days. I finished and asked, "Can you watch him for me?"

Arthur nodded. "Yeah, but only until tomorrow morning before the Council arrives. If they find out he's here, it could raise some eyebrows. You know what gossiping buggers those lot are."

"I'll be back before then. I need to find this guy. I just hope whoever ordered the hit hasn't killed him yet."

"You find him, you'll find the guy who supplied humans with Fixer guns. Sounds like a conspiracy, eh?"

"I know." I frowned. "That prospect hasn't cheered me any."

Arthur looked over at Jack. "All to get at a little boy, no less." He sighed. "Times've changed Lawson. They really have."

"Power, Arthur. It's all about power."

"It ought to be about the good of our society. Isn't that why folks like us exist?"

"That's what I thought . . . once."

He nodded and clapped me on the shoulder. "Find your man. The little lad will be all right here. I'll make sure he's fed and gets his head down for a few hours."

"Can't thank you enough, Arthur."

"You got revenge for Zero a few months ago. That's all the thanks I could ask. Zero too."

I nodded, but the hurt was still fresh. You don't get over friends like Zero for a long time.

And I knew Arthur hurt, too.

Chapter Eight

The Volvo felt empty without Jack riding next to me, and I grinned a bit in spite of myself. The little dude was growing on me. Still, I needed some alone time to go hunting. Arthur would keep him safe until I got back.

I was parked on Mission Hill—the highest point in the city, looking out over the city skyline. In the distance, the John Hancock and Prudential Tower poked out of the urban landscape and jutted skyward like tent poles holding up the night. Boston was a damned pretty town, especially at night.

I punched a number into my cell phone and waited for the ringing to start. The line was picked up after exactly one minute.

"Hello, Lawson."

The voice on the other end of the phone belonged to Benny the Phreak, one talented computer geek. When I say talented, I mean that Benny never left the house anymore.

Never showered, either, by the smell of his place the last time I'd been there, which wasn't very often.

"Benny, what's happening?"

"You tell me. You called."

Benny the Phreak didn't like wasting time when there were secret government files to be hacked or porn sites to be admired. I always kept the conversation to the minimum.

"I need a rundown of new patients into area hospitals for earlier this morning."

"How early?"

"Between one A.M. and five A.M."

"Which hospitals?"

"Start with the Longwood Medical area. They're close to the site where the guy would've been wounded. Expand outward from there."

"Any other parameters?"

"Bullet wounds ideally, but don't rule out lacerations or other penetrating wounds. Single white guy, age between eighteen and thirty-five."

"Got it."

"How long?"

"Twenty minutes."

I whistled. "Call me back."

I'd met Benny a few years back when I'd needed a pay phone and the only one available was being used by Benny to crack into the phone company's main computer and then hopscotch his way through other major corporations, finally ending up at the Pentagon. And like I said before, I maintain an extensive list of contacts with the kinds of skills I don't have ready access to. So I struck up the friendship and we've been in touch ever since.

But Benny didn't come cheap. His services and his expertise cost a lot, even if you had money to burn. But each time I used him, the Council never blinked when I filed the expense report.

Benny's age was almost indeterminable. I figured he was at least thirty years old, but the length of his matted salt-and-pepper beard, long stringy hair, and thick bottle glasses made it difficult to pinpoint exactly. Plus, with the exception of the whores who visited him on a regular basis when he wasn't pleasuring himself, no one really wanted to stay around ol' Benny long enough to ask.

He had money, though.

Did he ever. Benny'd made himself a fortune capitalizing on the fact that there were plenty of ugly people out there not getting a steady stream of sex. For them, masturbation was one of the few outlets they'd have. And Benny'd positioned himself perfectly by being the mastermind behind most of the larger porn sites on the Internet.

Not overtly, of course. Nothing Benny the Phreak ever did was overt. He'd built himself a shell company complete with a puppet administration that claimed to run the companies. But behind them was the ever-vigilant Benny the Phreak.

He'd told me once that computers were the only real friends he'd ever known. And he hadn't seemed particularly upset about it. He said that at least computers could be fixed and weren't given to the peculiarities of human companionship.

I figured it was only a matter of time before Benny invented a real cybersex machine. Believe me, he had the brains to do it. Then he'd cut out human interaction altogether.

At least the cyberwhore wouldn't complain about the smell.

After twenty minutes, the phone rang on cue.

I picked up. "Yeah."

"Okay, I got three possibles."

I grabbed a pen and paper. "Go."

"One named Victor Cavanaugh, who checked in at Beth Israel at three A.M. with a laceration that required stitches. Treated and released by five. Next, Fred Jones, bullet wound to the shoulder. He ran out of Mass General following the removal of the slug before the hospital could contact the cops. Finally, Chuck Derby required a surgical removal of various wooden objects at Beth Israel."

Wooden objects? "What time was Derby admitted?"

"Three-forty."

"Got any particulars on him?"

"Lessee, gave an address over the Back Bay. But the number seems too high to be legit. Hang on a second. . . ."

I heard some typing and some beeps followed by a quick chuckle. Benny came back on the line. "Address is a fake. Want me to run it down and find the real one?"

"Can you?"

A derisive snort filled the phone. "Can I? Hmph. Hang on."

The line went to hold and all of a sudden Benny's voice filled the phone, complete with mellow mood music I recognized as Kenny G. Benny was hawking fictitious breath mints. If I hadn't been in a hurry, I might have found it funny.

He came back on the line in five minutes, just as Kenny G was beginning to saw on my nerves. "Okay, I'm in the hospital security-camera log file. Lemme get last night's camera views up on screen here." More typing. More beeps. "Okay, fast-forwarding to this morning and . . . here comes our boy right on cue. Freeze that." I heard a chair swivel and a different scale of typing sounds.

"Okay, lemme hack into the Registry of Motor Vehicles computer here. Their system is so damned antiquated, it's pathetic. Call up the name Derby, and let's see if he used his real name. Oh, look at that—he did."

"You have his face shot to compare?"

"I do indeed. And, Houston, we have a match."

"And his real address?"

"Absosmurfly. Want it?"

"Please."

"Roslindale. Beech Street."

He read me off the number, and as he did so, I heard his door buzzer in the background.

"Am I interrupting something there, Benny?"

"Stay on the line much longer and you will be."

"Thanks for your help."

"You'll get the bill."

I disconnected and sat for another minute watching a plane make its final descent into Logan. Derby's wound sounded like one of my rounds. The wooden tips are designed to blossom on impact, spreading the wood like a fragmentation burst. On vampires, it makes one helluva lethal hurt. On humans, it probably felt like having your body riddled with splinters.

Not pleasant, but not deadly, either.

The address made me pause, though. Roslindale was five minutes from Jamaica Plain. The fact this guy basically lived in my backyard didn't buoy my spirits any.

I U-turned out of the New England Baptist Hospital's parking lot and dropped down behind the Veteran's Hospital on to South Huntington, followed it back to Center Street in Jamaica Plain, and then up toward West Roxbury and Roslindale.

On the way, I passed the Faulkner Hospital, where my father had worked for most of his life. He died young. Too young, in my opinion. We were just getting to that stage when fathers and sons become more like pals than elder and junior. I still think back, with a fondness I don't reserve for much else, on those few instances when we shared a beer and a hearty laugh about women.

Center Street dipped and then forked. To the right lay the VFW Parkway, pockmarked with potholes the size of small moon craters this time of year. Center Street continued on to the left, into Roslindale proper.

I slid the car to a slow stop a few houses before the address Benny had given me and killed the engine.

According to Hollywood movies and TV programs, cops and spies stake out a house for a grand total of thirty seconds before rushing in and kicking ass. Talk about so much bullshit. Do that in reality and you will live for a very short time.

And die for a very long one.

In reality, you need to adjust to the environment. The environment needs to adjust to you. That means you sit in the car for just as long as you can without looking suspicious. Then you check out the area and see if anything changed on your arrival. If it looks okay, then you exit the car and start your approach.

Slowly.

You do a lot of listening. The same way the sounds in a forest or jungle will change when the animals sense something amiss, so, too, do urban landscapes. A wise operator knows this and pays heed.

And while I am sometimes very short on wisdom, this was one area I observed the rules with a religious devotion normally reserved for maniacal cults in Middle America.

Nothing seemed to have changed since my arrival, so I stepped out into a slush puddle next to my Volvo and quietly closed the car door.

Derby's house looked like a two-family unit mashed into a triple-decker, but the second and third floors were dark.

According to Benny, Derby lived on the first floor. It was dark, too, except for one room toward the back of the house that glowed a dull yellow.

The streetlight in front looked like someone had either shot it out with a BB gun or chucked a rock hard enough to break the bulb. Whoever had done it, I was grateful to them for the additional cover of darkness.

Normally, dealing with humans doesn't concern me much. I can't really be killed conventionally. I've been shot, stabbed, and almost blown up. Sure, I can get hurt like a bastard, but killing me is another matter entirely. Over the years, vampires have built up incredible restorative powers.

Still, the fact that the goons from the other night were all equipped with Fixer guns put me on guard in a major way. Those bullets could kill me dead real fast. And I'm kind of addicted to living—at least right now—so I took my time getting close on the target.

First I had to get past the rusted old chain-link fence that seemed more a rarity these days than in the 1970s and 1980s. I lifted the latch, eased the gate open, and stepped through, careful to replace it just so.

The broken cement pathway in front of me leading down the side of the house was only about two feet wide and crowded with heavy-duty green plastic garbage containers. I dodged them as best I could, ducking under the various windows that my head skirted.

Finally, I got close enough to the lit window and stood on my tiptoes to pee inside.

And couldn't see anything, thanks to the heavy drapes that covered the window.

I sighed.

It would have been nice to see Derby sitting there perhaps in a recliner watching the football game and eating chips. I could have made my entry and put him down before he could utter a word.

Now I had to go in without any idea of where the guy could be.

No one ever said it would be easy.

I chose the back porch over the front because it afforded me more time and cover to pick the lock. Fortunately, like the front, this house had two doors going to both apartments. I got down close to Derby's lock, examined it, mentally pronounced it pickworthy, and set to the task.

My philosophy on picking locks had changed a lot over the past few months. I used to prefer just kicking the door in, storming the place, and getting the deed done quick.

Zero always preached the more relaxed sneak-and-peek entry and to that end had mastered picking almost every lock and defeating virtually every alarm system he could find. It was a respectable achievement, and since his death, I'd thrown myself into that same pursuit.

My skills were nowhere near as good as what his had been, but I was coming along. Needless to say, it took me a little while longer to get through the dead bolt.

But I got through all the same.

The back hall stank of old garbage, and the stench hit me like a wall. I sucked in hard and fast, trying to acclimate myself to the smell, but it was bad, anyway. To my enhanced olfactory sense, Derby must have dined almost exclusively on sardines, rotten lettuce, and spoiled milk with a healthy serving of whiskey.

A simple swinging wooden door led into the kitchen. I prayed the hinges wouldn't squeak too loud, especially since the place was almost eerily quiet. No television sets, no radios.

Stone dead.

I kept my pistol in what special ops folks like to call the

"low-ready" position, the muzzle aimed just below the imaginary horizon line in front of me. If a threat presented itself, I'd sight-acquire-fire and put the bad guy down fast.

I reminded myself I wasn't here to kill Derby and using the gun was a last resort. Some questions needed answering. And I wanted those answers pretty bad.

I took another foul-ridden breath and eased through the door.

The kitchen looked like a garbage Dumpster had exploded in it. The ambient light spilling out of the room next door illuminated piles of trash and dirty dishes. Empty beer bottles lay strewn about the counters, old pizza boxes with uneaten stale crusts loitered on what looked like a fifty-year-old gas stove, and a pile of newspapers sat by the refrigerator.

Place was a goddamned firetrap.

Pretty much exactly what I expected, too.

See, professional operators maintain discipline in every area of their lives. If Derby had been a top hitter, his place would be clean. But judging from how he and his gooney friends conducted themselves last night, the state of his dismal living quarters came as no shock.

I stood in the kitchen for three minutes.

Listening.

Cataloging the ambient sounds of the place. I wanted to make sure every creak and ping was carefully stored so I didn't freak out if they popped while I was there.

I also hoped to hear some noise that would help pinpoint Derby's location. But I got nothing. No floorboards creaked; no thumps bumped; no breathing breathed. Nothing.

And I didn't like it.

The lit room beckoned and I advanced toward it, still keeping the pistol ready to go. As the doorway opened in front of me, and I cut the pie, clearing the room of any potential threats—pieces of the room gradually revealed themselves.

The wide-screen TV probably cost at least $1,200 and looked out of place next to the faded yellow pinstripe wallpaper that peeled away from the corners and edges of the room. The pockmarked maroon rug showed holes of hardwood flooring in places. Yellowing newspapers littered the corners. Bloody bandages turned brownish from dried blood sat in a pile as a blue plaid recliner came into view with its back to me.

I moved into the room now, sniffing the air.

I could smell stale blood—that vague coppery tinge that would have been caked on his bloody bandages. But I caught a whiff of something else, too. Something . . . fresher.

That didn't make any sense, unless . . .

I swung the recliner around.

Derby's vacant eyes stared at me from behind the veil of death.

I sighed—lowered my pistol.

Shit.

I stooped closer and got a look at him. The entry wound looked neat, probably a .22. Whoever'd done it had put one clean into the middle of his forehead. I could tell from the discoloration on the chair behind his head that what few brains Derby'd once possessed had been blown out the back and now mixed with the blue material of the chair in some vague melange of grisly color.

The shooter'd been close, too. Derby's eyebrows had powder burns on them.

From the look on his face and the somewhat rigid state of his body, he might have been dead almost twelve hours. That meant, whoever he'd worked for had rolled up the operation and gotten that much of a jump on me.

And that wasn't good at all.

My one lead was sitting in a pile of his own shit and piss and blood and not telling me anything except that he hadn't chosen his employers very carefully.

I could have told him that.

Standing in that crappy apartment, I doubted Derby would have been smart enough to write anything down. Even dead, he didn't look like he and the alphabet had been on speaking terms.

But there might be something in the joint that could help me make a jump to the next possible lead. I've known professional trackers who use the same principle in their business. They follow a trail for as long as they can. If the tracks disappear, they cast around for a new track to continue the search. They start small and expand, hopefully finding the trail again. In the dog world, it's known as casting for scent.

In my world, it means I'm shit outta luck and damned desperate for anything fresh to go on.

It took me another twenty minutes to determine that most of Derby's worldly possessions amounted to the TV set, an imitation brown leather wallet made in Taiwan, a cellular phone, and a set of keys to a Ford Escort.

Both the TV and the cell phone were new. That told me old Derby had recently done some shopping. I found the receipt for the TV in the kitchen by the newspapers. Unfortunately, it had been paid for in cash. I hadn't been far off the mark in what the damned thing cost, either. Bully for me.

The cell phone held some promise, though.

Good old Benny the Phreak could probably hack the records and tell me who Derby had been calling or receiving calls from. For a price, of course.

I wiped the place down of my prints as much as possible.

It wasn't really necessary—I'm not listed in any computer files—but old habits keep me alive.

I turned off the light as a courtesy on the way out. I don't know too many dead folks who like to sit under the light like fries at a fast-food chain and bake away in a putrid mess.

According to my watch, it was closing on eleven o'clock. Time enough to grab Jack and get home for some much needed sleep.

It had been a long day, and until Benny the Phreak had a chance to get up close and personal with the cell phone, things didn't show much hope of looking up any time soon.

Still, it could have been worse.

I could be sitting in some crummy apartment in a recliner with the back of my head blown off.

Just like Derby.

Chapter Nine

Jack asked me the question the next morning over cereal, orange juice, and juice.

"When can I go home?"

I'd known it was coming. Hell, anyone in the kid's place would have asked it a thousand times before then.

But the question was a difficult one to answer. Partly because, until I got to the bottom of this thing and figured out who the bad guys were, Jack was still in a lot of danger.

Then there was the fact that the kid was growing on me.

I've been a loner most of my life. Never had any brothers or sisters. I grew up fending for myself—given the finer points of leading a worthy life by my father and mother—and that was it. Jack reminded me a lot of myself, but with glasses.

I made an executive decision I hoped I wouldn't regret. "We'll go back to your house after breakfast. But just to get some of your things. Until I can nab the guys who did this, you're still in danger."

"Because of my gift?"

I nodded. "Yeah, pal. Looks that way."

"Some gift," he said, and went back to munching his flakes.

I sighed. "You've got something a lot of people seem to want. I don't know who yet and I don't know what for, but I promise I'll find out."

He looked back up at me. "Then what?"

That one stopped me cold. I hadn't thought that far yet. The way this thing was unraveling, I felt like I was playing catch-up the entire way. The future was just that—a long way off. And right now, it was the last thing on my mind.

"How about we take that as it comes?"

"I guess." He chewed for another minute. "Are we going to see Mr. Dulton again?"

"You mean Arthur?" I smiled. "Sure, I don't see why not. You guys had fun last night?"

Jack nodded. "Yeah. He's not such a great cook, but he told me a lot of very cool stories about the old times. Some legends I never even heard of before."

"You probably heard some I haven't heard before, either."

"Mr. Dulton says most folks in our society don't know the old tales. He says that's one reason why people like you and him are needed. He said that if people respected the old traditions, they'd know the right thing to do all the time."

"Maybe they would, Jack. But unfortunately, we can't change everyone. Some folks will just go and do what they want with little concern for anything but their own personal gain. They'll do anything for any price. What makes us good is concern for others. We need to work together, help each other out."

He considered that. "I'd like to hear more stories about the old days. It sounds like a good time to have been alive."

I smiled. I felt the same way. Somehow Fixers and Elders like Wirek always felt like we were born at the wrong time. While the rest of our society wanted to move into the future, we were the holdouts. The preservers of the old ways.

In a lot of ways, the newer generations wanted nothing to do with the traditions. Some of the young folks even went so far as to have their canines ground down so they wouldn't look so pointy. It reached the point where it was almost a denial of our heritage. I shared Arthur's concern about it.

We washed the dishes together and then jumped in the Volvo for the ten-minute ride to Brookline. Jack spent most of the ride filling me in on some of Arthur's exploits as a Fixer. I wasn't quite sure if Arthur had embellished them for Jack's sake, but if the stories were half true, Arthur had been one hell of an operator.

Jack's house looked a lot different in the daylight. The trees that had yawned great shadows over the lawn the other night seemed friendlier now. And even the house itself didn't look nearly so deserted as the sun danced through clouds and brightened the melting snow.

"We'll park the next street over and then walk. We'll go in through the back door, okay?"

"I don't have the key."

"Not a problem. I can pick the lock."

"Really? Cool."

I looked at him. "Just remember, we've got to be quick. If the humans who live around here see us, they'll call the police and then we'll be in serious trouble."

"I won't be long."

I nodded, pulled the Volvo around and found us a two-hour parking spot on the next street. We got out, crunching ice and snow urderfoot. Jack fell in beside me and we walked together, neither of us saying much.

We cut across the backyard and came up to the back door. I tried the doorknob on a whim, but the cops must have locked it. I pulled out my picks and went to work. Two long minutes later, we were inside.

While Jack ran around gathering some things in a small gym bag, I looked the place over. Several indentations in the walls marked where the hit team had fired at us the other night. There must have been shell casings on the floor because small chalk circles were all that remained from the crime scene investigation unit.

I walked into Henry Watterson's study. Like some foreboding brown monument, a heavy oak desk squatted in the center of the room. I jimmied the top drawer open and rifled the contents. Stacks of overdue bills from the electric, cable, and phone company clogged the drawer. Notices of imminent shutoffs vied for space with bounced checks.

Obviously, there'd been some money problems.

Something about that didn't strike me as right.

According to the information I'd received from the Council, Watterson had been selling drugs, and plenty of them. A man with that much money doesn't get letters threatening shutoffs.

I heard Jack thumping back downstairs from the second floor and went to meet him. He'd added another bag to the one he'd filled already. I grinned. "You got enough stuff there?"

"The important stuff," he said. "I'll get the rest later."

I nodded. "Okay, let's get out of here."

We left the way we came, out the back door and through the yard over to the Volvo. A bright orange ticket flapped in the wind under my right windshield wiper. So much for two-hour parking. I slid it into the glove compartment. I'd mail it to Larazo later.

Once we were back on the Jamaicaway, I cleared my throat. "Did your father ever give you an allowance, Jack?"

He put his head down. "No."

I glanced over. "Sorry, I didn't mean—"

"We couldn't afford it." He shrugged. "I mean, Dad had the house, but he never seemed to make enough money for us."

"Business wasn't good?"

"I guess not. He used to sit up a lot at night in his study. I think he was just trying to figure a way to make more money. I used to lie in bed and listen to him sigh a lot."

"He couldn't get any help from anyone?"

"I don't know that he even asked," said Jack. "I think he was embarrassed."

"Yeah," I said. "That's understandable."

"My dad was a hard worker. But he never forgot to tuck me into bed." Jack sniffed and turned away. "I miss him a whole lot."

Watching Jack try to make peace with his father's death, one I was personally responsible for, didn't make me feel very good. In fact, I had a crummy feeling in the pit of my stomach that I didn't think was going to vanish any time soon.

I'd had that feeling before, and every time, my instinct was right. Not that being right was liable to make me feel better.

Not now.

And probably not for a very long time.

Chapter Ten

That evening, I dropped Jack off with Arthur again. Arthur seemed glad to see Jack, and Jack made me promise not to tell Arthur we'd stopped off for burgers down on Commonwealth Avenue beforehand.

Back in my car, I punched up Benny the Phreak on the cell. He answered quickly.

"Yo."

"It's me again. You busy?"

"Been expecting your call."

"Yeah?"

"See the paper today?"

"No."

"Derby had a small blurb in the Irish sports pages."

"That's not very politically correct of you, Benny."

"Fuck that, man. I'm Irish. I don't mind. Why should anyone else?"

"Anything unusual in the obit?"

"Just that he was dead. I figured it must have been a dead end. Figured you'd be calling if you'd found anything you needed me to run down for ya."

"You figured right. Can I swing by?"

"If you can stand the smell, man, help yourself. You know the address."

"Fifteen minutes."

Benny lived in a loft down near where Congress Street stopped looking financial and started looking old-abandoned-textile-warehouse-turned-expensive-condominium. Benny owned five such buildings. He kept the four surrounding him vacant and lived in the fifth.

I once asked him why he kept the other four empty, when he could have made a fortune renting them out. He told me he liked knowing who his neighbors were. Or in his case, weren't.

The Big Dig, Boston's bogus construction project that seemed to be taking longer than a walk to Pluto and had more cost overruns and corrupt officials than ants at a picnic in July, had scarred the waterfront section of town. Where once there were roads, now lived detours, dead ends, and the ubiquitous presence of cops on overtime. Trying to thread your way around down there took a lot of time and a lot of patience.

Boston drivers usually possessed neither.

What the area did have plenty of, at least down by where Benny lived, was parking. I found a spot half a block away and slid the Volvo into it easily. I'd upgraded to the Volvo after my Jetta began to disappoint me after only three years and 25,000 miles. First the door handles kept breaking. Next the transmission took forever to switch gears. Then the rubber molding along the doors kept falling off.

Finally, I gave in and bought myself the Volvo. Sure, it

was about two times as much as the Jetta, but you get what you pay for.

Benny lived in a brick and mortar building that at one time had lots of windows. Now they were blocked up on every floor except the second-to-top floor. There'd also been a few doors once, judging from the archways that were also blocked up.

Now the only way in was through a heavy steel-reinforced number with a small buzzer and intercom box to one side. Very sterile, but also very secure. Above the doorway, Benny'd installed a pinhole camera.

As I approached and reached for the buzzer, the door clicked open. I pulled the door, feeling it give and creak as the hinges turned.

Stairs led up immediately, giving you no other option than to climb. My footsteps echoed off the steel treads as I climbed to the second floor.

Here you could either climb another set of stairs or head down a hallway filled with doors. The hallway was one of Benny's traps. He'd built a maze of cutouts and dead ends in case someone broke in. The real path to his living quarters lay upstairs.

The third floor stopped on a landing that had enough space for one person to stand. Anyone else would have had to stand on the steps. A blank wall stood to the left beside another set of stairs leading up.

I stood at the blank wall and waited.

After a second, a hydraulic hiss sounded from somewhere on the other side and then the wall slid open with the exact same sound as when Captain Kirk used to walk on to the bridge of the *Enterprise*.

Ahead of me, the hallway was lit in a few places by lonely red lights in the wall. At the end of the hall, a single door waited.

A small silver nameplate read simply: BENNY THE PHREAK.

It opened as I came down the hallway.

And Benny the Phreak greeted me.

"Heya, dude."

If you were anyone to Benny the Phreak, he always called you "dude" in person. I was glad to see I still rated.

"Good to see you, Benny."

He pumped my hand once. Benny'd always had himself a firm handshake. I think it came from how many times a day he got it on with himself.

He backed away from the door and let me inside.

Beyond the door, everything just exploded outward. No walls separated any of the rooms. A bank of enormous bay windows showed off the city's financial-district skyline.

I'd once pointed out that he might have been susceptible to microwave audio surveillance, but he'd shown me the triple panes of bullet-resistant glass with white noise pumped in between them.

He'd left the walls exposed brick for that proper urban-loft feel. A few choice area rugs dotted the floor, but otherwise everything was imported hardwood Benny'd ordered specifically for his pad.

Computers covered nearly every piece of available space. Some sat in varying states of assembly or disrepair. Benny had learned all about computers the hard way: buying all the parts and assembling them by hand. It took a long time, sure, but he knew exactly how everything worked by the time he finished.

He began playing with computers over twenty years ago. Nowadays he still bought triples of new high-tech gadgets. One to play with, one to destroy, and one to rebuild from scratch. Schematics to Benny the Phreak were as boring as listening to a group of accountants discuss the benefits of the decimal system.

Sheets of computer printouts filled any gaps in the hardware spaces and littered the floor, overflowing from two giant dot-matrix printers Benny still loved and a series of trash cans and shredders.

I smelled stale pizza.

Benny cleared his throat. "So, what'd you bring me?"

I held out Derby's cell phone. "I need a history on it. All calls made from and received, complete with traces, addresses, names—"

"Jeez, you want DNA, too?"

"If you can get it, yeah. I'm stuck in a bad way and this phone is the only hope I've got right now."

He nodded. "Figured it mustta been serious if you volunteered to come around." He took the phone and headed over to his main computer console, a rack of four ultrapowerful consoles and servers, sat down in a captain's chair he'd purchased off a decommissioned battleship, and began typing.

I caught a whiff of mouthwash. That was a change. Benny used hygiene products as often as politicians told the truth.

"Listerine, Benny?"

He smiled. "Got some company coming by later."

"Not the usual talent, I take it."

He shook his head. "Nope. Got someone special coming by."

"Someone special?" I grinned. "You dog."

"Great girl. Met her in a chat room."

"She a lingerie model like all the rest of them?"

He pointed a finger at me. "Hey, some of them actually were." He swiveled around and plugged the cell phone into some kind of base unit and waited for it to beep. Then he swung back around to a keyboard and punched a few keys. One of his screens filled with scrolling pages of numbers.

He whistled. "Your boy did a lot of talking on the phone."

"I didn't think he had the phone all that long."

"Mmm." He punched some keys on another keyboard and watched the results on another screen. "Two months, according to the ol' database."

I peered closer. "You got the cell phone company's database up there?"

"Sure. It's not like they have incredible security. They forget that just because they read the Department of Defense Orange Book, everyone else can, too. And some of us read a helluva lot more than just that." He winked. "I know the guy who helped write it."

"Who bought the phone?"

He typed a few more lines and sat back. "Guy named Alexander Petrov." He looked up at me. "Ring any bells?"

I shook my head. "Wish it did."

He pointed. "Okay, we got all the numbers."

"Can you group the same numbers together with dates and times?"

"Of course."

I watched a half-dozen groups pop up onto the screen. "There." I pointed. "Late Saturday night and early Sunday morning."

Benny nodded. "Same number called once at eleven and again at one in the morning. So what?"

I scanned farther down and saw it. "And again at three-thirty." I patted him on the shoulder. "Can you trace that back?"

He nodded. In two minutes, one of the giant printers churned out a page with the numbers and back-trace information. "Courtesy of the wonderful phone company."

I looked at him. "You ever get any bills, Benny?"

"What an unusual question, dude." He grinned. "What do you think?"

"I think I'll look at this printout." I sat down in one of

the few chairs Benny kept around the apartment and looked down the list. It didn't take me long to realize that the same information kept popping up.

Everything led back to Alexander Petrov.

The address was bogus, though. It belonged to the Lenox Hotel, down on Boylston Street, across from the Boston Public Library in Copley Square. I should know the address—the bar makes a damned fine drink.

"Shit."

"What's wrong?"

"Address is a fake. Nothing concrete I can go on here."

He frowned. "Well, you still got the number."

"Yeah. So what?"

Benny put on a disapproving look that reminded me of a schoolteacher scolding a student. "Call it, dummy."

"Call it?"

"See who answers. Shake 'em up. Tell them you're coming for 'em, or something like that. Shit, dude, didn't they teach you anything in spy school?"

I grinned. For a smelly computer whiz-kid geek, Benny the Phreak had a pretty good head on his shoulders.

"Thanks, Benny." I started for the door.

"You forgetting something there, genius?"

I stopped. "Can you bill me?"

"Not the money, idiot." He tossed me Derby's phone. "Use that one to make the call. That way they can't trace it back to you, got it?"

I turned the phone over and put it in my pocket. "Yeah, I got it."

"Good, now get outta here—I gotta cook dinner."

"Cook dinner? Benny, you okay?"

"I'm fine. I just happen to like this girl, okay?"

"You never cooked me dinner."

He frowned. "Yeah, well, you don't look all that good in thigh-highs."

"And she does?"

Benny smiled. "Dude, she looks amazing. . . ."

Chapter Eleven

I like working alone.

Being a Fixer, it goes with the territory. We all operate alone. Out on the edge of our society, cloaked in shadows and doing things that normally don't get a lot of attention. We excel best when we're given an assignment and the freedom to do it however we know best. Fixers get results; then we disappear—waiting until we're called again.

But even though we operate alone, an integral part of our job relies on a network of information. I have my contacts, like Larazo and Benny the Phreak, who can get me information from a wide variety of sources, especially when it comes to humans.

But there are times when I need information about the vampire world. And that information usually comes from my Control.

Not having a Control deprived me of a valuable source of information. And since there aren't all that many Fixers, and since most Controls are drawn from retired Fixers, replacements aren't exactly easy to find.

That meant I'd have to rely on myself. Sometimes that's as much a blessing as it is a curse.

When Alexander Petrov's name kept popping up on Benny the Phreak's databases, it concerned me. Mostly because I've heard of Alexander Petrov before. Of course, I couldn't tell Benny that. See, Alexander Petrov isn't human.

Current lack of information notwithstanding, I knew quite a bit about the guy.

Petrov was a Fixer during one of the toughest times in history, during the Soviet years in Russia. Petrov worked almost exclusively in Moscow, but he also ranged into the Urals and other parts of Communist Eastern Europe. It was tough back then because the Communists kept a tighter rein on their societies than the West. That meant doing what Fixers do and keeping the Balance protected was a helluva lot tougher over there than it'd been over here, just due to his operational environment.

But Petrov managed it.

Hell, he excelled at it.

When the Berlin Wall came down and the Communists started seeing the writing on the wall, Petrov requested a transfer from the Council. With his record of service, it was granted quickly. Petrov became a Control in Paris. His sector had one of the top performance reviews for five years running.

He dropped out of sight after that, with most official stories painting him as a tired old Fixer who'd opted out of the game for retirement in a small French countryside town near Calais.

But official stories only hold so much water if you know nothing about the people the stories were about. For those of us who knew Petrov, we knew he'd never go into retirement quietly.

I met him once when I was on an assignment in Europe. I had to stop off in Paris for a layover and he insisted on meeting me. According to him, my reputation preceded me and he wanted to meet what he called "the best Fixer in the Western world."

So, after humping planes all day, I dropped into Orly and caught the Metro into Paris. He met me at the local pefect building, kind of a governmental sublevel in vampire society.

As in most cities across the world, the Council made sure we had some damned nice buildings. The one in Paris was no exception. Graceful archways merged with granite steps in a building just off the Champs d'Elysee.

Under a heavy downpour, Petrov ushered me into a hallway filled with local dignitaries in the vampire world. A massive banquet was under way. Petrov turned to me and smiled.

"When I heard you were gracing us with your presence, I simply couldn't *not* have a party."

If I'd had only half the brain Petrov clearly assumed, I might have fallen for such a stupid ruse. But standing there, dripping in jeans and a turtleneck and leather jacket, my mood was sour and my enthusiasm for being exposed as some sort of celebrity was not one bit enthralled.

Instead, I simply smiled and then used my body momentum to maneuver us both into a recessed corner of the hall. There I put my face a few inches from Petrov's and whispered very articulately: "Are you trying to blow my cover, you idiot?"

He blanched. Obviously, not operating under the pressure of Communism had dulled his intelligence. "I didn't mean to do any such thing."

"But you throw a party for me—a Fixer of all things?

Half of these people aren't even supposed to know I—that we—exist at all! And now you've gone and not only shown them that we do, but you've spotlighted me of all things."

Petrov frowned. "Lawson, are you saying you're not happy with the party?"

"That is exactly what I am saying, Alexander. This was a dumb thing to do. You know it. I know it. Now go find some other rube you can use to spotlight instead, tell them I'm not who you said I was, and let me get the hell out of here."

He might have been a dimwit for arranging the party, but Petrov showed he still had the charm so often vital to our work. Within minutes, the guests were toasting some young local governor who no doubt needed more friends than I ever wanted.

I disappeared out of the prefect building and hauled ass back to the airport, where I got a flight home. As luck would have it, McKinley, my old Control, picked me up at Logan and drove me home. He got to hear the entire account, and sighed when I finished.

"Some of us knew the change of environment would do him more harm than good."

"He's lucky I didn't do him more harm," I said. "I want a report filed."

McKinley shook his head. "Can't do that. Petrov's got too much juice."

"Juice?"

"Yeah, pal. Seventy plus years' hard service under the Commies can do that for a guy. You can't just go to the Council and tell them they were wrong about one of their star Fixers. They won't buy it, first of all."

"Not even from me?"

McKinley grunted. "Sorry, pal. You're good, no doubt,

but you got the personality of an old catcher's mitt that some dog shit on."

"Colorful."

He shot me his trademark slithery smile. "Truth is, the Council digs you about as much as they like hanging out in lumberyards."

"Your analogies need a lot of work, McKinley." But I let the damned thing go. And then Petrov disappeared about two years after that fateful Paris incident. No one knew where he disappeared to. I didn't particularly care where the hell he was, just so long as he wasn't around me any longer.

Now Alexander Petrov was surfacing.

And I didn't like what I was seeing through my periscope.

Now, sure, I didn't have much. But I did have a cell phone, a series of calls placed to that cell phone that led back to Petrov, and a trio of humans with Fixer guns. And since all roads right now led back to the man of the hour, he and I were gonna have to have ourselves a chat.

I used Derby's cell phone and dialed Petrov's number. It took him ten rings to answer.

"Yes?"

"Alexander Petrov."

"Yes. This is he. Who am I talking to?"

"You once called me 'the best Fixer in the Western world.' "

There was a slight pause and then a chuckle. "Lawson?"

"The same."

"My goodness, that was years ago when we last met." There was a pause. "Well, it's nice to hear from you. How ever did you get this number?"

From the sound of the background noise, he must have been in a car. "You wouldn't believe me if I told you. We need to talk, Petrov."

"I'm on a bit of an errand right now. Can it wait?"

" 'Fraid not."

"Pity. What's it about, then?"

"Oh, hell, not all that much. But we could start with you supplying three humans with Fixer guns and sending them on an unsanctioned hit for starters." I took a breath. "That's a pretty big no-no."

He actually chuckled. "That's a pretty big accusation, Lawson. You have proof, I assume-witnesses, testimonials, that type of thing, yes?"

"The one witness I had is now deceased. A nice neat roll-up job, too. He got head-jobbed out in Roslindale. Must have been days ago by the smell of him."

"Hmm, that's a shame."

"Yeah, I was all broken up about it. Fortunately, I don't need witnesses to do my job. You know that, Petrov."

"I do, indeed. Make your point quickly, Lawson. I'm late for dinner."

"What do you want with the kid?"

He laughed again. "Haven't you figured that out yet? Haven't you witnessed what he's capable of?"

"I've seen it, yeah. The kid's special. So what?"

"I've been employed to bring that boy to some very powerful people. People who wish to use his power."

"For what?"

"I couldn't really say, Lawson. Nor would I." He laughed again, and it was really starting to annoy the hell out of me. "I must say, though, you've made my job a lot easier calling me like this. I had no idea who it was who intervened the other night. I actually thought the little boy might have done the job himself before escaping. Now, though . . . Well, this changes quite a bit."

"Yeah?"

"Indeed. Now I know you have him."

"I wouldn't try to get him if I were you, Petrov."

"I'm afraid I don't have any choice. A job is a job, as they say." He paused. "By chance, are you still living in Jamaica Plain?"

That was supposed to be classified information. But if he knew that, then there didn't seem much point in disputing it. "Yep."

"I admire your honesty, Lawson. A lesser man would have attempted to lie."

"I've never been a lesser man than you, Petrov."

"Perhaps. Perhaps not. Tell me, is the boy there now?"

"Knowing me like you do, what do you think?"

"No. I didn't think you'd leave him alone. Still, he must be with someone. Or do you have him with you now?"

"No."

"No to the first question or the second?"

"Pick one."

"I don't have time for games. I could make you rich, Lawson. Do you know that? Give him to me and I'll see to it that you reap a fortune."

"I'm not a big fan of selling little kids, Petrov. And money's only good if you live to spend it."

"I'd heard you were incorruptible. I'd hoped that might not be true. But I see it is."

"Whoever gave you your information was thorough. Congratulations."

"You're going to make this difficult, aren't you?"

"You bet."

Another pause. "I see you're using Derby's old phone. That's quite a nice trick. I assume you know the location of Derby's calls to me?"

"You could assume that."

"I've checked out of that hotel. It didn't quite suit my needs."

"Well, aren't we in a 'quid pro quo' kind of mood tonight."

"You were honest with me, Lawson. The least I can do is extend you the same courtesy."

"Damned kind of you. Don't expect it to have any bearing on your final judgment, however."

"I wouldn't dream of it. But don't you go expecting any quarter from my side of the table, either."

"Standard rules of the game, Petrov. Be seeing you."

I disconnected and pressed my back farther into the leather of the driver's seat, trying to stretch the lower back muscles. I'd tensed up during the call.

At once, a heavy breath shuddered out of me. Making the phone call was probably not the smartest move I'd ever made. I'd disadvantaged myself and Petrov knew it. He had one up on me because he knew where I lived and I had no clue how to find him apart from his cell phone. Even if I had access to triangulation equipment to pinpoint his location, it'd be one helluva pain to set up. And since Benny the Phreak was the only guy I knew capable of it, the money involved would be extreme.

Petrov would try his luck at my place. That much was fairly certain. I'd do the same in his place. And even if I'd told him Jack wasn't there, he couldn't afford not to check out the possibility.

That put me into a bit of a quandary. If I couldn't keep Jack at my place, and Arthur couldn't keep him at the Council building during the business hours, I'd need to find some place else to stash the little guy.

And the only obvious choice didn't make me feel any better.

Chapter Twelve

The prospect of Petrov staking my place out didn't warm my heart any. And bringing Jack back there would only be putting his life in unnecessary danger.

So I wasn't in much of a good mood when I rang the bell at Wirek's place.

To my surprise, he just buzzed us in.

No negotiating through the rusted grille of the outside intercom.

No snarled strings of profanity.

Just a quick click and we were inside.

Surprise nailed me again, once we crested the steps and found Wirek waiting for us. He'd cleaned himself up. Showered and obviously shaved, he looked almost normal in jeans and a flannel shirt. He stood back and let us in.

"I was wondering when you'd come back."

"You knew we'd be back?"

He shrugged. "I'd be a fool to claim the alcohol hasn't

dulled my senses somewhat, but it hasn't killed them all. I can still . . . sense things on occasion.'' He looked down at Jack. ''Nice to see you again. You must be tired.''

Jack's response was a stifled yawn and a shy grin. Wirek led him to what I assumed was a spare bedroom and reemerged three minutes later.

''Little guy can sleep, huh?''

''His schedule's been a little off lately. Hit teams and whatnot.''

Wirek nodded. ''I'd guess. Find anything out?''

''Some. Ever hear of an Alexander Petrov?''

''Should I?''

''Maybe. He worked as a Fixer behind the Iron Curtain back when the Communists were in fashion. As a reward for service under duress, he was promoted to Control of Paris. He disappeared a few years back.''

''You mean he just vanished?''

''Went to ground, yeah.''

''And now he's resurfaced.''

''I spoke with him earlier tonight.''

''How'd you manage that?''

''I got his cell phone number. He said he was working for someone else. His job is to get Jack and bring him in. That's why he subcontracted out to a bunch of humans.''

''Plausible deniability.''

''Yeah. Except for the guns. He wouldn't be able to explain that.''

''So he knows you know he's after the boy.''

''Worse, he knows where I live.''

''How's he know that? I thought you guys kept your stuff classified.''

''We do. But an ex-Fixer knows all the tricks. He's probably got some informational pipeline that scored him the info.''

"You can't go home," said Wirek.

"Not with Jack, anyway. That's why I brought him here."

"You shouldn't go home at all."

I grunted. "And disappoint Petrov's reception party? That'd be rude."

"I'll look after Jack." He nodded at me. "Who looks after you?"

"Lady Luck when she remembers."

"She remember you often?"

"Doesn't feel like it."

He pointed at the kitchen. "Coffee?"

"No. But I'll take some tea."

I stood and followed him around the apartment. He'd cleaned the place up, too. Even the kitchen, small as it was, looked recently scrubbed. I smiled. "You've been busy."

"Like I said, I knew you'd be back and that I'd be having a guest."

"That some kind of special ability peculiar to Elders?"

He shrugged. "Not really. Anybody can do it. It's just a matter of rediscovering innate abilities that have lain dormant for a long time. You get in touch with that aspect of yourself and things begin to . . . come to you."

"Sounds like a lot of mystical mumbo jumbo."

Wirek frowned. "You're one to talk. From what I've heard about you, you're very much into martial arts."

"Yeah. It's for self-protection."

"Not self-defense?"

"Self-defense is what happens when you're too stupid to see the warning signs that always precede a violent encounter."

"What kind of warning signs?"

"You know, environmental changes, subtle energy shifts, intention . . . You start to pick up on it—" I stopped and looked at Wirek. He smiled at me.

"See? You know exactly what I'm talking about."

"Maybe." I wasn't convinced. There's a big difference between sensing something when your life is on the line as opposed to just plucking it out of the air when you're relaxed. At least, as far as I knew.

"What about the Sargoth a few months back? That doesn't exactly fit into the realm of normal society, does it?"

"No." Maybe the old guy had something after all.

Wirek passed me the cup of tea. "The boy, he has a special gift, as I told you. I didn't want to upset him. But the power he wields is great. If he knows how to properly use it, that power can be used to great good. But if the wrong people can subvert him, bend him to their cause, that would be bad. Very bad."

"I don't think the folks Petrov works for would qualify as decent people. Not if they're trying so hard to either kidnap Jack or kill him."

Wirek shook his head. "Shame. It's always so sad to hear of a Fixer who's sold out. I wonder what caused it."

I stirred some sugar into the mug. "Can't say. But I've got to get to Petrov and then get beyond him if I'm going to figure this mess out."

"And how will you do that?"

I took a sip of the black pekoe tea and felt its warmth course down my throat, warming my insides. "Might as well go crash my own party."

"Are you sure that's a wise move, Lawson? If something happens to you, I'm not sure how long I can keep the boy hidden."

"I'm not sure anything I do qualifies as a wise move, Wirek. But I don't have much of a choice right now. If there was another way, I'd take it."

"At least finish your tea," said Wirek.

* * *

I parked my Volvo two streets over from mine.

I blew hot breath into the crisp, cold night air, listening to sounds echo off the houses all tucked away for a few hours' sleep. The air smelled of grimy snow and slush, the way winter air always does after a snowstorm. Underfoot, my feet mashed ice crystals together in a steady cacophony of crunches. Overhead, the new moon bled darkness into the night and I blended with it—stealing through backyards and over fences, until I, at last, reached my street.

I moved slow.

Snow and slush, like crisp autumn leaves, has a way of alerting people you are coming. And I definitely didn't want anyone to know I was in the area.

So I went from a walk, to a crawl, to a very slow form of pulling myself along the ground using my arms. It's a method I learned at the martial arts school I study at, over in Allston. And I've used it enough times to be thankful I learned it.

Cover and concealment are also difficult during the winter months when most of the foliage is, well, exfoliated. Unless you live in an area surrounded by evergreens, there was not going to be much shrubbery worth hiding in.

Fortunately for me, my neighbor loves rhododendrons and planted a solid wall of them in front of his house. I slid into them, feeling their branches yield to my presence.

I sat still.

Breathing.

Even inhalations and exhalations—tasting, listening, and feeling the surrounding area. I let my jaw hang slack, opening the auditory canals a little bit more.

It took twenty minutes.

Three.

Again.

Petrov obviously preferred threesomes. I wondered if they were human or vampire, but figured they must have been more human riffraff. Petrov wouldn't be able to hire vampires without word getting back to the Council and, hopefully, then to me.

Humans or not, they'd still probably have Fixer guns. That made them dangerous.

I spotted the first one easily enough. No one on my street owns a red Toyota. And in the darkened interior of the car, a bright red cinder from a cigarette burned—a trail of smoke wafted out of a cracked window.

More amateurs.

I sighed. It must be getting harder to find true professionals. A real pro would never smoke in a car. Hell, he wouldn't smoke to begin with. Smoking shows a lack of discipline. It's a weakness most operatives can't afford.

I spotted the second one sitting ten feet off the ground in the branches of the linden tree next door to my house. Maybe he thought it was a nifty position.

It was stupid.

Hiding in trees limits your ability to move or stay still. I noticed him when the branches moved out of rhythm with the breezes.

Goon number three showed the most, albeit limited, sense by simply strolling along the sidewalk from one end of the street to the other and back again.

He looked like a sentry out on such a cold night. If any of my neighbors spotted him, they'd call the cops. My neighbors are like that.

Still, compared to Einstein and Copernicus, he had the ability to move quickly and freely. That made him the most dangerous.

Part of me wondered if this was truly a serious attempt

at staking my pad out. I wondered if there were more of them hidden outside. I chucked that theory. Something told me this was all there was.

The easiest option would have been to pull out and wait for them to get tired and leave. Surveillance is boring work. Boredom makes you lazy. No matter how alert you are when you come on duty, you get tired real fast. And if Petrov had no bench strength—which I doubted he did—all I'd have to do was wait them out.

Unfortunately, easy and I haven't been on speaking terms for as long as I can remember. Pain-in-the-ass and I are great friends, though.

Lucky me.

And right now, PITA was telling me to go get Petrov.

I needed to get past the three stooges and have myself a heart-to-heart with the ex-Fixer.

That meant taking them out.

Stroller boy would go down first.

I waited until he reached one end of the street and then I carefully slithered my way to the opposite end, working through front and side yards as quietly as possible.

I found the perfect ambush spot beyond the curve in the street. Once he passed that point, the other two wouldn't be able to see him. I just hoped they didn't have radio contact.

He came quietly.

His footsteps like a soft whisper against the wind, even with the snow and ice covering everything. His stride made me think he might be a cut above the other two. He walked on the balls of his feet, the way dancers and thieves do.

I waited until he drew parallel to the tree trunk I'd hidden behind and then clotheslined him with my right forearm, already moving behind him to catch his body and drag him into the shadows of my neighbor's yard.

It doesn't sound particularly romantic to say I just stepped out from behind a tree and rammed my forearm into his throat, but I'll let you in on a secret: simplicity works.

Most amateurs prefer elaborate ambushes, which simply don't work. I subscribe to the "Keep It Simple, Stupid" school of thought.

I frisked the stroller under cover of the bushes and found him packing a Fixer gun and a hypodermic syringe. I frowned. Was Petrov hiring junkies now? Nah, probably not. I decided it was a knockout drug of some sort.

Next, I stripped the stroller of his jacket and tried to make my hair resemble his as much as possible. That was kind of tough. I keep my hair real short.

Then I simply began walking back toward the other two like I was the stroller.

Now the fun really began.

I'd have to take out the other two almost simultaneously without alerting anyone else who might be watching. That's tough. Even for me.

Tarzan must have heard me coming, because the branches started moving again. The linden trees on my street were planted close to a hundred years ago, which means they have nice thick trunks. I stopped next to the trunk and sighed.

A gnarled voice dripped down from above. "You okay?"

I coughed. "Yeah."

"See anything?"

"No."

"Want a smoke?"

I coughed again. "Yeah." Sure, come give me one of your cancer sticks. Please . . . oh, pretty please. . . .

I saw a hiking boot appear, followed by the other, then two legs as Tarzan shinned down the tree. His back was to me and he jumped the last two feet, came down with a dull thud.

He turned—facing me—surprise already registering.

"What—"

I jammed the hypodermic into his stomach and pressed the plunger down, hoping whatever the needle contained acted fast. I needed this guy out quick.

It must have been strong stuff.

The guy's legs buckled and he slumped back against the tree.

Unfortunately, we were both visible to the guy in the car. I heard the door open. He came running.

"What the fuck?"

He whispered quietly.

I smiled.

He must have assumed the guy in the tree was having a problem, because he didn't pay any attention to me at all. He just stooped, trying to get his arms around the guy's chest to help him back on his feet.

"What happened?"

Thank god for amateurs. "The same thing that's happening to you. " I chopped down on the side of his neck with the edge of my hand and watched the lights in his eyes blink out.

It took me two minutes to drag them both into my neighbor's shrubs, bind them with their belts and shoelaces, then work my way over to my porch.

I needed some supplies inside and then I'd collect the three goons. Then I'd interrogate them, find Petrov, and settle this damned thing once and for all.

I slid my key into the lock and turned.

Shit.

It was open.

I'm really anal retentive about locking my door. My home is one of the few places where I can relax. It's sacred to me. So, finding the front door unlocked meant that someone had violated my sanctum sanctorum.

Not a smart move.

For anyone.

I climbed the steps to the second floor. My cats, Mimi and Phoebe, who usually thump down the steps to greet me when they hear the door open, were nowhere to be seen.

Something had spooked them.

True, it doesn't take much to scare Phoebe. She's about as schizo as a cat can get. I was betting she was buried under the covers upstairs in my bedroom.

But Mimi's the guardian of the house when I'm out. Hell, I didn't spend hours wrestling with her for nothing. She could fight.

Her absence meant she was equally spooked.

I don't like it when someone scares my cats.

My house sat in darkness. The automatic lights hadn't come on, or else they'd been unplugged.

Darkness doesn't bother me. And after being outside in the cold and wet snow, my night vision was acute. I began scanning the place as I crested the stairs.

Naturally, as I started into the living room, the lights suddenly exploded, bathing the house in bright light. I squinted reflexively, sand in that brief second, a kick slammed into me from behind. My legs buckled.

And a gun rammed its way into the small of my back.

"Good evening, Lawson. Don't you think it's about time we had a talk?"

I looked up, finally adjusting to the brightness.

Petrov sat before me in my favorite leather wraparound armchair.

Smiling and drinking a glass of my juice, of all things.

The bastard looked a helluva lot more relaxed than I was just then.

Chapter Thirteen

"It's a comfortable chair."

"So glad you like it."

Petrov leaned forward so I could see that he was holding a pistol aimed at my heart. That made one in front of me and the goon's gun behind me. Not good odds.

He smiled. "Now, Lawson, can you blame me for waiting for you here? After all, you did call me." He took a sip of juice and smacked his lips. "Very nice."

"You leave any for me?"

"That should be the least of your worries."

"Guy comes into my house, uses my favorite chair, and drinks my juice . . . real nice." I sighed.

"You're upset," said Petrov. "It's understandable. I feel the same way about my home."

"I'm not mad about you being here and using my stuff, Petrov. That's rude, true. But I can tolerate rudeness."

"Can you?"

"Yeah. What gets me mad, though, is *why* you're here. You sold out. And treason isn't something I tolerate."

"Wrong, Lawson. I didn't betray anything or anyone. I was betrayed."

"What the hell does that mean?"

"The Council turned its back on me. Turned me out into the cold, as it were."

I pointed at the less comfortable chair across from Petrov. "You mind if I sit?"

He nodded. "Please."

I sat and looked at him. "That's ridiculous. You were their shining star. Why would they do that?"

"There was a situation over in Paris."

"What kind of situation?"

"I wouldn't expect you to know about it, Lawson; no one ever did. But when it was over, I was out."

I did recall hearing about another Control being put into place a few years back, but I'd thought that was due to Petrov's sudden disappearance.

He sighed. "They sold everyone on some silly story that I'd just opted to take my retirement and get out of the business. When in reality, I was being turned out to keep an embarrassing situation from coming to light."

"So clue me in. What happened?"

"One of the Council members was having an illicit affair with a human. I found out."

"How?"

"She was French. As you know, the Controls for most cities have access to a lot of information. I was doing routine reports one day, checking travel logs, that sort of thing, and I noticed a name kept popping up in my files. It was the name of this Council member. He was flying over here three times a month."

"Bullshit. He would have used a cover name—"

"Perhaps not. Why should he suspect he was being surveilled? He was, after all, a member of the Council, our illustrious governing board. Shouldn't he be above such speculation? Shouldn't he be beyond reproach?"

As much as it bugged the hell out of me, Petrov had a point. Council members tended to either fall into one of two categories: hardworking and dedicated to vampire society or egotistical as holy hell. The latter outnumbered the former.

"So, what then—you followed him?"

Petrov nodded. "I located his mistress. But I've been in love enough times in my life to know that this wasn't just a casual tryst. It was a full-blown love affair. He was as serious about her as she was about him. Obviously, the ramifications were enormous. A Council member accused of one of our highest crimes wouldn't wash well with the vampire society at large. There'd be endless investigations, calls for reform, a nightmare in short."

"Let me guess: you made the mistake of telling someone."

Petrov cocked his head. "Mistake? That's a curious statement coming from someone like you. I would have thought you'd understand."

I might have, too. Once. But I had other reasons now. Reasons I wasn't about to cue Petrov in on.

"I meant mistake in the sense that the gravity of who it was would have possibly made you second-guess your course of action."

He thought about that over another sip of my juice. "Maybe I should have. But I didn't. Maybe I was a bit too full of myself, after everything I'd been through. I might have thought myself above such perils." He nodded. "It was my mistake, as you say."

"So they tossed you out for reporting the crime?"

"They told me that I'd been incorrect in my appraisal of the situation. That the Council member was actually working on some top secret operation. As if they could feed me that drivel and expect me to believe it. You know as well as I do, Lawson, that after everything we see, we become jaded. Bullshit, as it were, does not wash with us."

"True enough."

"I insisted otherwise and we went back and forth. I kept pressing them for an inquiry. They refused. I threatened to go public—"

"What?"

"That may not have been wise."

"No shit, Sherlock. No one ever goes public about who we are and what we do. I thought I explained that to you back in Paris."

He finished my juice. I wondered if he'd wash the glass. Probably not. "They finally reached their limit with me. Told me I was out. Just like that. No ceremony, no thank-you-very-much. Just a quick wad of cash in an envelope, a full pension, and then a swift kick in the backside. I was out for doing what I'd been trained to do."

"Not exactly."

"Excuse me?"

"If you'd done what you were trained to do, you would have executed the Council member for his crimes."

Petrov smiled. "You have a point?"

"Do I need one? We aren't here to discuss your past actions. For all I know, you might have wanted to expose that Council member as a way to earn more stars. But I don't really care about that. Them putting you out to the pasture doesn't give you the right to turn against the laws you helped protect."

"Doesn't it? What if I felt those laws were a sham? Obviously, if they only apply to some of our society, what good are they at all?"

"Because they help keep order. Without them, we'd perish."

"Oh, Lawson, that is such naïveté."

"Is it? Do you really believe human society would integrate and accept vampires as part of its own? We're fundamentally different and yet we share a common ancestry. But the differences are too great. We'd be hunted down."

"We don't know that."

"It's not something we have to experience to figure out if it's true or not."

Petrov clicked his tongue against the roof of his mouth, making a popping noise. "I see we are at a bit of an impasse on that topic, anyway."

"All right, then, let's move on. Who are you working for?"

"Where is the boy?"

I looked at him and he at me. "He's safe," I said at last.

"That's not what I asked, Lawson."

"But that is what I answered. Your turn."

"I'm working for some incredibly powerful people, Lawson. Much more powerful than you could imagine."

"Tell me who."

"Where is the Invoker?"

I shook my head. "Forget it. I'll figure it out, anyway. Eventually. You know I will."

"Yes." He sighed. "I knew you would be difficult. I actually hoped to get in and out of this city without interacting with you. I've seen your service record, Lawson. I know what a formidable opponent you can be. Butting heads with you is not the preferable option here."

"What is?"

"You letting me get my job done."

"Not in my town, Petrov."

"My employers are wealthy. Could you be tempted with money?"

"You asked me that question already."

"I'm asking it again."

"Then I'll give you the same response. If you really saw my service record, you already know the answer to that question."

"Well, it was worth a shot." He leveled the gun on me. "You don't leave me much choice."

I felt the goon behind me move away, giving Petrov clearance for the shot. I shifted. "You're going to shoot me?"

"You have a better plan?"

"You can't kill me, Petrov. You need me to find the boy. Otherwise, you still lose."

"You don't think I could find the boy on my own without your help?"

"Maybe you could, but it'd take far too long. You said yourself you want to be done with this and get out of here. Boston's a pretty big town. I could have stashed the kid anywhere and you'd never find him."

The gun lowered slightly. "You are right, of course. I probably would not be able to find him. It would take me weeks of searching. And I am not the most patient man."

I nodded.

He smiled. "Which is exactly why I am going to shoot you."

The gun came up, and even as I started to move, I heard the muffled pop—suppressor?—and felt the impact center mass in my chest.

Heat blossomed, spreading the pain—

and I was already

trip
falling
to
the
floor
—gone.

Chapter Fourteen

When I woke up, I wasn't in a soft white linen hospital bed.

Nor was I surrounded by a fleet of buxom nurses dressed in those great uniforms of yore.

So much for this being a dream.

Instead, it felt like my entire body was being dragged inch by inch over a bed of nails and broken shards of glass. Possibly with the oil of chili peppers smeared over the points and edges.

I felt that good.

My head swam lazy circles around a giant buzzing sound that seemed rooted to the space between my ears. My eyes took forever to focus.

I guessed whatever Petrov shot me with, it was one helluva powerful tranquilizer. It would have had to be, to take out a vampire.

As awareness seeped back into my body, pins and needles

shot along my arms. I tried to flex, but realized my hands were shackled to a metal grate and then the wall behind me. My arms and legs were akimbo.

Even with my eyes closed, I knew we weren't in my house anymore. I don't like dungeons, and S and M has never done a damned thing for me.

I tried opening my eyes again. Light poured in, making me squint hard to shield myself. That must have been part of the reason why my head hurt so much. There was a zillion-candlepower light fixated on my skull.

My tongue felt thick and heavy. I smacked my lips a few times and got a bucket of water thrown in my face as a reward. I shook my head and tried to get some of the water into my mouth.

The air smelled cold and dry, yet musty. We must have been deep underground.

"Lawson, nice of you to join us at long last."

I coughed a bit, but kept my head down. "Wanna turn off that fucking light? I can't see a damned thing."

Petrov chuckled and I thought I sensed more than one person in here with him. "Not just yet, Lawson. Maybe if you tell us what we need to know, maybe then I'll turn them off."

"Who's 'we'?"

"Some people very interested in your little friend. Now are you going to help us?"

"Can't do much for you with that light giving me a severe headache. Turn it off. Then we'll see."

I heard whispering and some of it seemed strained. Finally, there was a pause and I heard a click. The blinding light went away. I blinked a few times and finally raised my head.

Stone walls surrounded me on all sides, except for a doorway to my left. A dim electric bulb burned overhead, casting a pathetic amount of light in the room. That was okay with me, I preferred the darkness. Behind me, I could hear water running down the wall from when I'd been doused.

In front of me, Petrov stood alone.

"Your team sure vanished fast. Where'd they go?"

"It would probably be better if you did not see them, Lawson. Anonymity is priceless, don't you agree?"

"I wouldn't know. I can't seem to keep strangers out of my house."

He chuckled. "I enjoy your sense of humor, you know that? Has anyone ever told you your mirth is one of your best qualities?"

"Just a few people I killed."

"And the way you deadpan . . . amazing." He clapped his hands together. "Now, really, Lawson. In all seriousness, I need to know where you have stowed the boy."

"Thanks for turning out the light. But forget it."

He shook his head. "I am not a cruel man. I hope you can understand that." He walked around me. I tried to follow his movements, but my head only turns so far.

He stopped again in front of me. "But alas, I do have a job here and you are making things much more difficult than they have to be." He leaned closer to me. "The mission must succeed. I know you understand that, don't you?"

"Whatever."

"You know that I have to do what I have to do to get what I need."

He had a way with words and I suspected he'd done a lot of work with to hypnotic speech. My head continued swimming from the drugs. That and the fact that I was manacled to the wall didn't make me optimistic about my current situation.

Petrov's face loomed closer to mine. "Lawson, can you really blame me for feeling the way I feel? Can you discount the rage I felt when the Council turned on me? After everything I'd done for them, after all the sacrifices I made all those years. You know what I'm talking about; you've done the same. How would you feel if it happened to you?"

"It's never happened to me."

"You've never felt any rage toward the Council?"

"So, what if I have? You and I are completely different. There is nothing that would ever make me sell out what I've worked my whole life for."

"We're not so different, Lawson."

"I'm willing to bet that we are."

The slap smacked my jaw and sent my head slamming into the metal grate behind me. Petrov could hit. I saw stars briefly, tasted the coppery tinge of blood in my mouth. I worked some saliva around with my tongue to coagulate it faster.

"That the best you got?"

Petrov chuckled. "That hurt you. I know it did."

I said nothing. Was there really much to say?

Petrov sighed. "Very well, Lawson, you leave me no alternative." He clapped his hands once.

A door opened to my left side and I saw two men enter. They were two of the guys I'd knocked out outside of my house. I should have killed them.

One of them rolled in something that looked like an old gasoline generator, complete with the pull-string starter. They positioned this close enough to the metal grate so that two cables could be clamped to my rack with giant alligator clips.

Then the other man placed his hand on my forehead and pushed it back into the metal frame. His friend affixed a leather bandanna and tied it so my head was tight against the frame.

This was not looking good.

I've never had the pleasure of getting acquainted with torture. With good reason. My work dictates the ability to get in, do the job, and get out before anyone knows that I've been there. I make the kills neat and quick. Capture isn't something that I'm ever in the mood for.

When I'd gone through Fixer training, torture was a subject they touched on only briefly. And what they told us hit home pretty hard. Basically, what it came down to was that everyone has a limit. No one lasts forever. Eventually, you break. A skillful torturer knows just how far he can take a victim and then hovers at that point between where the pain becomes too intense the victim falls into merciful unconsciousness and where it is sheer agony. Then the endless repetition of questioning begins, the pain grows and subsides in waves. In the end, it's all you can do to keep breathing, let alone hold on to secrets.

Petrov knew this, since he'd gone through the same kind of training I had. But I also suspected he might have some nasty shit up his sleeve since he'd served behind the Iron Curtain. During the Cold War years, the Communists had devised some pretty nefarious techniques for information extraction.

Electrocution torture would produce massive pain, but Petrov had to be careful at the same time. He could easily shock my heart into arrhythmia and I could turn into a vegetable before he got what he needed.

One of the goons looked at Petrov.

Petrov looked at me. "Last chance."

I said nothing. Just stared straight ahead.

Petrov nodded once. The goon jerked the starter cable. Instantly, the generator coughed once and began churning. Petrov walked over and looked at the dials, fiddled with one of them, then walked back toward me.

"You know this will hurt worse than anything you've ever felt before, don't you?"

I kept mum. I was too busy trying to control my breathing and my heart rate. I began counting my breaths, withdrawing my awareness into the protective inner oasis I've mentally tried to perfect for years. The theory was, if I could focus myself so internally that exterior stimuli didn't register, I might have a chance at withstanding the pain.

Dimly now, I saw Petrov shake his head once and then mutter something to the two goons.

The first jolt of electricity raced across the tightly wound steel springs and through my body. I arched my back, drawing my lips taut against my teeth. Sweat began oozing out of my pores.

But I held.

Inside myself I saw the effects of the voltage. Somewhere off in the distance, I felt the thousands of nerve endings firing off messages to my brain, all reading the same thing: pain.

But somehow my breathing and slowed heart rate allowed me to remain deeply detached.

Petrov must have ordered the voltage increased.

Because the next bolt of electricity chopped right through any inner peace I was maintaining. And I screamed.

I felt my muscles and ligaments stretched tight. I felt the sweat cascading down my body, soaking me through, and the gasps of air rushing in and out of my lungs.

Everything exploded.

They hit me with another jolt and again my body slammed out and then back against the frame. If they hadn't tied my head down, I might have knocked myself out from the concussion. Agonizing waves of pain rushed over me.

"Enough."

The current vanished and I slumped slightly, sucking in lungfuls of air. Petrov's face reappeared before my eyes.

"Tell me, Lawson." He patted my face. "Tell me where the boy is hiding."

I coughed, tasting blood and saliva.

Petrov pulled back. "Again."

Another two-ton truck of juice smacked me silly and I convulsed again. I struggled to regulate my breathing. That isolated inner peace was what I needed if I hoped to get out of this.

The current vanished. The generator must have died.

I steeled myself and planted my tongue against the roof of my mouth. I inhaled through my nose and out through my mouth. In and out. Inhale-exhale-inhale-exhale.

"Lawson."

Petrov's voice seemed to float within my skull.

"Lawson."

Inhale-exhale-inhale-exhale.

"Where is the boy?"

I just kept breathing. Eyes closed, always breathing.

"Tell me where he is."

And then I slowed my respirations.

I heard the generator turn over and start running again. Petrov's voice wafted over the noise. "Hit him."

This time, the jolt did not make me scream. Physically, it did the same thing to my body, but I was no longer there. Far off, almost cut off from the corporeal sensations that were racking my every nerve.

The brain itself feels no pain. And the spirit, if you can access it, feels no pain, either.

That's where I kept myself.

And a strange thing happened as I kept breathing slower and slower. I felt my heartbeat slow as well. Dramatically. But I just kept breathing.

Far off now, I heard Petrov's voice shouting at me as they sent more juice into my body. Heard him screaming.

But it had no effect.

And then my heart slowed even more in time with my breathing, which was now so slow I thought I must have been breathing perhaps once every minute.

It got quiet.

Real quiet.

I heard mumbling, muttering—felt the physical sensation of my eyelids being opened, of a hand on my chest—then release.

From my vantage point somewhere deep inside the peaceful oasis of my inner self, I felt my body slump to the ground, but I felt no pain as my flesh struck the wet stone floor.

And then I was being dragged away, down a long, winding corridor with few lights.

I thought I might have overdone the breathing bit.

Thought I might have damaged myself.

Hell, I thought I was dead.

Chapter Fifteen

Vampires are a bitch to kill.

So while electrocution might well have killed a human—being that I was of more unconventional stock—I survived the torture session. Even though it felt like I was more than half dead.

If Petrov was concerned about arrhythmia, he certainly didn't show it during that bout. Maybe he wasn't concerned at all. Maybe all he wanted was the information and he didn't care how he got it.

That made me feel even better.

Petrov knew I must have somehow found a way to combat the electricity. I heard vague shouting. Things sounded like a television set was turned up too loud in another room.

I felt strong hands grab my body and begin dragging it away. Petrov officially ended the first torture session. I knew there'd be more.

Prisoners of war and survival experts will tell you the

best time for an escape attempt is as soon as possible after you are captured. The farther down the chain you get, the more organized things become. Better organization means your chances of escape dwindle.

So even though I felt like I'd just been passed down someone's small intestine and shit out into a putrid toilet bowl, I knew I had gained a very small window of opportunity.

And if I had any hope of getting out of this alive, it was time to open that window a bit more.

I started with the breathing.

I increased my respirations, dragging my awareness back up to the physical level. As I did, I felt the flush of blood seeping back toward my skin, warming me.

The next sensation I felt was more acute pain.

After all, it hurt like a bastard being dragged down a stone corridor. Then the lasting effects of the electric torture had left my mouth scarred and bloody. I could smell what must have been body hair burned off.

Then my hearing returned.

"This guy stinks." I must have pissed myself at some point during the session.

I opened my eyes. Each of Petrov's goons had one of my arms.

The other one coughed. "Sooner we get him to the cell, the better."

I sped up my respirations, causing my heart rate to follow suit.

Adrenaline dripped into my bloodstream.

I got that woozy feeling.

Expectation.

One of the goons dropped my right arm as we stopped.

"I got the door."

Now.

I came alive and executed a front roll.

My body momentum broke the other goon's hold on my arm. He started to reach for me—everything seemed to move real slow. . . .

I came out of the roll and brought my fist straight up under his jaw, slamming his head back at a sharp forty-five-degree angle and into the wall behind him.

He slid down to the floor, out cold.

Behind me, the second goon dropped the keys and started to rush me.

I shot my left elbow into his solar plexus, then heard a dull crack of shattered bone.

He staggered back.

I jammed the edge of my hand into the base of his neck.

Grabbed him around the nape—jerked him down to my lifting knee strike.

Another sick crack as his face bounced off my knee.

He slumped over to one side of the corridor, eyes open and head bent at an obscene angle.

I checked his pulse—nothing.

I turned my attention back to the first guy. He was dazed—I'd probably given him a concussion. I got behind him, grabbed his jaw and jerked his head up and to the side.

Veterbrae popped like bubble wrap as his neck broke.

Necessity dictated I kill them. I'd let them live earlier and it had almost cost me my life. I don't like making the same mistakes twice.

I leaned back against the wall and sucked in some air, feeling the adrenaline wane.

But I couldn't afford much rest.

With the two goons dead and out of the way, another series of problems immediately surfaced: Where the hell was I? And how the hell was I going to get out?

And just another small item plagued me as well: where was Petrov?

No time to waste, I came off the wall, frisked the goons but found nothing I could use as a weapon. That wasn't really a problem. I'm quite comfortable using my body to inflict damage.

I started back up the corridor.

Streaks of darkening blood scarred the coarse ground. I looked down at my chest and saw the dirt encrusted valleys scoring my upper torso.

How delightful.

I came to an intersection.

And a decision.

I didn't remember making a turn when we came from the cell, so I let my intuition guide me. I went left.

After two more minutes of stealing along the corridor, I saw roughly hewn granite steps leading up. I stayed close to the wall as the staircase curved upward. Ahead of me, lights cast long shadows that I stayed in, trying to keep myself concealed as much as possible.

The stairs ended.

I made the landing.

Wherever I was being held, it was huge. I thought it might have been an old mansion, probably on the outskirts of the city. I racked my brain trying to remember if I'd heard of any such places.

My brain told me to leave a message. It would get back to me later after a serious helping of aspirins and sleep.

Boston's an old town. Mansions and vast estates come with the territory. Hell, there are all sorts of nasties prowling the catacombs at Downtown Crossing.

I could be anywhere.

The floor that merged with the landing felt cool under my bare feet. I looked down at mauve terra-cotta tiles and smiled. Tiles help keep things nice and quiet.

I moved into another corridor.

This must have been the basement proper. I'd been held in a subbasement. I kept moving. There had to be another set of steps leading up.

Sure enough, I found them at the other end of the hallway. This time, they were wooden.

I paused.

Wood is tricky.

Wood creaks.

Wood tells everyone that someone is coming.

I like arriving unannounced.

I don't like wood.

Especially when I am walking on it in my bare feet. Cripes, I hoped there weren't any splinters poking out, this was going to be the shortest escape in history.

There are plenty of techniques for ascending wooden stairs without making noise. All of them are difficult at best. The easiest method and one of the fastest is to stay close to the wall side of the stairs, where your weight is least likely to produce creaks and squeals as the wood shifts under you.

I discarded that in favor of using an ancient technique I learned in my martial arts classes. The technique of *yoko aruki* is one of those many methods employed by the ninja intelligence-operatives of feudal Japan. Sideways walking, as it translates, allows you to maintain better environmental awareness, balance, stability, and make less noise simultaneously.

I started up the steps, leading with my left side. My arms were out in a reverse hugging position, gripping the wall and acting as feelers.

I eased my feet up the stairs, shifting as fast as I could without making much noise.

I began to sweat.

Tiny lightbulbs, like what you see on Christmas trees, helped bathe the staircase in deep shadow interspersed with small pockets of light.

I kept my breathing even.

I kept moving.

If I stopped and let my weight settle, I'd make noise.

At the top, I paused.

A door barred my way.

It looked like an ordinary oak wooden door with elaborate molding. It even had a glass doorknob, like the kind I have at my home in Jamaica Plain.

I stooped to examine the lock. There was a key sitting inside. Was the door itself locked? Who was beyond the door? Guards? Petrov?

Sweat oozed like salty grout, burning its way into the long lines of cuts marring my chest and stomach. I wiped my eyes with one grimy hand.

I knelt down on the landing and looked under the edge of the doorjamb. There was just enough space for me to make out a carpeted hallway on the other side.

Otherwise, I couldn't see anything.

No feet connected to guards.

No shadows.

I took a breath. Time to open the door.

Slowly, slowly, ever so slowly, I turned the knob.

And pushed.

The door didn't budge.

Shit.

I stood there cursing in over a dozen languages, until I noticed the molding around the door. Then I cursed myself in another dozen languages and tried the door again.

This time, I pulled.

The door clicked open.

I craned my head to check the hallway.

Empty.

I stepped onto the thick blue pile carpeting, feeling it cushion my battered feet. I looked left and right. More decisions.

The corridor led both ways with no windows in sight. In fact, aside from a lot of other doors, the place seemed vacant of detail. Old faded wallpaper adorned the walls, but that was it. No pictures, no paintings. Nothing.

Martha Stewart would shit herself twice and die of horror if she saw this place.

I pulled the door shut behind me and locked it. Better safe than sorry.

I pocketed the key and made my choice. Left was working for me so far. I'd stick with it. I headed down the corridor again using the *yoko aruki* walking and stayed close to the wall.

At the end of the hallway, it opened to the left again. I started down it and almost bumped into a large floor plant that barred my path.

I sighed, boxed around the pot, and kept moving.

That's when the entire place went crazy.

An alarm from somewhere deep inside the house began screaming. For the first time, I noticed small speakers nestled into corners of the ceilings. The entire joint was wired.

I abandoned my eminently stealthy demeanor in favor of something else that works well for me: running.

Ahead of me, a single door beckoned and I yanked it open. I was in what looked like a coat closet. The damn house had secret passageways. Great. I didn't need to get lost right now.

I pushed through a maze of coats, yanked the door in

front of me open, and stepped out into a reception hall. I'd emerged from under the stairs and was situated near two large doors.

Did they lead outside?

I heard shouts coming from behind me—in front of me. Footsteps trampled the stairs above, descending fast. The place was lousy with people.

I whirled around in search of a hiding place, but there was nothing. With no choice left, I dived for the door and jerked it open.

Outside!

Cold night air whipped around me, stinging my skin and shrinking my pores. I was hardly dressed for the February night. But that seemed to be the least of my worries right now.

Now all the voices were behind me.

And they were growing louder.

I ran down the steps, ignoring the paved, plowed driveway, and ducked right, heading toward a mass of pine trees ahead of me. My bruised feet crunched snow and stones underfoot, ripping my soles open.

Nothing like leaving a blood trail.

Escape and evasion is one of those things you hope you never have to do. The advantage always goes to the hunters. They have more resources and strength to call upon. In most cases, like mine, they know the lay of the land. I didn't. They knew where the exits were. I didn't. They could coordinate a search. I had no clue what was around the next corner.

Great odds, huh?

I made the pine trees and scooted behind a trunk about forty feet in, poked my head out and tried to see what the hunter force looked like.

Five men spilled out of the house, hit the gravel circular drive and paused. All had guns out. One of them gave directions and they fanned out. Two of them headed toward my direction.

I ducked back. They'd seal off the driveway first, since it probably led to a gate. It made sense. If they were dealing with someone else. Humans and animals always take the least path of resistance. Normally, it's also the fastest.

But I'm neither animal nor human.

I'd go out another way.

I ran through the pine trees, away from what I thought would be the location of the gate. The ground here was a mixture of melting snow, damp muddy soil, and soft pine needles. It would make tracking me harder. If I could find a fence and get over it to the streets beyond, I'd make it.

I hoped the fence wasn't electrified. I had enough singed hair to last a lifetime.

I pushed through the thickening grove of trees. Pine needles clawed at my face and exposed skin, while the cold burned my ears and made my sinuses run down my face. Snot froze on crusty blood, and sweat broke out on my chest. I was all set for my centerfold shoot tonight, no doubt.

Breathing was tougher out here and my adrenaline levels had spiked again for the umpteenth time tonight.

I heard some crunching a few hundred yards behind me.

My pursuers.

I paused and listened to their footfalls. They were cautious. Tentative. They weren't on to me yet. They probably thought I'd head for the gate.

I considered taking them out, too, but decided against it. Killing them would waste valuable time and alert the others that I wasn't where they thought I was. All I needed to do was get over the wall and I'd be home free.

Hopefully.

I edged my way through another two hundred yards of pine trees and finally ran face-first into a brick wall.

And another problem.

The damned wall was a good twelve feet high.

I looked back. No room to run and try some of that *shotenjutsu* vertical wall climbing I'd been itching to try out for some time. But there were thick branches that would get me closer to the wall.

I shinned up the nearest tree.

Crunching footsteps suddenly sounded closer than they should have.

I stopped.

The whispered voices and bouncing flashlight beam came out of nowhere. I hugged the tree trunk about ten feet off the ground and slowed my breathing down.

". . . already gone, for crying out loud."

". . . waste of damned time. It's fucking freezing out here."

"Check the wall and we'll make our way back to the gate. That way, they can't say we didn't check."

The flashlight stopped at the base of the wall.

"See something?"

Two heads in knit caps poked out of the darkness below me. One of them stooped and looked at the ground. After a minute, he stood.

"Nah, it's nothing."

"Well, hurry up, then, and let's go. My balls are gonna drop off if I stay out here much longer."

They pushed through the tree branches to my left and kept talking. I waited until they were gone and then climbed a few feet higher.

I could see over the wall.

Boston's skyline sat in the distance.

Where the hell was I?

No time to lose, I reached out and grabbed the upper lip of the wall and pulled myself on top of it. Crouching, I looked down along the outside, checking to see if any of Petrov's people were posted outside the property.

Nothing.

The neighborhood was dotted with similarly elaborate mansions on both sides of the street. Petrov might not want to call too much attention by posting people outside the perimeter.

My luck.

I took a breath and dropped down to the ground on the other side. Twelve-foot drops don't take any wind out of me, but I exhaled on contact, anyway, out of instinct—felt the sting on the undersides of my feet and rolled to compensate.

A damned good thing I did too—the bullet that splanged off the wall, close to my head, barely missed me.

I ran before I knew I was running. My bare feet clawing up the sidewalk made me wince from the pain. I kept my head low as another round zoomed past me.

Someone had apparently decided I was better off dead than alive. I wondered if Petrov had sanctioned it.

I zigzagged through some parked cars.

Footsteps behind me. Maybe three sets.

This was not good. I hadn't had any juice in almost eighteen hours and my energy level was sapped. A prolonged fight or race for my life would leave me dying if I wasn't careful.

I flew into another yard, down a winding side pathway,

heard a dog start barking, then hit another fence, which was fortunately only about eight feet high.

This time, I'd had enough space to build momentum and basically used that to run right up the wall and over the other side.

I landed on brown grass and snow, which felt better to my feet than cement. I was suddenly in a busier section of town.

My lungs felt like fire.

My vision blurred.

I bent over, trying to catch my breath.

And came back up, ready to run some more.

Ahead of me, I caught sight of a convenience store. If I could get there—

Voices behind me sent more adrenaline surging into my bloodstream. It'd take me a while to recoup all that I'd used tonight.

I ran for the store.

My legs felt like wet noodles dragging me down to the sidewalk. And then, right in front of me with its white light on—

a taxi.

I fell for the door, fumbling with the latch.

Why wouldn't it open?

Voices—

—shots.

Splang!

Too close.

A click. The door unlocking.

I fell inside, jerking the door shut behind me.

"Where to, buddy?"

"Drive! Just drive!" I ducked down as the cabbie put the pedal to the floor and we screeched away from the sidewalk.

Away from my pursuers.

Away from Petrov.

I leaned back into the vinyl bench seat and gulped air like a newborn suckling his first breast.

Alive.

Still.

Chapter Sixteen

It took the taxi twenty minutes to drive into Boston.

As we passed some familiar streets, I finally knew where I'd been held: on the Newton/Chestnut Hill line, an area with lots of big houses, tree-lined streets, and money.

I tried memorizing the details of the area as we drove. I'd need them later on when I went back to discuss things with Petrov—on my terms.

The cabbie kept stealing glances in the rearview mirror at me. "You, uh . . . okay there, Mac?"

I looked down at my chest and stomach. I was covered in dirt, blood, sweat, and oozing wounds. I must have looked like hell.

"I'm all right. I'll be better when I can get cleaned up."

He nodded. "No shit."

I directed him to Wirek's place. Ordinarily, that goes against pretty much all of trade craft rules. But the fact of the matter was that I was half naked, cold, wounded, and had no cash with me. Petrov still had my wallet. That wasn't so much of a problem as it was a temporary inconvenience. I had doubles of everything back at my place.

But I'd need to pay the cabbie. After all, he'd pretty much saved my life.

We rolled off Storrow Drive down by Mass General Hospital and under the Red Line station. We swerved into the circle by the liquor store and I told him to stop.

He looked back over the seat. "Lemme guess: you ain't got your money with you."

"Good guess. You wait here; I'll get you some."

He frowned. "Yeah, sure. . . ."

"I'm not lying. My friend lives around here. Just give me a minute to get some cash off him."

He eyed me some more. "I'll wait. You don't come back down, I call the cops."

I almost smiled. After the night I'd had, there wasn't much Boston's "boys in blue" could do that would scare me.

I stepped out of the cab and into a puddle by the curb. I shook my foot loose of the junk and leaned on Wirek's buzzer. The cold February night swirled around me. I hoped Wirek was awake.

Thankfully, he was quick on the door release.

I shot upstairs. Wirek met me at the door.

"What the hell?"

"I need twenty bucks."

He frowned. "Looks like you need more than that, pal." He vanished back inside the apartment and returned in a few seconds. He tossed me a T-shirt. "Try that on for starters."

I pulled the shirt on. "The money?"

He handed me a twenty. "Get a receipt."

I laughed, went back downstairs, and paid the cabbie.

"Tell your dispatch you dropped me off a few blocks, away, all right?"

By the time I got back upstairs, Wirek had already drawn a bath. Steam poured out of the bathroom. And despite the dirty grout, a tub never looked so inviting.

Wirek came out. "Get yourself cleaned up. And pay attention to those wounds. Jesus, what the hell—" He stopped. "Never mind. Get cleaned up first. We can talk afterward."

I slid my stinking pants off along with my jockey shorts and Wirek's T-shirt. Stepping into the hot bath felt real good. And then it hurt like hell as soon as the water touched my fresh wounds.

I grimaced but sank into the tub just the same, closing my eyes, inhaling the steam and trying hard to put tonight out of my mind—just for a little bit.

It took me a while to clean out the deep cuts on my torso. Small embedded stones took forever to pick out. By the time I was done, I was bleeding again, but only a little bit. It stained the foggy water as I soaped up one last time and then pulled the plug.

I saw the gauze and tape on the vanity and grinned. Wirek was remarkably well supplied. I dressed the wound first and then finished toweling off.

Wirek knocked on the door. "Got some stuff here for you to put on."

I opened the door and took the clothes. He nodded at my chest. "Clean?"

"Yeah."

"There's shorts and another T-shirt there oughtta fit you. I don't have much else. You're bigger than I am, so pants are out."

"This is fine. Gimme a minute and I'll be out."

I slid into the clothes. Worn as they were, they felt soft going on.

Wirek sat nursing a cup of coffee on the couch when I came out. "Got some more on the stove, if you're interested."

"Tea?"

"Bags in the cupboard. Help yourself."

I fixed myself a cup and then sat down in his recliner. It eased back, elevating my legs. "Damn, that feels good."

"Looks like I could offer you a porcupine pillow and that'd be better than what you went through tonight."

"Just about."

"I'm guessing the recon of your house didn't go so well."

I toasted him with my mug. "You are wise beyond your years."

"Yeah, I know." He took a sip of coffee. "Tell me about it."

I did. When I finished, he just looked at me and shook his head. "Helluva night."

"Understatement."

"How's your back?"

"Why?"

"Electrical burns. You got any?"

"Don't think so. I don't feel it."

"Good. It's bad enough you'll have some scars on your chest for a while." He sighed. "So, what now?"

"I don't know."

"Well, you can't go home. Petrov will keep a watch on your place. That's elementary. Plus, if what you said is true, he'll be gunning for the boy even more now."

"And now he's likely pretty pissed off I escaped."

"And how," said Wirek. "You need a plan, my friend."

"I need sleep." I looked at the tea and frowned. "And juice. You got any?"

"Juice?"

"Blood."

He grinned. "That's right. I remember hearing you called it that." He chuckled and walked to the kitchen. I watched him go and didn't say anything. I didn't particularly feel like explaining myself to him right then.

He returned with a tall glass filled with blood. I drank it down straight, feeling the life force hit me a few seconds later.

I brought the glass away from my lips. "Thanks. I haven't had anything all day."

"Christ, Lawson, you gotta take better care of yourself. You can't go out looking for the kind of trouble Petrov brings on without nourishing up first. Take some responsibility, would you?"

I smiled. Hearing that kind of talk from a drunk like Wirek was strangely ironic. I told him as much.

"Recovering alcoholic to you." He thumbed at the guest room, where Jack was sleeping. "It's a bad example for the kid, drinking all that tequila."

"Does this couch fold out into a bed or what?"

He rolled his eyes. "Don't tell me I just inherited another houseguest."

"Like you said, I can't go home. I need to get some rest. Tonight took a lot out of me."

"Yeah, you really look like shit."

"As appraised by the resident expert." I grinned. "You mind?"

"I got no choice." He got up and found some musty, old blue blankets and sheets. "I'll keep the heat up tonight to compensate for my lack of linens."

"How's Jack?"

"Amazing."

"Excuse me?"

Wirek stopped fitting a pillowcase. "I said he's amazing. We did some practicing tonight."

"What kind of practicing?"

"Nothing spectacular, just basic stuff to get the kid on his feet. He needs to learn how to control what he can do. He's got more natural talent than anyone I've ever seen with regard to that kind of ability."

"You've seen a lot?"

Wirek shrugged. "Some. A long time ago. No one like the boy. His power comes to him like a breath of air."

"How does he do it?"

Wirek finished with the pillows. "It's just a matter of getting in touch and in sync with the proper energies is all. The boy there does it simply by emotion."

"You mean if he likes something?"

"No, more like if he's worried, concerned, angry . . . that type of thing."

"Makes sense. Back at his house on Saturday, he was really worried, all right. Those guys were going to kill us."

"Exactly. I led him through some simple channeling exercises tonight that don't rely so much on emotion as they do sheer intent. If he can be trained to invoke the spirit energies with intention rather than emotion, he'll be much more powerful. And more in control."

"Where'd you learn how to do this?"

He eyed me. "Wasn't always a drunk, you know. I did some traveling a while back. You pick up things."

"How long do you think it will take him to get a handle on his power?"

Wirek eased himself back into his recliner. "Could take years, could take days. I don't really know. I've never worked with a protégé before. After all, this isn't really my gig. The boy needs formal training."

"There's formal training for this?"

Wirek smiled. "You don't know everything about our society, Lawson. Try to remember that."

"So what is it, a special school or something?"

"Yes. Like the Fixer training you went through, there's a school for gifted children like the boy. The training is arduous by any standards, but they come out with the control necessary."

"And then what?"

"They fulfill other job functions in our society."

"Jobs? Invoking spirits is a job?"

"It can be," said Wirek. "It just depends on your perspective."

I lay down on the couch. The blankets felt great against my skin. "Kid took his dad's death pretty well, all things considered."

"No other family?"

I sighed. "Nope. Mom died when he was younger. It's just been him and his father for the last few years."

Wirek was quiet for a minute. "Want to tell me about the father?"

I sat up. "Who told you?"

"I did some checking."

I shot a glance at Jack's room. "Keep your voice down, he'll hear us."

"What did they tell you about him?"

"I thought it was just another assignment, for God's sake. His dossier must have been bogus. According to what I was given, he'd been dealing drugs all over town." I shook my head. "You know the sentence that one carries."

Wirek nodded. "If you get an assignment, the sentence is pretty standard."

"They must have set him up. Told him to go out there where I was waiting. Told him anything to get him where I'd find him. They knew I'd do the job without question."

"Well, you have been on thin ice with them lately. Whoever set him up knew that much about you."

"How the hell do you know I'm on thin ice?"

Wirek chuckled. "Lawson, I might have been a drunk, but I'm not a fool. I know a few folks who still roam the halls of power. I hear things." He jabbed a finger at me. "You, my friend, fell in love with a human."

I took a sip of my tea. Cold. I looked at Wirek. "Yes, I did."

He chuckled. "Ain't moral ambiguities a bitch?"

"My whole life has become a bit of a bitch as of late," I said. "Moral ambiguities notwithstanding."

"Still involved with her?"

I looked at him. "You really want me to answer that?"

"I think you just did." He looked away. "You gonna tell the boy?"

"What would you do in my situation?"

Wirek shrugged. "I'm not you."

"Pretend."

"Some other time."

I frowned. "You know what his father said to me as he lay dying? He said, 'Protect my son.' He knew, Wirek. He knew he'd been set up as soon as I told him the Council sent me. Looking back on it now, I know he realized it. I thought he was just being noble—you know, the final request? Hell, he knew someone sold him out."

Wirek was quiet for a few moments. "I guess that I wouldn't tell the boy. At least not right now. Maybe some day you'll have to. But that's not one of those things I'd be in a rush to confess."

"Confessions are never my strong point."

"You said the order came from the Council?"

"They all do."

"Good point," said Wirek. "Still, it means only one thing: someone on the Council is dirty."

"Yeah, especially since they'd be the only ones to have

knowledge of an Invoker in the vicinity. That's not common knowledge, after all."

"Other members of the Council may not even know."

I took a final gulp of cold tea. "And they must have contacted Petrov. Arranged for him to grab Jack while I was doing the real dirty work by getting rid of his father. That way, there'd be no one to raise a stink."

"The boy would, in effect, disappear."

I didn't like the feeling of being used for someone's ulterior motives. I especially didn't like the feeling of knowing that I'd killed Jack's last real family. I'd deal with the second thing in my own way, in my own time.

But I'd deal with the first thing a lot sooner.

"I suppose the logical step is to find out whose house you were in tonight."

I nodded. "Newton. On the edge of Brookline and Chestnut Hill."

Wirek looked pained. "I know where it is, Lawson." He mused for a second. "Lots of expensive houses out there."

"I don't think it was Petrov's place."

"Why not?"

"Too showy. Petrov's here to do a job, not set up residence in some fancy part of town. The little I know about him, I know he likes to maintain a low profile unless he's on home turf."

"He say anything to you tonight that you can remember?"

"Spoke a lot about being turned out by the Council. He had some dirt about a Council member. They hushed it up and flushed him out of the service."

Wirek pursed his lips. "Vengeance factors always complicate things."

"Cover-ups do, too."

"Some of us have never looked at the Council as the pinnacle of upstanding citizenship. Not by a long shot."

I nodded. "I've become a bit jaded about them myself lately."

Wirek smiled. "I'll bet." He began ticking off things on his fingers. "What have we got, then: a traitor in the Council who wants to use the boy for his own purposes, which, as of right now, are indeterminable. And a former Fixer whose out to grab the boy at any cost, killing whoever gets in his way."

I grinned. "I've noticed something odd about you, Wirek."

"Only one thing? You've got a long way to go."

"You can go from the most guttural slang to erudite speech with ease. But you aren't often consistent with it. You bounce around quite a bit."

Wirek cocked an eyebrow. "What does that have to do with the price of bananas in Belize?"

"Not a damned thing. I'm just making a small observation."

"Damned small." Wirek stood and stretched a bit, yawning as he did so. "Get some sleep, Mr. Fixer, you've had a long night. And before this talks really gets philosophical, I'm hitting the rack."

I lay back down, pulling the blankets up.

Wirek turned off the lights and left the room.

In the darkness, bits of light filtered in from the streets, making shadows dance across the walls. I lay there watching them, thinking about Petrov, the Council, and Jack.

Then I thought about Talya.

I thought about her eyes, her smile, the softness of her lips. The way she felt when we made love. The warmth we'd shared for such a short time a few months back.

I missed her.

Falling in love with a human woman was one of the cardinal sins in vampire society. Seduction as a means of getting juice was perfectly fine. But love? No way.

I told the Council it was over. Hell, Talya walked away from me the last time I saw her.

But it was a ruse.

As far as operatives go, Talya was one of the best. And as far as women go, she was tops in my book. I'd be damned if the Council could make me give her up.

I thought about her for a long time. Having her with me now would be a big help. She'd have some great ideas on how to proceed.

As I started to drift off, I saw her face in my mind. Smiling. Sensual. Serious. All at once. I kept that image as long as I could.

And then I fell asleep.

Chapter Seventeen

There's a saying I once heard that went something along the lines of when you're in deep shit and you've got nowhere to turn, the best thing to do is attack.

Waking up the next morning, I realized my options were about as limited as a castrated midget making a career as a porn actor. Actually, mine seemed worse.

And attacking was the best option.

But in order to attack, I needed information. Specifically, I needed the address of where I'd been held the night before. Only after I had that information could I do what I did best: be the fly in the ointment, the sand in the machinery, and the massive speed bump in the middle of the road.

In order to get that kind of information, I'd need Arthur's help. I wasn't sure how thrilled he'd be about that.

I found out in a hurry later that evening when I showed up at the Council building after five o'clock. When I told Arthur what I needed, he crinkled his forehead and snorted.

"Can't do it, lad. The information's stored on a computer."

"I can break into the computer."

"Not bloody likely. It'd be password protected. It's not some silly door you can kick in."

"Just get me to the computer, Arthur. I can handle the rest."

"And what if they've a log that tracks users? Or an alarm? They'd know I let ya in and I'd be cooked." He leaned closer to me. "Lawson, I like my job. Believe it or not. It suits me."

I laid a hand on his shoulder. "Arthur, relax. I know exactly what I'm doing."

"Oh, ya do, do ya?"

"Sure."

He snorted again. "Ya know how many frickin' times I said exactly that same thing?" He grinned. "Usually, it was right before a whole bungload of bells and whistles went screeching off."

"I promise that won't happen."

"I made promises, too, Lawson. And then I broke 'em even faster."

"Arthur, I can do it. Just let me have a crack at it."

"You've no idea what the setup is like."

"But I've got you. You know what the setup is like."

"Oh, sure, drag me right down with ya, is that it?"

"There won't be any dragging down, Arthur."

"Ya damned right there won't be." He eyed me. "You sure you can do it?"

"Honest? No."

"Damn it, Lawson, you're supposed to lie." He sighed.

"The only way this whole mess could be happening is if someone on the Council is dirty, Arthur. We've got one traitor, maybe more, in our midst. It's our duty to root them out."

"All right, all right. Don't you lecture me about duty."

"Sorry."

"All right."

I smiled. "All right?"

"Yeah. If there's one thing I can't stand it's a traitor in the ranks. But you'd better be right about this. If it turns out everyone on the Council's clean, you owe me."

"You got it."

He gestured for me to follow him. "All right, let's make this fast. Come with me."

I'd been in the Council building a few times before, but the place never failed to astonish me. From the outside, it seemed so much smaller, but inside it was a veritable maze of deep, carpeted hallways, rich mahogany walls, and subdued lighting that cast long shadows against a backdrop of old framed portraits and worn leather furniture.

Arthur led me past the stairway that, I knew, wound downstairs to the Council chambers proper. Zero and I had broken in their only a few months back. I sighed, remembering his friendship, and kept walking.

Ahead of us, the corridor forked and we headed left. Ten feet farther on, we came to a door. Arthur withdrew a key and unlocked it. Inside, there was a hum of computer equipment and the temperature seemed a bit cooler than the rest of the house.

"Watch your step," said Arthur, pointing. "Floor's raised."

I stepped up and onto the white-tiled flooring. Green and yellow lights blinked on and off across the room. Arthur flipped the light switch.

Rows of computers lined the room. Probably twenty in all. I whistled. Arthur nodded.

"Heart and soul of the Council's information network. Updates, news, intelligence—it all comes in through here. This is the origin of your assignments. Dossiers on almost every member of our society are stored here as well. All in all, rather impressive, wouldn't you say?"

"Very." I walked around the terminals. "They have off-site storage as well?"

"Yeah. Don't know where. Probably manned by some Loyalists."

I nodded. Loyalists were the very few humans who knew about our existence. For reason I didn't know much about, they agreed to work for us. I know some of them died a few months back, victims of my oldest enemy, Cosgrove. I wondered how many were left.

I pointed at one of the terminals. "So how do we do this?"

" 'We'?" Arthur grinned. "My dear boy, you are very much on your own for this part of your mission. I shall simply point you in the right direction. That computer over there is what you are looking for." He twirled the key. "I can give you ten minutes to find what you need and then I'll be back to lock up. Any longer than that in here and automatic video surveillance gets triggered."

"Why only after ten minutes?"

Arthur shrugged. "I check the room throughout the night. Guess they got tired of seeing me pop onto the screen." He turned and walked out.

The computer he'd pointed me to looked more like an old 286 PC than the rest of the top-of-the-line models on the floor. Its luminescent green monitor came to life when I hit the enter button. A small cursor blinked at the left of the screen.

I checked my watch. Two minutes had already elapsed.

I typed in "addresses."

The computer beeped and asked me for a log-in code.

Crap.

I wished like hell I could have called Benny the Phreak. After all, the guy could crack anything in five minutes flat. Probably faster. And since I'd already burned enough cash using his services this week so far, I figured another couple grand wouldn't hurt.

Unfortunately, Benny would have been able to see the files I was looking at. Then he might start asking some questions. Questions he shouldn't be asking.

Benny was trustworthy. To a point. Beyond that, human curiosity might dictate my killing him. And since I thought he was more useful alive than dead, he'd have to stay out of this caper.

Four minutes gone.

I typed in "guest."

The computer buzzed and told me it was an incorrect log-in. The cursor reappeared asking again.

This time I typed in "user."

Buzz.

Another wrong guess.

Five minutes gone and I sat there muttering obscenities. Did Arthur know the password? It had to be simple. Too many passwords tended to confuse people. It had to be something they could recall easily.

I suddenly had a flash. Since this was supposed to be a secure installation, maybe they weren't too anal about codes being left out in the open.

I turned over the keyboard.

And saw a piece of paper taped to the underside. I sighed and typed in "varot," which I thought meant "truth" in the old language. Whatever it meant, it was obviously the right code, judging by the series of beeps that erupted from the terminal. Instantly, the screen filled with names and numbers.

A quick glance at my watch told me I had three minutes to pore through this junk and find what I needed. I tried sorting the material using the Council as a keyword, but got junk. There were only six members of the Council. The computer had given me a list of two hundred. Unless they were grouped together with the local governments around the world. I typed in ''council-Boston'' and hit enter.

Six names and addresses popped onto the screen.

I hit the print command key and heard a printer pop to life across the room. Two minutes left.

I logged off the terminal and dashed to the other side of the room. The printer was blinking, but nothing was coming out. A yellow light on the side blinked, laughing at me.

It needed paper.

I ran around the room looking for a box of paper, but couldn't find any. Finally, I saw a closet and yanked it open, jerked a ream out of an open box and ran back to the printer.

The tray bounced once as I ripped it out and stuffed a few sheets into it before ramming it home. Instantly, the printer began whirring and printing out the list.

One minute.

The sheet emerged from the spool in slow motion, slowly bleeding into the receptacle.

Thirty seconds.

I ripped the paper out of the printer, ran over to the light switch, shut it off, and tripped out of the room with ten seconds to spare.

Across the hall, Arthur leaned against the wall.

''Find what ya needed, then?''

I exhaled in a rush. ''Whoever said technology would

make life easier didn't know what the fuck they were talking about."

Arthur smiled. "I've often thought the very same thing."

Six names and addresses.

Not bad duty trying to sift through them. But the fact that at least one of them was in all likelihood a traitor made the task hard.

Seated inside my Volvo, I scanned the list and found only one that came close to being in Newton. A woman named Arvella. She lived at an address that bordered Newton and Chestnut Hill. A ritzy part of town where the houses were few and far between, and neighbors didn't ask very many questions.

I drove back to Wirek's place and parked the Volvo around on Charles Street, amazed I found a metered space. Parking down here was always a bitch.

Wirek and Jack were seated on his couch when I opened the door. Jack's eyes were closed. Wirek spoke to him in quiet tones. In the old language.

I'm not much of a history buff. Never have been. I know the barest of facts about my people, but that's never been a problem in my line of work. My job doesn't demand a lot of book knowledge.

But lately I'd found myself becoming more interested in it. Probably because of my old friend Zero. He'd introduced me to some interesting things during our years together.

It was Zero who suggested I study the old language. I knew a few rudimentary phrases, but nothing I could converse with. It occurred to me how strange it was that I spoke over a dozen human languages, but I'd neglected my own.

Wirek looked up as I came in, motioning me to sit down

in the easy chair. I did so, watching Jack all the while. Wirek continued speaking to him.

The temperature in the room grew warm. It felt like a spring breeze at first, but then the intensity of it increased. I felt a line of perspiration break out along my forehead.

Wirek kept talking.

Jack sat still, although his brow was creased—furrowed in deep concentration.

I shifted, trying to get some air under my shirt. It got hotter.

And then, with a simple rush of energy, we were no longer alone in the room. I turned as it rushed past me and then hovered in front of Jack. A bulbous globule of energy. Maybe a spirit.

Jack opened his eyes. Wirek kept speaking in hushed tones. Jack nodded and then closed his eyes again. I thought I saw a brief flutter of an eyelid and then the globe zipped across the room, hovering near the kitchen. Another flutter and it came right back.

This went on for several minutes. Jack seemed to be controlling the energy-spirit thing with his mind, using techniques that Wirek was teaching him.

The energy ball transfixed me. It swirled, transformed, and intermingled all within the space of the sphere. It was like looking into a cloudy crystal ball and seeing anything your imagination wanted to see. At times, I thought I saw a face; other times, it was a swirl of clouds. It sparked and crackled from time to time, usually when Jack gave it a command that sent it spinning off to other parts of the apartment.

After ten minutes of sitting in the stifling heat, there was another rush and the energy vanished. Instantly, a coolness filled the room, relieving the oppressive heat.

I leaned back in the chair, exhaling in a rush. "That was damned impressive."

Jack started and opened his eyes. "Oh . . . hi, Lawson."

"Sorry, slick, didn't mean to scare you."

Wirek beamed like a proud parent. "He's come so far in such a short period of time."

Jack looked at him. "With your help."

"Maybe," said Wirek. "Unfortunately, I'm about out of useful ideas. I have only a little information about the training of Invokers. You need proper schooling, my boy. Only then will you be able to adequately control the spirit energies. Only then will you fully realize your true birthright."

I pulled out the sheet of paper from my back pocket. "Got the information I needed."

Wirek nodded. He looked at Jack. "Go wash your hands with cold water now, like I told you about."

Jack left the room and Wirek moved over closer to me. "He's doing amazingly well. I'm surprised, frankly."

"Why so?"

Wirek shrugged. "He's young. He's lost his father in the last few days. He's unschooled. Those three factors should be inhibiting his ability to control the energy. But it's almost as if it's enhanced it, instead."

"That a good thing or a bad thing?"

"Good. Definitely good. It means he has the discipline of mind to block out the unnecessary emotional flux that could act against him. The most important attribute of an Invoker is the steadfastness of mind and spirit. They must fuse as one and be almost inviolate. Only when that occurs can the Invoker truly control the spirits."

"So I guess now would probably not be the best time to talk to him about his father, huh?"

Wirek snapped around. "Don't even consider it just yet.

If he's not ready for it, it could backlash on him." He pointed at the paper. "What'd you find out?"

"Only one lives near Newton. A woman named Arvella."

Wirek sucked in a breath and then exhaled it in a stream. "Shit."

"Well, that answers my next question. You know her, apparently."

"I wish I didn't."

"Want to explain that to me? I couldn't get the dossier in time. I can use all the information I can get about her."

Wirek got up and walked to the window, peering out of the worn yellow curtains. "Arvella is one of the oldest Council members. She's always had a fascination for the old ways. Needless to say, she's one of the few who does."

I knew what he meant. Despite the Council's obvious public stance on preserving the old ways, most of the members favored a push into the future and considered the ancient traditions something more for formality than actual usage.

"What's her background?"

Wirek let the curtain fall back into place. "She is also . . . an Invoker."

"Oh, crap. You mean she can do what Jack was doing here?"

"And more," said Wirek. "She is one of the best, too, from what I hear." He sighed. "This is bad, Lawson. This is very bad."

"Want to elaborate on that whole 'bad' thing for me? You seem to forget I'm just a dumb Fixer."

"I'm not forgetting." Wirek slumped into the couch. "If Arvella is involved in this, it must mean she needs the boy for something special. Before I thought someone might have desired to have the boy summon the spirits for other reasons."

"And now?"

"If Arvella is involved, it can only be something much more sinister. An Invoker of her skill would have little need of the boy's powers. After all, she can invoke with far greater skill than he."

"Well, what's she want with him, then?"

Wirek shook his head. "I don't know." He frowned. "I feel like I'm missing something. Could be all that damned tequila messing with my head."

"How long has Arvella been on the Council?"

"Could be almost twenty years now." Wirek scratched his crotch. "Before that, she was the headmistress of the school for Invokers."

"This is getting better by the minute."

"And her family line goes back, way back. I don't have to tell you how much that means."

"Usually means the family has an even greater chance of being dirty."

"Sounds like we've had similar experiences."

"More than I care to recount right now."

Wirek nodded and then his head snapped up. "Wait a minute. What's today's date?"

"The eighteenth of February—"

"No, no, no. What's today's date in the old calendar?"

"Hell, if I know. I only go by the same one humans do. I thought we all did. It tends to keep things simpler."

"Sure it does. But it also keeps us from remembering the important days in our own tradition. And that may be just what Arvella wants." He went to his desk and flipped open a worn leather book. After a few minutes, he whistled.

"What?"

"The New Year."

"What about it? It happened a month or so back."

Wirek shook his head. "I'm not talking about the human

New Year. I'm talking about ours. The New Year in our tradition occurs next week."

"So. Big deal."

"Lawson, it's not just a new year. It's the start of the New Millennium."

"Oh. Okay. Well, what's so special about that?"

"It is the one day when the spirit energies converge at one point in the space-time continuum. An Invoker with great enough ability would have the power to bring all that energy onto this plane."

" 'Space-time,' Wirek? What the hell are you talking about? You're starting to sound like some bad sci-fi novel."

"Oh, Lawson, stop being naive! You know as well as I do the energies exist. Spirits don't die when they pass; they simply move on to another state of being. You've seen what Jack can do. You've run into the Sargoth before. You know what can happen." He nodded his head. "It makes perfect sense."

"I'm glad it does to you. I'm still lost."

"Don't you see? Arvella obviously knows about the millennium coming. She knows about Jack. She's trying to bridge the spirit world, bring it here. If she's successful, she can wreak untold havoc. Conceivably, she could take over the world using the spirits."

"Where does Jack fit into the picture?"

"We already discussed the fact that he has an incredible degree of natural talent. He's blessed with a raw power. Sure, it's unmolded, undisciplined. But that may be just what Arvella needs. If she can use Jack to help her bring the spirits into alignment, under her control—"

"Bad, huh?"

Wirek nodded. "Real bad."

"And you said this millennium is happening . . . when?"

"Next week."

"So they'll be pulling out all the stops to try to get Jack before then, huh?"

"Count on it." Wirek came back to the couch and sat down. "We'll have to be very careful."

"I'm already being careful. I'm not sure what else I can do and still try to track down these traitors."

"But we'll have to be careful on a whole new level. We aren't dealing with your ordinary thugs. Arvella being involved means this thing takes on a whole new dimension. A bad—"

But he never finished his sentence.

Because at that moment, the front door of his apartment imploded, showering the room with splinters, dust, and gas.

And even as I fell from the sofa, trying to claw my way to where I knew Jack was, I was already losing ... consciousness.

Chapter Eighteen

The two times I've had the distinct displeasure of being caught in explosions hasn't changed my opinion about the experience much: loosely speaking, it sucks.

Vampires can withstand a lot of damage.

But that doesn't mean we don't feel pain.

So, while the only real danger would have been wooden splinters fragmenting into my body, there was still one helluva concussion wave that knocked me senseless.

Consciousness came flooding back into my skull twenty minutes after the door blew apart. It felt more like my head was being used to batter down a castle wall.

Groggy.

Aching.

"Wake up, Lawson."

I opened my eyes. Wirek knelt over me with a wet navy blue facecloth and slapped it on my forehead. The damp coolness felt good.

I looked up at him. "What the hell happened?" Fuzzy memories of men dressed in black with gas masks wafted back into my mind.

"They got Jack." Wirek handed me a small glass of juice. "That's what happened."

"How?" I drank the juice, feeling a lot better, but only physically.

"Because I'm a damned fool." He sighed. "I should have thought of it. He must have transmitted when I had him practicing his powers."

I sat up and leaned against the wall. "What the hell does that mean?"

"When you develop certain powers—humans call it psychic abilities—they often act as kind of a beacon. Your presence becomes known to others who have similar abilities."

"You mean she tracked him the way we'd trace a phone call?"

"That's a simplified way of putting it, but yes."

"Shit." I got to my feet, feeling pretty woozy. I didn't want to puke. Puking blood leaves the kind of bad taste you simply do not want to have lingering in your mouth. "How come they didn't waste us?"

"I don't know."

That didn't make sense to me. If I'd been in their position, I would have killed anybody I perceived as a threat. Being left alive, while a good thing, also bothered me a great deal.

"That doesn't make sense," I said.

Wirek shrugged. "What the hell, Lawson. I don't know why they didn't kill us. Maybe they had orders not to. Maybe they want us to come find him."

"A challenge? Is that Arvella's style?"

"Dunno. Is it Petrov's?"

"Could be. I doubt it, though. I think he'd opt for the easy route if there was one."

"Well," Wirek responded, grinning, "we can always ask them, I suppose."

"We've got to get Jack back."

"How we gonna do that?" Wirek frowned. "We don't know where they are, Lawson."

"We've got Arvella's address. That's as good a place to start as any."

"They'll expect us to do that."

"Might be why they left us alive."

"I'm not really keen on walking into ambushes."

I grinned. "Good. Neither am I. Let's get going."

"We're really gonna do this?"

"Sure, haven't you ever done anything like this before?"

Wirek frowned. "Lawson, I was an Elder. Violence and I have never gotten along all that well. I'm into books, booze, and broads, not guns, gore, and gambling with my life."

"Well, there's no time like the present to start acquiring a taste for it." I started for the door. Wirek followed slowly behind me.

"Just the two of us, huh? Against all of them."

"We need to make a few stops first."

"Fine," said Wirek. "The more stops we make, the better I'll feel."

I would have liked to have Arthur along on this jaunt, but if he suddenly disappeared from his job at the Council, Arvella and company would have had advanced warning. And the best way to attack is always when it's a surprise.

Or possibly a surprise.

I wasn't kidding myself. There was a damned good chance

we'd walk right into a bushwhack. But Lady Luck hadn't changed the deck lately and the only choice she'd dealt me was the one I'd have to go with.

I risked stopping off at my house.

I didn't think Petrov would bother with anyone there, since they had Jack now. And I needed to feed my cats.

Wirek whistled when we drove up. "Nice pad."

"Family house," I said. "My ancestors built this when we came over from Germany."

"The molding, woodwork . . . Real craftsmen, huh?"

I nodded. "Built a bunch just like it all over the city."

"You own 'em all?"

"No way. Just this one. But they built it for the family. Not for sale. It'll stay in the family forever as far as I'm concerned. My father loved this house. He worked his ass off making sure it was always the best-looking one on the street."

"Do the landscaping yourself?"

"I used to. Schedule's kind of busy nowadays, what with chasing child kidnappers and traitors all over town."

"Damned inconsiderate of them to cut into your garden time like that."

"You said it. Nowadays I hire some of the local kids to mow the lawn, plant a few shrubs, that kind of thing."

I led the way inside and up to the second floor. I heard the chirps from Mimi and Phoebe before we crested the stairs. Phoebe got a look at Wirek and freaked out, running for the upstairs bedroom.

"Schizophrenic," I said. "Doesn't like strangers much."

"A schizophrenic cat? Never heard of such a thing."

"You have now."

In the kitchen, I opened two cans of catfish and plopped them into the bowl. Phoebe reappeared. Her appetite always did win out over her various phobias.

Mimi seemed more interested in nuzzling me and getting some quality affection in. I spent a few minutes with her and then nudged her toward the food dish before Phoebe polished it all off and added another layer of fat to her already ample midsection.

Wirek checked out the Japanese paintings in my sitting room. "So, what are we getting here?"

"Weapons," I said. "You ever do any shooting?"

"Long time ago. Long time. Years. I think it was called a musket back then."

I nodded. "Well, here's hoping you haven't forgotten." I went into the study and pulled a section of the white bookcase aside. A hollowed-out nook behind the books served as my gun safe. I unlocked it and swung the heavy steel door open.

"Holy shit," said Wirek.

I smiled. I'm not a gun freak. As far as I'm concerned, most important thing about weapons is they do what they're supposed to do. Namely, go bang and launch a projectile at a bad guy. I don't care what the rate of fire is, how many feet per second the rounds go, or any of that stuff. If it holds bullets and fires when I pull the trigger, we can do business.

But even I recognize the need for superior firepower. And heading out to Arvella's estate, thick as it was liable to be with bad guys, we were definitely going to need more than just pistols.

I took out a Mossberg shotgun and handed it to Wirek. "Here, you don't need to be a marksman to use this. Just point and it'll spray enough shot to cover a room." I popped a box of rounds into his hand. "Loads underneath."

"A shotgun? It just sprays buckshot, doesn't it?"

"Not these rounds. Think of them more as hardened BB pellets of various hardwoods. Nasty shock to our kind, I'll tell you."

"What if they're not vampires?"

"You get hit with that stuff, no matter what you are, you'll go down. The closer the better, by the way. Don't shoot if you aren't within about fifteen feet. Any farther away and the spread fans out too much to do much damage."

"What about you?"

I reached back into the safe and took out the Heckler & Koch MP5. It had been modified some time back by the Fixer armorer here in town. It shot 9mm rounds of the same variety that I carried in my pistol. Wooden tips that exploded and fragmented on impact. Again, a nasty shock to a vampire, and a bad case of splinters for humans.

I took four extra clips of thirty rounds each and tucked them into the assault bag I kept in the safe as well.

Wirek hefted the shotgun. "This is kind of heavy."

"You'll be fine." I handed him a pistol. "Backup. Don't use it unless you have to. And for God's sake, don't shoot me in the back."

Wirek looked down at the two guns he held and shook his head. "Life sure does have a way of fucking with you sometimes, doesn't it?"

"Be grateful you don't get it every day like me."

Wirek chuckled. "Once an Elder, then a drunk. Now a gun-toting fool who's probably going to get his ass shot off." He looked at me. "How the hell do you do this shit?"

"It's my job." I shut the gun safe and replaced the bookshelves. "Come on. We don't have much time."

Wirek tagged along behind me. "So, what's the plan?"

I stopped. "Thinking up the plan was your job."

His eyes widened. "What?"

I clapped him on the shoulder. "Forget it, it was just a joke. We'll discuss our options in the car."

Chapter Nineteen

Going into combat is funny.

Especially when you know it's coming.

Little things that might barely have registered a moment earlier suddenly took on a new light. Potholes, as common as bad drivers in Boston during the winter months, seemed to sprout everywhere, causing me to slalom the car like an Olympic hopeful. Specks of dried brown slush at the fringes of the windshield loomed larger, reminding me the Volvo was overdue for a cleaning.

But overhead, the gray afternoon dissolving into a dark navy blue evening sky looked more beautiful than usual.

Wirek kept his thoughts to himself.

I looked over a few times, but he seemed still, internally focused no doubt. Part of me found it hard to believe that he'd never been in a fight before. Sure, he was an ex-Elder, one of those chosen members of vampire society who preserves the old ways and passes on his knowledge to others. But looking at Wirek, I always got the impression there was a lot more to him than met the eye.

The traffic on Hammond Pond Parkway crawled during the rush hour commute. We inched along. Slowly.

Wirek perked up. "Well, what's the plan?"

"I'm working on it."

"You're working on it?"

"Yeah. I'll have something put together by the time we get there."

"Uh . . . okay." He turned back to the window.

"Tell me something, Wirek."

He looked over at me. "Yeah?"

"What made you give it up?"

"Give what up?"

"Being an Elder. Something must have caused you to retire. What was it?"

"Kind of personal, don't you think?"

"You don't feel like sharing?"

"It's a long story."

I pointed at the bumper-to-bumper traffic. "We going anywhere fast?"

He sighed. "You're a pushy bastard, Lawson."

"I've been told that, yeah."

"Being an Elder is a lot like being a Fixer, you know? You don't really ever 'give it up,' per se. Once you're in, you're always in . . . except in extraordinary circumstances."

"All right, but you've never acted like much of an Elder around me. I mean, my impression was that you guys were all holier-than-thou."

" 'Holier-than-thou'?"

"Considering what kind of knowledge you have, yeah."

"We've got the same knowledge anyone else in our society could have if they read the same books, Lawson. We're not so special."

"I don't buy that. I know there are some elements to being an Elder that are pretty damned special."

"What we are," said Wirek, "is a fucking endangered species."

"Why so?"

He sighed. "You know how many people want to become Elders? Not many."

"You don't exactly advertise, though, do you?" I looked at him.

"No. We're chosen. Like Fixers. Like Invokers. Like other traditions. But telling someone what the profession entails can be a real downer. Most of our kind want nothing to do with it."

"Really?" I worked my way into the left lane and managed to gain three feet of road.

"Our people have in so many ways rejected the old traditions. They're focused on tomorrow. Always tomorrow. Can they get a bigger house? Can they get more money? They raise children on television and video games without so much as an ounce of discipline. Have you seen the new cars and minivans that have television sets in them? It's like another excuse not to even talk to your children. Our kind are growing up with no sense of history. The failings of humans are all around us. And I guess in some ways it's impossible to escape their influence."

"Is that what made you so disenchanted?"

"Not exactly. I realized a long time ago the ways were changing. Oh, sure, there are holdouts. Certain aspects of our society will always stay attuned to the laws of nature and our old ways, but there are so very few of us in those secret circles. . . . We're a minority."

"A powerful minority, though."

"Minorities usually are. It's why those in the majority fear them. They know the power they wield."

"Go on." A giant Ford Suburban cut me off and I briefly considered flipping him the bird. I decided against it. I didn't think road rage was popular with Wirek.

He continued. "For me, the turning point came a few years back when I began seeing how much corruption extended its evil hands into the most sacred aspects of our society. I saw members of the local governments delve into things that warrant them a visit by one of your colleagues, Lawson. And I saw members of the Council turn a blind eye to it, simply because it wasn't deemed as necessary for intervention."

"You're being too general. What was it in particular that made you change your mind?"

Wirek sighed. "You don't let up too easy, do you?"

"Persistence is a virtue in my line of work."

"Hmph. I guess." He fiddled with the heater. "Well, Mr. Persistence, all new Elders are apprenticed to an old member for on-the-job training. In my case, I got paired with an Elder years older than I was or even am right now. This guy was ancient. I remember the first time I saw him: he had flaps of skin hanging off, sheets of freckled flesh. His hair exploded out of his head like some kind of strange Albert Einstein look. He always kept a pipe hanging off his lower lip. I used to think it was going to fall off, but it never did."

"Nifty trick."

Wirek looked at me, but he didn't comment on my choice of words. "He spent years schooling me, carefully imparting his wisdom of times past. The laws, the lore, the virtues . . . even the vices of our people. His knowledge seemed boundless. He knew whole tomes by heart, could recite every legend in the old language. He amazed me.

"I used to think how lucky I was to have found a teacher like him. It was so rare to actually find an Elder so old and so . . . unscathed by the ways of society. I sponged off this guy. Soaked up everything he had to teach me and then asked for more. And I learned it all. In a relatively short time, I was appointed to a rank of some importance within the Elder community."

"You have ranks?"

"Like bishops in human churches, yes. I was known as the *Kaldak* for the Northeast."

" *'Kaldak'?"*

"It means 'one endowed with the ages.' "

"Okay."

"I came to Boston to work directly with the Council. And I was still young enough to feel proud of my accomplishment. There's nothing wrong with a little pride, you know. If you've worked hard for something, made sacrifices and relinquished a lot of yourself, there's nothing wrong with sitting back for a moment to appreciate the view."

"I've done that on occasion."

Wirek nodded. "So you know what I mean. Anyway, I came to Boston full of ideas about how to save our race. I proposed a series of outlines and initiatives aimed at bringing us back around to the old ways. I wanted our kind to disdain human vices. Embrace the past, I said. Reject the future. It seemed sound at the time, but I know now it was foolish naïveté. Call it youthful idealism if you want, whatever the case, it was stupid."

"Maybe not so stupid, Wirek. It sounds like a respectable ideal."

"Maybe to some extent it was. But it was flawed at the same time. I addressed the Council one day. I was giving a nonsense report on some trivial matter. The Council members seemed uninterested in it. No doubt, I was equally uninterested. The subject of who I studied under came up."

"Didn't they know ahead of time?"

"Not necessarily. Elders keep a very low profile. I was appointed not by the Council, but by the governing body of Elders."

I kept silent. The traffic was moving again and I worked hard to keep us in the steady flow toward Newton.

"I told them all about my great teacher," said Wirek. "I spewed such idol worship I must have really sounded fanatical. But I'd trained under a man I truly believed was great. He was someone to look up to, a pillar of our community.

"Anyway, when I finished, they all sat there with smiles on their faces. I asked them what they thought was so funny. They told me, Lawson, that the man I studied with, the Elder of Elders, the one I so desperately wanted to emulate—they told me he had recently been killed by a Fixer."

"For what reason?"

Wirek looked out the window. "For molesting a young child. Turned out he was a pedophile."

My stomach turned over. Pedophiles in my book rank even lower than racists and terrorists. And that is serious scum.

Wirek kept going. "It apparently wasn't the first time. He'd done it for years. While I was studying with him, even. But he'd never touched me. Hell, I never even suspected anything was amiss."

He looked at me now. "Do you know what it's like to have every one of your dreams dashed so completely in the space of just a few precious seconds? Knowing that you will never, ever feel the same about anything? That you'll never look at things the same way?"

"Possibly."

"Well, I became a jaded, cynical bastard in the space of about thirty seconds. I wanted so much to not believe their lies. I wanted to walk out of there, to try and rationalize their contempt as jealousy of the great man my tutor was." He cleared his throat. I kept looking straight ahead.

"But they weren't lies, Lawson. They told me the truth. And they destroyed me in the process."

He sighed. "Perhaps it was my fault. If I hadn't built him up so much in my mind, if I hadn't worshiped him so completely, maybe I wouldn't have been so devastated. But I was."

I wove around a double-parked red Toyota in Newton Center. "I'm sorry."

Wirek ignored me. "I turned to the bottle. I started drinking every ideal I'd once espoused into liquid oblivion. If it was a vice, I embraced it. Certainly not to the depraved extent that my teacher had. I could never do that."

Thank god. I couldn't tolerate Wirek if he'd molested kids.

"But I took drugs, drank, smoked, cavorted with hundreds of human women, let myself go and generally became a slovenly pig." He tapped the dashboard. "And all the while I blamed my former teacher. I blamed him for everything I did. Anytime I needed an excuse, he was there to take the fall. But it wasn't really his fault. Oh, sure, he did the worst things imaginable and I certainly would never condone them. But in terms of my own behavior, he wasn't to blame. Only I was. You understand that, Lawson?"

"I think so."

He looked at me for a second before nodding. "There's a cult of victimization that runs rampant in every society. And if it grows unchecked long enough, it will gain momentum and carry everyone along with it. When people start looking for excuses to shirk responsibility, when they start blaming something else for a lack of discipline, you know it's almost too late."

"We may be too late then."

Wirek nodded. "It's possible. But if enough people stay true to the laws of personal discipline and the laws of nature, there will always be hope. Even if there's just a few of us left."

"I don't know how much of an upstanding member of society I've been, Wirek. I wouldn't go using me as an example."

He smiled for the first time in several minutes. "I don't think your love for a human excludes you from the good vampire club, Lawson."

"The Council may not agree with your assessment."

"To hell with the Council. For the most part, they're hypocrites. Endowed with the power of massive bureaucracies, there's no telling what kind of damage they can do."

"I'd agree with the hypocrisy part of that."

"So, what'd they tell you? You had to get rid of her, right? It was either that or they'd kick you out of the service? Maybe even send another Fixer to pay you a visit?"

"Something like that."

"Indeed. And you told them you'd break it off, right?"

"You're the one with all the information, Wirek. You tell me."

"All right, that's just what you did. And you might have meant it, I don't know. But love has a way of bypassing all that silly crap the Council imposes on us, doesn't it?"

"What do you mean?"

"What I mean, Lawson, is that you still love her. And if I'm still the keen judge of character I used to be, she still loves you. Hell, you two probably have some sort of arrangement worked out—no, don't go telling me, I don't want to know for certain. But don't think for a second that you're not a good man in spite of your transgression. True love obeys no laws, even the ones you hold up."

"Thanks."

"Thanks nothing. Zero wouldn't have been your friend if you weren't a decent guy. And I happen to know that among the Fixers I've liked best, the temptation to fool around and fall in love with human women has usually been too great to resist. Hell, Zero fell in love and married one of them. Talk about balls on that guy." He sighed. "Damn, I miss that bastard."

"You and I both. So you knew about his marriage?"

"I was a character witness at his hearing. Zero and I, we go way back. Maybe I'll even tell you about it sometime. Provided you get me through this crap we're about to undertake in one piece."

"Deal. So, what made you come out of your hermitage?"

"Why, the very boy we're going to rescue, Lawson. I would have thought that was obvious."

"Not necessarily."

He smiled. "I see in Jack the same way I used to be. His eyes, if you look into them, they hold that same idealism I once cherished. There's some real power behind his spirit. He can do great good for our people. Maybe I saw that and wanted to help him. Maybe I'm still working through my mistakes. I don't really know."

"On the subject of your mistakes, you ever have any regrets about your life? Would you have done things differently knowing what you know now?"

Wirek turned down the heater. "I used to ask myself that very same question all the time, usually when I was coming down off some cheap high and sleeping off a hangover. It's funny how when you sink into oblivion you become real philosophical. The best thinkers in this world are the drunks and addicts. They see the bottom of the barrel—hell, they live it. And they come up with some pretty profound shit while they're down there."

I didn't say anything. Personally, I've known some pretty

stupid drunks and addicts who couldn't reason their way out of a See Dick Run–level book.

"But to answer our question, no, I wouldn't do anything differently. I'm a firm believer in the power of experience. We go through bad shit so it tests us. Sometimes we get hit hard and sink like stones. Other times we float to the top and face that adversity head-on. I've done some things in hindsight that look bad. But I don't regret any of them. Life wasn't meant to be regretted. It was meant to be lived. That means we take the good and the bad with equanimity. I think that's where true courage and discipline come from. That ability to meet the bad, to take it on regardless of fear."

"Glad to hear you say that, Wirek."

"Yeah?"

I slowed the car down next to the curb on the tree-lined street. Overhead, the first stars began poking out in the darkness. "Yeah. Because we're about to experience some decidedly bad shit."

Wirek looked at me. I nodded.

"We're here."

Chapter Twenty

I parked around the corner from the main house and gate.

Wirek looked at the walled compound. ''Impressive.''

''You should see the inside of the place. It's pretty sweet.''

''I never would have figured Arvella for having enough money to buy a place like this.''

''No?'' I slid the car into park and leaned back into the leather seat, trying to stretch and release some of the tension that had begun creeping into my body.

''Uh-uh. The Arvella I knew wasn't into material possessions.''

''Times change, apparently. The mansion house is a real spread. Mahogany wood paneling, carpeted hallways, the works. And I didn't even have the guided tour.''

''Well, maybe they'll oblige you this go around, huh?''

''Yeah, maybe.''

Wirek shifted. ''So, when do we go?''

I checked the dashboard clock. ''A few more minutes. I

want it a little darker outside." I closed my eyes. "Keep an eye out, will ya?"

"You're sleeping?"

I opened one eye. "I wouldn't call it that. I'm just resting before we go in."

"How can you even think about that? I'm scared shitless." He shifted in his seat, trying to cross his legs and failing. He sighed. "I'd kill for some tequila right now."

"I'm always nervous before something like this."

"You don't seem to be."

"This is just how I try to deal with it is all. It doesn't work for everyone. Hell, I'm not even sure if it works for me. But everyone has a little ritual they go through before combat."

"I never knew there were so many requirements."

"Neither did I," I said, recalling the first time I'd ever gone into the shit. I'd had Zero with me back then. He'd been my mentor. He guided me through the preassault jitters that kept me up most of the night before puking my guts out. I smiled at the thought. How long ago was that faraway evening back in Alexandria?

Wirek fiddled with the radio. "You mind?"

"Knock yourself out. No boy bands, though."

"What the hell is a boy band?"

"A manufactured teen-idol musical group that generates untold profits for the people who back them."

"See?" said Wirek. "First Internet porn and now this. . . . Damn, I've missed out on everything."

I couldn't tell if he was joking or not, so I smiled halfway in apprcciation. Behind my closed eyes, I was rehearsing how we'd hit the house. If I'd been by myself or someone who was in decent shape, we might have gone over the wall. But with Wirek in tow, we'd have to hit the front gate and do a frontal approach. We'd lose surprise pretty quick, but then again, I felt pretty certain they wouldn't kill Jack. They needed him alive, apparently. That gave us a certain measure of advantage. But only a damned small one.

Wirek passed a classical music station in favor of a thudding techno bass line. I opened my eyes. "You like this?"

He was bopping in the front seat. "This stuff is great. Total body syncopation. I love it."

Jesus. I had a nine-hundred-year old ex-Elder in the front seat of my Volvo who happened to love techno music. If my life got any more bizarre, I was gonna need help living it.

I watched twenty minutes tick away to nothing. I reached behind my seat for the assault bag. I unzipped it. We'd take out the guns once we were closer to the gate. I didn't think the local cops would appreciate a pair of vampires walking down a side street armed to the teeth, no pun intended.

I looked at the dashboard clock. "Time."

Wirek snapped off the radio and I watched the apprehension flood back into his body. I clapped him on the shoulder again. "Relax and follow my lead. You'll do fine."

He just looked at me.

But there was nothing left to say.

I opened the car door and got out.

The cold February night air embraced us. My breath stained the air in front of my face with a gray mist. I could feel my heartbeat tick up a notch. Wirek got out of the car and pulled his jacket tighter around him.

We walked the street over toward the main gate. There seemed to be very little activity on the street. Good. I took a quick peek around the corner and saw nothing out of the ordinary. Hopefully, we'd be crashing the party unexpected.

I knelt down, pulled Wirek's shotgun out and handed it to him. He took it and ratcheted a round in the chamber. In the crisp night air, the ratcheting sounded like a sharp crack that echoed all over the street, louder than I hoped it was.

I took out the MP5 and a small surprise I'd brought along for the front gate.

I took the lead and approached carefully, trying to keep my shadow from looming ahead of me. But the streetlight overhead wasn't being cooperative, so my shadow reached the gate about two seconds before I did.

No matter. It was too late to back out.

I reached the gate.

The heavy iron bars were a formidable obstacle. Temporarily. I slid the package in my hand in between the brick wall and the gate hinges, flipped the tiny switch, then beat a hasty retreat back toward where Wirek squatted on the cold sidewalk.

I counted back in my head.

I turned—the explosion rocked the gate. Surprise vanished.

We moved.

The small block of plastic explosive had tossed the gate aside easily, creating a nice hole for us to get through.

"Don't bunch up," I said. Then we passed through onto the grounds.

Wirek fanned right. I swept left.

I spotted the first guard and brought him down with a triburst from the MP5. On my right, I heard Wirek blast away with the Mossberg. Two guards fell writhing in pain. Vampires.

Another guard appeared at the mansion doorway. I brought the MP5 up, sighted and fired. The gun kicked slightly as three rounds rocketed toward my target. He caught them square in the forehead and sagged against the doorway, blood streaming everywhere.

Wirek and I reached the house, stepped over his body, and slid inside.

Absolute quiet enveloped us like a thick wool blanket, blotting out everything. I looked at Wirek. He frowned. I almost smiled at the sight of the old guy hefting the shotgun. But he looked more confident now. That was good. Part of me had been concerned he might freeze up.

I moved toward the staircase. Maybe they were holding Jack downstairs in the subbasement. I opened the secret door and led the way through to the other corridor with the muzzle of the MP5 taking point.

The quiet followed us.

Wirek looked at me. "I don't like this."

I nodded. We were either being set up for a massive ambush or something was definitely wrong. The resistance at the front gate had been remarkably light. Not that I was complaining.

But it didn't make sense.

We kept moving.

Together we threaded our way through all of the rooms, checking all of the niches and nooks. Wirek kept up a running commentary about the portraits on the walls. He knew a lot of them, apparently.

"Nothing like seeing your former peers immortalized on canvas."

I said nothing. I'm not much for talking when I'm working.

At the red carpeted hallway, I tried all the doors until we'd cleared them all and only one was left. The subbasement.

Unlocked.

We went down the stairs.

At the bottom, it remained quiet. Wirek looked at me. "This where you were held?"

"Yeah."

"Nice atmosphere," said Wirek.

I took one corridor. Wirek took the other. We met up two minutes later outside the cell I'd been held in. Wirek was out of breath.

"Nothing here."

I frowned again.

The place was empty.

Wirek let the muzzle of the shotgun dip toward the floor. "What the hell is going on?"

"We're too late," I said.

"What do you mean we're too late? Where the hell would they go? This is the address you got out of the Council's database, right?"

"Yeah, it is. But they aren't here"

"It doesn't add up," said Wirek. "Arvella needs the boy for her ceremony and doesn't have much time. Why wouldn't she do the ceremony here?"

I leaned against the wall. "Unless . . ."

"What?"

"You mentioned that Arvella was once the headmistress of the Invoker school, isn't that right?"

Wirek nodded. "Sure, that was back years ago, though. Besides, they moved that school after she left. The new headmaster wanted it closer to the rest of our society, not far off in some remote vista."

"Where is it?"

"Now? The Canadian Rockies."

"Where was it when Arvella was in charge?"

"Way the hell out there. In the Himalayas."

"The Himalayas? Why so far away?"

"Apparently, Arvella thought the sanctity of the Invoker tradition needed to be preserved and kept cloistered from the temptations of modern society. Plus, I think she was originally from there, a long time back."

I looked at him. "What are the odds?"

"That she's brought Jack there?" He shrugged. "Cripes, I dunno. But she sure as hell ain't here."

"We're running out of time. If she's out of the country already, that gives her a huge head start. We're playing catch-up again and I hate that."

"In that case, we'd better get ourselves on a plane."

"Yeah. But first we need to make sure we're not being played for fools."

"How you gonna figure that out?"

"We find Petrov and persuade him to tell us."

"You know where he is?"

"No, but if he isn't anywhere that we can find him, it might mean he went with her."

"That's a pretty tenuous assumption, Lawson."

"Well, it would at least mean we might be on the right track."

"Why," said Wirek, "does that not make me feel any better?"

"It doesn't make me feel any better, either, but we don't have any other choice."

Chapter Twenty-one

I called Petrov's number as soon as we cleared the mansion. I got a polite message informing me that the service had been disconnected. That figured.

Wirek stowed the guns in the trunk of the Volvo. "We should get going."

"Time's wasting, huh?"

He shrugged. "Figuring travel time to get to where we need to be? Oh, yeah."

I sighed. "This school, the Invoker academy or whatever you call it—you know where it is?"

"Sure."

I wasn't convinced. "I mean exactly, Wirek. The Himalayas are a lot of ground to cover. We can't just drop in over there and spend six days dicking around."

"I can find it. It's been years since I visited, but I think my memory is still pretty sharp."

"All right. How much prep time do you figure we need?"

"We'll need some gear," said Wirek.

"Yeah. My house first, then yours. We can grab a taxi to the airport from there."

We drove back to my place and quickly cleaned the guns before stowing them back in the safe. I would have loved to bring them along, but they were obviously out. I can carry a gun through most security checkpoints because I know how the security works—or rather doesn't work. But I'd never been to Nepal before and I didn't want to risk a search that would flag us and alert Arvella we were on scene.

Fortunately, in my line of work, I have other weapons I can use besides firearms. Downstairs in my basement, I unlocked the antique wooden chest my ancestors carted their carpentry tools from Germany in. I'd put the tools into other chests over the years. Now I keep my treasured belongings in the ornate chest.

Unwrapping the handmade wooden *bokken* that had been carved for me some years back by a famous weaponsmith in Japan brought out a flood of memories. The pure hardwood lignum vitae gleamed in the dim light as my mind flashed back to when I'd used it to kill my oldest enemy, Cosgrove, just a few months previously.

Now I was getting ready to use it again.

Some things never change.

I unwrapped the folded steel *tanto* as well, another gift from the same weaponsmith. I laid both the *bokken* and the *tanto* into my long luggage bag.

I packed some winter gear, not knowing how potentially bad the weather might be in Nepal. Wirek assured me it might actually be temperate over there, but I've learned to go with my instinct and felt we might need the extra warmth.

Finally, I dropped a note in the mail to my neighbor so she could check in and feed Mimi and Phoebe while I was gone.

We zoomed back to Wirek's place and he grabbed some supplies as well. I saw him covertly stow his hip flask in his carry-on bag. I hoped he wouldn't be drinking himself silly on the flight over.

"You ready?"

He nodded. "What about the Council?"

"What about 'em?"

"You planning on telling them where we're headed?"

"Hell, no. If Arvella has any allies, they'd alert her. I don't want her knowing we're coming until we're already there."

Getting to Logan Airport took almost as much time as the actual flight. With construction from the Big Dig still sucking billions of tax dollars out of the commonwealth, new routes and detours sprung up faster than horny eighteen-year-olds at spring break.

Northwest Airlines booked us on the next flight to Osaka, Japan, with a minor stopover in the Twin Cities, Minneapolis and St. Paul. I'd flown Northwest before on several trips to Japan. Overall, their service was decent, but listening to the flight attendants scurry up and down the aisle asking if you wanted *ocha,* the bitter Japanese green tea, got a bit old after a while.

Wirek sacked out as soon as we got airborne. I had to keep reminding myself of how old he truly was. Vampires tend to live for about five hundred years, given that a daily ingestion of life force from humans slows down our metabolic rates substantially. Wirek was pushing double our normal life expectancy.

Add to that the fact that he'd gone into combat for the first time this evening and come through perfectly intact. Hell, he deserved a long sleep.

Flight time from Minneapolis to Osaka was a solid twelve hours. I punched up the video projector attached to my seat and saw they were playing the latest teen comedy as the in-flight movie. It's a decent flick. The first time you see it. On this flight, however, the damned displays broke down, so every time you turned it on, the same movie came on. So much for keeping myself amused.

I considered our present situation, mulling over the factors that led us to being on board a transpacific airplane. Normally, I would have liked a lot more prep time. Chasing traitors halfway across the world wasn't exactly the kind of thing I like to do on the fly. But time was something we were all short on.

I couldn't let Arvella have Jack.

Watching the cloud layers pass by my window like balls of soft cotton candy pulled apart by kids at a carnival eventually lulled me off to sleep.

I woke up a few hours later. Wirek's elbow kept denting my side.

"Want some dinner?"

I stretched. "Does it really qualify as dinner?"

He glanced down. "Some kind of chicken, I think. Red potatoes. Asparagus. All served in a rectangular plastic container." He grinned. "Ain't technology grand?"

"I hate asparagus."

I took a sip of bottled water and caught a whiff of the chicken. It actually smelled good. Wirek grabbed one of the flight attendants and scored me a tray of food.

After the carrot cake, I settled back. Wirek nudged me again. I looked. He had the hip flask in his hand.

"Want a hit of the good stuff?"

"No." I frowned. "I don't drink tequila."

He shook his head. "Stupid. I told you I was through with the booze, remember?"

"Then what's in that?"

"It's—what the hell did you call it? Juice?"

I leaned over. "Blood?"

"Yeah, genius."

Shit, in my rush to get us to the airport, I'd completely forgotten about the need for nourishment. Thank god for Wirek. Without him, we'd probably have had to borrow some from a passenger. And getting kinky in the cramped bathroom of a 747 at 35,000 feet might sound good in the pages of a sex magazine, but it sucks in real life.

I took the flask and put it to my lips. I sucked down a few gulps of the coppery blood. It flowed thicker than I like it.

I winced. "Did it coagulate?"

Wirek took the flask back. "It's unrefrigerated. Plus, the altitude affects it, too. Don't be fussy."

I felt the surge of energy come on and sighed. "Thanks. I needed that."

"Forgot, didn't ya?"

"Yeah. Been a while since I had to travel out of the country. I'm used to being close to home."

"We might find supplies a little tight over there." He looked at me. "Will that be a problem?"

"I remember how to hunt, for crying out loud." But inside I winced again. I prefer getting my blood from a blood bank in Boston staffed by vampires. Given my job, I don't have a lot of time to go hunting fresh juice.

Truthfully, I don't relish what I have to subsist on. I'm a vampire and it goes without saying that you have to drink juice. But I don't like it. Never have.

Wirek was still looking at me.

"What?"

"Got some real distaste playing across your face there, Lawson."

"Must be the chicken."

He nodded slowly and went back to reading the in-flight magazine. I went back to sleep.

Osaka's airport was much the same as I remembered it from a few years previously. Japanese airports are designed to make passengers feel like hamsters in a Habitrail. Clear tubes and walkways herd you exactly where you need to go and nowhere else. It's good security, but it also leaves you uncomfortable.

We humped a Royal Nepal Airways flight out of Osaka. The flight itself felt surreal. Flight attendants spoke at least four languages and pampered everyone. A sense of peace permeated the plane, even over the whine of the jet engines.

By the time we touched down in Kathmandu, we'd been in the air for close to twenty-four hours. I felt like shit. Long flights wring me out and leave very little behind.

Tribhuvan Airport bustled. Smaller than a lot of other international airports, Tribhuvan nonetheless had the usual assortment of newsstands and small eateries. And it had a lot of crowds. Nepalese and Indians accounted for most of the traffic, but a sizable mix of Westerners loitered around as well.

I wanted to get out of the whirling maelstrom as fast as possible. I let Wirek take the lead, since he'd been there before. He guided us past our other passengers and we reached the customs desk quickly.

While Wirek chatted pleasantly with the officials in fluent Nepali, our bags got a brief going-over. Speaking the home language is always a plus when you enter a foreign nation.

We got our visas and a big smile.

"Good to go," said Wirek.

It's also a plus having authentic passports, courtesy of the vampires who work for the State Department.

"I need a shower and some serious rack time."

Wirek nodded. "We'll grab a hotel. We can get started in the morning."

We walked outside.

A cool breeze whipped around us as evening descended. Wirek took a deep breath and exhaled.

"Ah . . . you smell it?"

I took a whiff. The air stank of sewage. "Christ, is that what I think it is?"

He nodded. "You bet. Welcome to the top of the world."

"I always thought shit flowed downhill."

He laughed. "We'll get a ricksha."

I pointed at the long line of taxis. "What's wrong with grabbing a cab?"

"We're going to Thamel, that's why."

"Thamel?"

"Old part of town. Think of it as tourist central. Streets there are only wide enough for one car and congestion is fierce. A ricksha's a safer bet for getting to the hotel." He winked at me. "Unless you want to get stuck in a traffic jam."

He wandered over to a wrinkled old man who looked almost as old as Wirek himself. A minute passed. Wirek asked a few questions and then motioned me into the back of the carriage.

Our trip to the hotel gave me an eyeful of Kathmandu life. Small shops bordered the roads and streets, each wedged right up against each other, smashed together like so many sardines. Traders and merchants filled the streets. But many of the shops looked closed.

"Most folks hit the rack by ten," said Wirek. "Nightlife is limited."

"Good thing we're not here for that," I said.

The old man pulling the ricksha sang while he ran, his

voice keeping an off-kilter cadence to the *clickety-clack* of the wheels that bounced over small bumps and raised whorls of dust in our wake. The whole city seemed caked in dust. That and the ever-present smell of sewage made me wish we'd opted for the taxi, instead.

But then the roads grew suddenly narrow.

"Thamel," said Wirek.

Wirek had called it right.

The place overflowed with people. Long lines of cars beeped at each other while rickshas scooted here and there, intermixed with streams of people bustling and hustling everywhere, ferrying foods and goods back and forth, like so many ants rushing in and out of their burrows.

We reached the hotel. Wirek paid the rickshaman, then hurried us inside. "We've still got time for some dinner. You interested?"

"What kind of meal are we talking about?"

He eyed me. "Some Nepalese cuisine." Then he grinned. "We don't need more of that just yet. Let's get some normal food and plot out a course to the school."

We entrusted our bags to a young porter Wirek tipped with a twenty-dollar bill. The porter's eyes went wide. Wirek laughed as he hurried off to deposit our bags in our rooms.

"Kid'll do anything to make sure our stuff is safe. Let's go."

We got sucked back into the street flow. Wirek steered us to a small eatery called the Blue Note.

"Looks American."

"Ex-pat runs it, last I knew of," said Wirek. "Food's good stuff. Very Nepali, though."

We sat down to a meal of chilled chicken and San Miguel beer, which, I've found, tends to pop up in the most unlikely of areas. The chicken tasted a helluva lot better than the Northwest cuisine.

Wirek produced a map from his cargo pants pocket and opened it on the table. He looked around at the rest of the restaurant. Trekkers from all over the world seemed to be planning their trips here tonight.

"Thamel tends to be the jump point for most of these folks," said Wirek in a whisper. "Let's hope no one wants to join our jaunt."

I sucked down some beer. "So, where are we going?"

Wirek stabbed the upper corner of the map with his finger. "Mustang."

"Nice car," I said. I kill myself sometimes.

"It's a semirestricted zone in Nepal," said Wireck, ignoring my bad joke. "Foreigners aren't even supposed to go there without a local liaison officer tagging along to make sure you don't break any of the rules."

"What kind of rules?"

"You can't give kids anything—they might turn into beggars. No trash on the trails. You can't stay with the locals in their houses, you have to bring your own tent, that sort of thing."

"Why's it so restricted?"

"Look at the map, hotshot. See how the entire region juts into Tibet? For years it was a staging area for the Khampa guerrillas that used to fight for Tibet's freedom from the Chinese. They used Mustang to hop back and forth over the border harassing Chinese troops. They were backed by the American CIA during the 1960s and 1970s. CIA gave 'em guns and money. The Nepali government finally cracked down."

"Why so?"

"Shit, Lawson, they're not fools. They know that they're kind of in a hairy situation. They got a million Chinese troops a few miles north of here all ready to pour over the border. They aren't going to risk their sovereign state for a bunch of guerrillas. They restricted travel there."

"So, how are we gonna get there?"

"Well, you're supposed to have a special permit ahead of time, but obviously we didn't have time to file for one. And they only allow about one thousand foreigners to visit there each year." Wirek drank some tea. "Luckily, I know a fellow here in town who can get us what we need."

"What about the tagalong officer? Any way we can ditch him?"

Wirek nodded. "Not a problem. Most of the officers can be bought off." He folded the map. "We'll fly out of here tomorrow to Jomsom and have to walk from there. Figure about six days to reach the school."

"Are you kidding me? That's cutting it pretty damned close to the wire."

"There's no other choice. Helicopter rides are out-of-this-world expensive. Plus, the two of us would attract too much attention. We'll just have to hustle."

"You up for that?"

"Hey, I can hold my own."

"If you say so."

"I do."

"Okay, just checking. Don't freak out on me."

"You just worry about dealing with the high-altitude acclimatization and I'll worry about keeping up."

"Acclimatization?"

"Yeah, cowboy, we're traveling into the upper altitudes. That's one reason why the trek takes so long. Bodies don't get used to the change in altitude for a few days, even ours. Don't expect to get much sleep."

"If we're humping packs and walking our asses off, I'm not concerned about sleep."

Wirek grinned. "You will be."

"Once we reach Mustang Province, our destination is Lo Monthang. We'll be able to get to the school easily enough from there. It's disguised as a Tibetan Buddhist temple. And since there are two other gorgeous temples up there, the school never gets any attention because from the outside it looks like shit."

"What's Lo Monthang like?"

"It's like shit," said Wirek. "No running water, no electricity, no telephones—it's Old World. The two temples date back about five hundred years and the city predates them by a few hundred as well. Not much has changed there. It's mud brick that's got an adobelike consistency. Dusty dirt lanes—"

"I'm getting used to that."

"And no plumbing facilities to speak of. Which reminds me, you'd better stock up on toilet paper back at the hotel."

"What the hell are you talking about?"

"Toilet paper is unheard of in this part of the world, friend. Out in the countryside, they use their left hand and a jar of water to clean themselves."

"Great. I'm loving this country already."

"Well, if things go well, we'll be back in the States in a week or so. Once we get the boy, we'll have to hustle out of there pretty fast, so maybe we can arrange a chopper out of Lo Monthang to Jomsom. That might be good. I'll arrange that as well."

I finished my San Miguel. "Great. Sounds great."

Wirek looked at me. "You'll love this, trust me."

"Can't wait." I fished some money out of my pocket and left a wad on the table. "Ready to head back to the hotel?"

"Not just yet. You go on ahead. I'll take care of a few other things we need. I'll catch up with you later, but if you don't hear from me, plan to be at the airport for seven A.M. so we can get to Jomsom."

"Seven A.M.? I'd been looking forward to some hearty sleep.

Wirek nodded. "It's for the boy, Lawson. Keep telling yourself that."

"Yeah," I said. But it didn't make it any easier.

Chapter Twenty-two

I woke up at quarter to six the next morning, rolled out of my fluffy bed, and padded into the small bathroom to wash up. The small porcelain sink spilled out brown-tinged water that eventually ran clear. I sighed.

Wirek's bed looked like it hadn't been slept in.

I wondered where he had spent the previous night.

By six-fifteen, he hadn't appeared. I locked the door and called the porter, who got our stuff downstairs. I gave him another twenty and asked him to fetch a ricksha.

It then took me another five minutes to mime to the rickshaman that I needed to go back to the airport. By the time we got there at quarter to seven, the city was already hopping.

I hopped off the ricksha, just shy of a deranged taxi driver who swerved to avoid hitting the elderly driver. I hauled our gear down and looked around.

No Wirek.

Fortunately, a wiry security guard by the front entrance pointed me to the Royal Nepal Airlines gate for a flight to Jomsom. As I approached the ticket counter, I saw Wirek waving me over.

He still wore the same outfit he'd had on the day before, the one he'd flown over from the States in. I wrinkled my nose at the thought of how bad he must smell. Of course, by then, the pervasive stench of sewage in the city had acclimated my nose. I wasn't sure if Wirek's body odor would be able to penetrate.

"Where the hell did you go last night?"

He grinned. "I told you I had some things to take care of. What's the big deal?"

"The big deal is you left me at the hotel. I might not have been able to find my way here. Remember? I don't speak Nepalese."

"It's actually called Nepali."

"Whatever."

Wirek frowned. "C'mon, Lawson, gimme a break. You're a big boy. You know how to find your way around, even if you don't speak the lingo. I told you the timings. You're here. What's the problem?"

"Forget it." I sighed. Third World countries and I don't really get along all that well.

"I got the tickets already," said Wirek. He handed me one. "I hope you're not claustrophobic."

"What the hell does that mean?"

"Our plane's a small twin-engine job for the run up to Jomsom. She looks old."

"Great. Killed halfway around the frickin' world because the damned plane crashed. That makes perfect sense."

Wirek grabbed his bag and mine. "C'mon. Let's get on board."

We walked through the security checkpoint and out onto the tarmac. Wirek wasn't joking. The plane didn't look old.

It looked ancient.

I walked around the outside of it, wondering whether the propellers were taped on or not.

From the outside, it looked like it might hold twenty people. Inside, reality told me that ten would be pushing its maximum capacity, including our luggage. A flight attendant dressed for outdoor survival helped us with our bags.

"Interesting uniform," I said to Wirek.

Wirek promptly babbled something off to her and she smiled and spoke to him for a minute. He turned back to me. "You're right," he said.

"About what?"

"She's dressed that way in case they have to ditch the plane. Skirts aren't too practical for parachuting out of planes."

I scrunched myself into the window seat behind the propeller and sighed. "Great."

Wirek plopped down next to me. "How come you always take the window?"

"It's spiritual."

"Spiritual?"

"Absolutely. I will spend the entire length of the trip willing the wings and propellers to work properly."

Wirek grinned. "Fair enough."

The engines started with a bang.

It scared the crap out of me.

I watched the flight attendant close the door and strap herself into a folding chair that faced us.

I leaned over to Wirek. "Does she pitch the peanuts to us when it's snack time?"

Wirek ignored me. He was studying his map again. I looked back out the window, gave a silent prayer to the twenty thousand various deities I know about, then watched the prop on my side start to turn.

Somehow we managed to jump ahead of the major carriers lining up on the runway and take off on schedule. I settled down once we were airborne, but I wasn't looking forward to the landing.

"How long is the flight?"

Wirek checked his watch. "Maybe an hour or so. It's been a while since I was here last. Things have changed."

"How so?"

"There were no planes back then. You walked everywhere or got a horse if you were lucky. And rich. I was neither."

"How long were you here for?"

"A few years." He went back to the map.

I closed my eyes.

Just as I started to relax, we hit turbulence. Mild at first, it soon turned into jolting swells of air pressure that tossed us all over the sky. I lost track of how many times my stomach remained on the ceiling while the rest of me dropped like a stone.

Thankfully, we hadn't gotten our peanuts yet.

Wirek remained completely unfazed by the entire event. For someone who might not have flown in Nepal before, he seemed remarkably at ease with the whole process. I think he was the only one who was.

Even our flight attendant looked upset.

Ten minutes after it started, we got through the worst of it. The pilot announced that we'd be descending into Jomsom within a few minutes. That was good news because I didn't know how much longer I could stand being on such a small plane.

Jomsom paled in comparison to Kathmandu. In fact, the airport looked like little more than a few mud huts and a wind sock. It brought back memories of when I'd flown onto the island of Palawan in the Philippines. That airport was an open-air hut, a wind sock, and a stretch of hardened dirt scraped out of the jungle. It looked like something used by drug traffickers.

We started our descent. I watched the mud houses grow larger.

We bumped, rattled, and eventually skidded to a stop about thirty feet from the closest hut. Some of the other passengers on the flight with us got to their feet slowly, obviously nauseated from the roller-coaster ride.

Outside, the sun shone bright and dust whorls settled as the props wound down to a stop. Around us, the flat, featureless stretch of northern desert loomed; in the distance, green meadows and snow-peaked mountains stood out against the contrast of bright blue sky.

Wirek handed me my bag. "Let's get going. We need to get our transportation squared away."

"I thought we were walking."

"Walking takes six days, unless you push it hard. We don't have six days. We've got four. And we need to reach Lo Monthang within three so we can figure out how we're going to tackle Arvella. If we walk, we might as well go home now."

"What are our choices? You said flying in was out of the question—"

"Horses," said Wirek. "We can ride most of the way. It's just a matter of finding someone who'll let us borrow some."

"You know anyone up here who would?"

"Most of the folks I did know are probably dead by now. And the local vampire population—they're known as *yidam* in this part of the world—is remarkably secret about itself. We probably wouldn't know them unless we saw their mark."

"And it's not like they walk around topless here, either."

"Exactly," said Wirek. "Our best bet is to press on, find someone with horses, and get cracking."

It was too bad, actually, because the help of local vampires could have saved us a lot of effort. But at the same time, it might have been better this way. If the locals knew a couple of out-of-town vampires had just shown up, word might spread. And we could walk into a pretty bad ambush up in the hills.

The air felt cooler up here. By comparison, Kathmandu had been very comfortable. Warm in some ways. Jomsom, at a higher elevation, felt tinged by the winds off the mountains in the distance.

Jomsom's streets were all dirt. I saw a few telephone lines, but nothing that made me think of the place as a technological hotbed of activity. Wirek steered us down several twisting alleyways until we came to a place called Saano's.

It might have been a bar, but the Pepsi-Cola sign so common in Third World countries told me they offered more than alcohol.

"Inside," said Wirek. "Stay quiet and let me do the talking, okay?"

"Sure thing, Ben Kenobi."

"Ben Kenobi?"

"Movie reference. Not important."

Darkness slid over us as we entered, reinforcing a sentiment I have about all Third World drinking establishments. The less you can see, the more dangerous it's liable to be.

Wirek worked us over to the bar and began speaking in rapid-fire Nepali. I looked around and saw a huge curved knife hanging behind the bar.

It was a *kukri,* the symbol of the legendary Gurkha fighters of Nepal. But the town of Gurkha was to the south, north of Kathmandu. I was surprised to see a veteran so far up north as we were.

After five minutes of talking, Wirek turned and offered me a glass of something.

"What's this?"

"House special, drink it up."

I tilted the glass back and felt the liquid burn my throat as it went down. I coughed once and the entire bar erupted into peals of laughter.

"Shit."

The barman gestured animatedly to the patrons and yelled something. They laughed even more. Then the barman looked back at me.

"You like?"

"Wonderful," I said with a smile. "Can I have another?"

He roared. "You bet."

I looked at Wirek. "He speaks English?"

" 'Course he does. You see that *kukri?* He's a Gurkha."

"I figured that one out."

"Well, then you should have known he'd speak English. It's a requirement for them. In order to serve with the British, they have to speak the tongue. Makes sense, doesn't it?"

"Finish your drink, Wirek."

I tossed down another glass of the molten fire and held out my hand to the barman. "I'm Lawson."

He grabbed it and pumped it twice. "Saano."

"What's that Nepali for?"

" 'Small.' "

I smiled. Saano was the complete opposite of his name. While he might have stood five feet eight inches in height, he was easily over 220 pounds. He looked six feet wide. And all of it pure muscle. The guy was anything but small.

I pointed at the *kukri.* "How long did you serve?"

"Twenty years. Borneo, Malaysia, Oman, Yemen—you

name it, I saw it. Then I came back here and opened this joint up." He looked around and leaned in closer. "You and Wirek headed up north, eh?"

"Yeah."

"Best be careful up there. Rumors say there's some strange activity going on. They say even the Tibetan Buddhists up there are running scared."

"Yeah?"

He nodded. "Believe it. News travels fast in these parts." He leaned over the bar. "Wirek tells me you guys need transportation and a guide."

"A guide?" I looked at Wirek, who nodded. "Yeah, I guess."

Saano smiled. "I'm your man."

"You? What about your bar here?"

"What about it?" Saano shrugged. "I'm restless. I've been tending bar here for years since I retired from the service."

"How much?"

Saano grinned. "Cost of supplies, that's it."

"That's it? Nothing in it for you?"

"Plenty in it for me," said Saano. "I'm itching for a little adventure."

"How do you know it'll be an adventure?"

He smiled, but it was a wary smile. "Because, Mr. Lawson, I have heard the rumors." He downed a glass of the same stuff he'd given me and winced. "And they aren't pretty."

Chapter Twenty-three

Saano managed to secure three horses for us in far less time than I would have thought possible. While he went to find us some supplies, Wirek and I got our packs secured.

"Why isn't this guy charging us anything?" I asked Wirek.

Wirek tightened a strap on the underside of his chestnut-colored mare. "Said he'll do it for the love of a good adventure. My guess is he gets tired seeing nothing but bar brawls. The chance to escort us up north must have made him happy."

"Seems strange to me," I said.

Wirek sighed. "Maybe he's an adrenaline junkie like you."

"I'm not an adrenaline junkie."

"No?"

I shook my head. "Any adrenaline I get goes along with the job."

"But you don't exactly shy away from it."

"I don't know if I can and still do my job."

Wirek considered that. "Fair enough."

"How come Saano can't go up there on his own anytime he wants?"

"Maybe because Lo Monthang isn't exactly high on anyone's list of must-see spots. No plumbing, no electricity, remember? It's harsh living any way you look at it."

I let the subject drop. Saano came sauntering back with a few sacks full of stuff, which he secured to his own black horse. I noticed his *kukri* hung in a leather scabbard at his side. I noticed him looking at my *bokken,* which I'd strapped across my back.

"A wooden sword?"

I shrugged. "It has its uses."

He nodded. "Maybe you'll find a reason to use it up north then, eh?" He looked at Wirek. "Are we ready?"

"Yeah."

Saano nudged his horse. "Then let's get going, boys. Time's wasting. And you've got a schedule to keep."

Riding out of Jomsom was a lot less stressful than arriving had been. Saano led us out on a well-worn trail that paralleled a range of flat-topped hills to our left. Vegetation seemed limited to some sparse shrubbery, small wispy trees, and moss. I was grateful we were riding, since breathing seemed to be giving me some trouble. Wirek must have noticed because he pulled in alongside me.

"You'll get used to the altitude within a day or so. Just bear in mind the closer we get to Lo Monthang, the higher in altitude we'll be, so take it easy."

"What about the horses? Do they suffer?"

Saano heard me and laughed. "They're used to the route. I borrowed them from a merchant who treks all over the country. He promised they'd last us—no problem. Then he patted the side of his leg where the *kukri* was strapped. "Besides, if they falter, we can always have fresh meat."

I frowned. "Don't think I'd be interested in horse meat, Saano."

He laughed again. "Let me tell you something, Mr. Lawson, you been in some of the places I've been and know what real hunger is, you'd relish a fresh course of horse meat."

"I don't know that horse would satisfy my appetite," I said.

Saano turned slightly in his saddle. "No. I see maybe it wouldn't." He laughed again. "That's okay. There is always food to eat along the way to Lo Monthang."

I looked at Wirek again, but he was already lost in the landscape. I supposed he was seeing a lot of land that he'd traveled many years ago. Being here must have brought back a lot of memories.

By two in the afternoon, we'd traveled a fair clip. Saano knew the countryside inside out and led us off the well-worn trail and onto smaller ones that hadn't seen nearly the amount of traffic the first trail had.

"That one," he said, pointing to the trail we'd just left. "It has too many trekkers on it. We haven't seen any yet, but they will be there farther up north. They get in the way." He nodded ahead. "This trail will get us to your destination faster and without the interruptions."

Wirek nodded. "That's good. We're not interested in interruptions."

"So, why are you both going to Lo Monthang?"

The question came out of nowhere. Wirek and I hadn't really agreed on much of a script. He'd told me before we went into Saano's bar that he'd do the talking, so I hung back and let him take the lead on this.

"We want to see the temples, of course," he told Saano.

"You can see temples in Kathmandu," said Saano.

"Not like the temples in Lo Monthang," said Wirek. "My friend here," he said, pointing to me, "is interested in history, and the temples up north are among the oldest in the country."

"Mr. Lawson is a historian who carries a wooden sword on his back?" He chuckled and muttered something in Nepali. I looked at Wirek.

"He said, 'Foreigners always lie.' "

I nodded. "What do you think we want to do up in Lo Monthang, Saano?"

He shrugged. "Maybe it's not my place to ask the question in the first place. You hired me only to be your guide and that is what I will do." He smiled. "But maybe I also have an idea about your trip up north. After all, I did not stay alive so long in the Gurkha regiment by being stupid."

"Tell us about the rumors, Saano," said Wirek.

Saano nodded. "They started a few weeks ago. At first, we dismissed them as some silly foreigner climber drunk on the atmosphere and altitude. They sometimes wander back weird from an aborted climb." He looked at me. "The altitude, it can do things to a man."

He shrugged. "This one, though, he comes into my bar and tells us about bad weather on the outskirts of Lo Monthang. He had been trekking by himself—not smart this one—and the weather forced him to find shelter. He saw a cave and he entered it, not knowing where it led.

"He told us that in the middle of the night—in the middle of a blinding snowstorm with thunder—that he heard strange voices from farther back in the cave. He followed them, tripping over the stones in the dark, but then he saw a light ahead. What he discovered, he said, were people in flowing robes with spirits flying around them."

"Spirits?"

Saano nodded. "Like I said, probably drunk on the altitude. So we gave him some food and drink and sent him on his way back home to wherever he came from. But then we started hearing other things from Sherpas and merchants coming down from the north. They said that during the night, some of the party would be attacked by a creature they could not see. A creature that bit them. Drew blood, it did."

Saano kept his face forward. "The stories began to increase in number. So much so that I know plenty of people who stopped journeying up there because of it. And you know, to make someone that scared—someone who makes their living from trading with the people up there—that they would not venture there anymore, well, I think, Mr. Lawson and Mr. Wirek, that there must be something definitely evil living up there."

He shrugged again. "Maybe it is the yeti."

" 'The abominable snowman'?" I asked.

Saano nodded. "Maybe. But I think not. Yeti is not a violent creature like that. So I ask myself what it could possibly be. I've thought about it a great deal lately. And then two strangers come into my bar wanting to see about getting a guide for that place. And I think to myself maybe there is a good reason to go along on that trip. Maybe these strangers know what lives up there, what is scaring the people. And maybe it's time for Saano to take back down his knife and journey with them to defeat this evil creature."

I doubted Saano would be much help against Arvella and her followers. It sounded like they had the place pretty well sealed up.

Wirek cleared his throat. "What about the monks that live in the temples up there? Has anyone heard from them?"

Saano nodded. "They say that during the day everything is fine. But at night, the doors and windows of the temple are locked tight. And the townsfolk who live by the temples will not journey out after dark, either. And they will not open the door for anyone, even if they sound like they are in mortal danger."

I frowned. It sounded like Arvella had the locals paralyzed with fear and she was sending out her followers to hunt at night. It was definitely strange for me to think about a community of vampires that still clung to the old ways. Most of the vampires in society nowadays had scorned the old hunts.

But then again, we were in some seriously old country. And if Wirek had been correct in his assessment of Arvella, she was definitely interested in keeping the traditions alive. Even if it meant killing off the local human population.

"You know," said Saano. "It almost sounds to me like the *yidam.*"

That word struck a chord with me and I remembered Wirek said it was Nepali for "vampire." Wirek laughed.

"Vampires? Come on, Saano. You don't believe that, do you?"

Saano turned in his saddle again and pointed at me. "I'm not the one with the wooden sword." He turned back around and urged his horse forward. "Besides, I have seen plenty of things that most people would not believe. I am a very superstitious man and I have had good reason to be."

"Seen a lot up here, have you?" I asked.

"Nepal is an ancient land. She borders Tibet, China, India—some of the oldest land in the world. We have legends that no one else knows about. Except maybe the yeti. Everyone knows about them."

"Them?"

Saano shrugged. "Of course. They are a community of creatures like any other. They must have more than one to survive, you know?" He nodded. "I have seen them. Once, during a climb far up north on the Tibetan side of the mountains. I had crossed over illegally, not at the border crossing with the Chinese. But I had found my own way across. A pass that seemed almost invisible, unless you stumbled on it as I did.

"Partway though, I came upon some tracks unlike any I had ever seen before. Bigger, far bigger, than a man's foot, with spread toes. I followed them for as long as I could before having to pitch camp for the night. While I huddled around a fire I'd been able to start underneath a rock overhang, I heard the cries. Such cries. Like an animal in pain. They howled above the roar of the wind, filling me with fear. I drew my knife as the cries got closer. I thought for sure they must be coming to kill me. Perhaps I had encroached on their land and had not known it. The cries got closer, but my eyes could not penetrate the darkness because of my fire.

"And then the smell came to me. Such an awful smell, like unwashed yaks that have been covered in their own dung. Ungodly smell. It was awful. Then just outside the range of my vision, I sensed them moving. They seemed curious. I was terrified." He looked at us. "Believe me, I have faced many enemies with just my trusty knife and never been as scared as I was that night. I thought I would surely die."

"What happened?"

"I stayed standing throughout the entire night, waiting for their attack, waiting for them to kill me and drag me off to some unknown part of the mountains. There are places up there no one knows about, where they would surely have left my body when they were through with it."

He shrugged. "But they never attacked. In the morning, as the first rays of the sun came over the mountaintops, I could see them leaving. Furry, covered with hair. There were two of them that night. The tracks I found that morning confirmed it."

"What did you do?"

Saano chuckled. "I had two choices: either follow the tracks and confront them or go home." He looked at us. "I went home. There comes a time when a warrior must acknowledge that he might be defeated by a better enemy than he. This was that time. The yeti could have killed me that night. I was in their territory. But they didn't. And I am very good at listening to warnings. Now I leave the yeti alone and urge anyone with a desire to see them to do the same."

Wirek whistled. "That's a helluva story."

"It was a helluva scare," said Saano. "It certainly made me respect the things that don't lend themselves to ordinary thought."

Things that don't lend themselves to ordinary thought. It was an interesting concept. Wirek and I both belonged to that category. I wondered if Saano knew that. Part of me sensed that he did. Another part chalked it up as just native suspicion about foreigners.

Of course, wearing the *bokken* on my back probably didn't help.

Chapter Twenty-four

"We'll camp here for the night," Saano announced a few hours later when the sun had begun its westward retreat across the sky. He led us into a shallow depression, a few yards off the winding trail we'd followed for most of the afternoon. Small tufts of grass blanketed the ground and several large boulders formed a protective border.

We dismounted. Saano promptly disappeared to find some firewood. Wirek got out his map and confirmed that if we kept to the pace Saano had set, we'd reach the outskirts of Lo Monthang in two more days.

"It's a tough schedule he'll have us on, but we don't have any choice."

I nodded, getting the tent from Saano's horse. Wirek and I managed to get it up in a few minutes. Pronouncing it worthy of habitation, I slid our gear inside the flaps.

"Lawson." Wirek motioned me over to his horse and withdrew the silver flask. "Quick, before he gets back."

I took a much needed hit of juice and felt my strength wax again. It had been almost twenty-four hours since we'd last fed and both of us were in need of some sustenance. I passed it back to Wirek, who had a long drag, and then I took one more before he packed it away.

"Gotta conserve," he said with a smile. "Otherwise, we might have to hit Saano up for some."

"Some what?"

Saano had reappeared suddenly from behind the horses.

"Christ," said Wirek. "You're one stealthy bastard."

Saano nodded. "It helped while I was in the army." He held up his arms. They were filled with short, broken-up pieces of dried wood. "Got us enough for most of the night, I should think."

He dropped it to the side and took the horses over to a small outcropping of rocks, securing the reins to the largest boulder, and let them graze awhile on the small lichens and scrub grasses that grew up between the cracks. Then he brought them a feed bag and scattered some among the horses.

I gathered some rocks for a fire circle. I felt like a small child again, going camping for the first time. I wished this trip were that innocent.

Saano joined me. Together we found enough rocks for a large shallow circle. Then Saano dug out a pouch from inside his shirt.

"Lint bag," he explained. "Gets the fire going faster."

Sure enough, placed a small pile of furry threads into the center, then built a small tepee of twigs around it, with a few thicker pieces around that. Then he took out his *kukri* and a piece of what I assumed was flint and struck it once, aiming it perfectly into the lint. Within a few short seconds, the spark caught to the lint and licked its way through the twigs to the thicker branches. The crackling and popping of dry wood catching fire brought back more camping memories.

The air around us filled with a delicate scent of wood smoke. I thought I smelled peat smoke. Wirek wandered over with his sleeping bag and sat down next to us.

"Smells good," he said.

Saano smiled. "Some of the kindling are sticks of incense. Up here, fire is a spiritual activity. It's our savior as much as a means to keep ourselves warm. We always light some incense to pay homage to the gods."

A breeze blew over the hills behind us, rustling the tent flaps and making the flames twist and dance in the coming darkness. I leaned back into the hard ground, feeling my back and legs relax some. Above us, the first stars began to peek out of the sky.

Saano produced a pipe, packed it with a wad of tobacco, then took a long, thin stick out of the fire and lit the bowl. He closed his eyes and inhaled deep, finally exhaling a long stream of white smoke into the air.

"Ah, that's good," he said. "Nothing like a smoke after a long day's ride." He turned to Wirek and offered him the pipe. Wirek took a drag and then passed it to me. As much as I hate smoking, I figured it would be rude to reject the pipe. So I took a drag, but inhaled only so far before exhaling it again.

I had to admit the taste of whatever Saano stocked in the pipe tasted good. And the effects of the nicotine relaxed me even more.

Saano pointed to the sky. "Do you see that star, there?" He smiled. "When I was a child, my mother would tell me stories about a warrior god who would race across the sky at night chasing his enemies. But they always managed to stay just out of his reach. As hard as he would try to catch them, they would try just as hard to get away. They always succeeded. My mother told me that if the warrior managed to ever catch them, it would mean the end of the chase . . . the end of the world."

I followed his hand moving across the sky. "Look there, you see how much closer those stars are? The warrior god is finally catching up with his enemies."

Wirek frowned. "So, what? The world is coming to an end?"

Saano looked out into the night. "It is probably just an old legend." He glanced over at the horses and then back at us. "Of course, it might not be after all. Maybe there is more to it than old legend. Maybe we'll find out someday, eh?"

I nodded. "Maybe we will."

Wirek cleared his throat. "What's for dinner?"

Saano laughed. "Food! Yes, that's what we need." He jumped to his feet. "Forgive me for getting so sentimental on you." He rummaged through his pack, producing several carefully wrapped packages.

From one, he produced what looked like cured meat. He jammed some meat on to the end of three blunt sticks and then settled them over a forked twig above the fire.

From another package, he pulled out three small loaves of dark bread and placed these on the rocks closest to the flames. After five minutes, he proclaimed that dinner was served and handed us each a skewered meat stick and a loaf of bread.

I bit into the meat, surprised at how tender and tasty it was. I could tell Wirek was equally impressed.

"What is this?" he asked around a mouthful of meat.

"Yak," said Saano. He looked at me. "You like it?"

"Never had it before," I said. "But it's not bad."

"The bread," said Saano, "is an old family recipe. Secret

ingredients and all. My mother taught me when she realized she'd never have a daughter. Try it."

I did. As soon as I swallowed the flaky piece, I felt like an energy volt had hit me. I felt strangely rejuvenated.

"That's amazing," I said.

Wirek had a funny look on his face. "Very tasty," he said.

Saano only smiled. "Ah, such secrets. You know, the world revolves on such things. It's not money or love at all. It's intrigue. Curiosity. Even suspicion. That paranoia, doubt . . . it's what makes us quest on for the answers to our very souls."

I chewed some more of the bread, feeling even better about the dinner and the trip in general. We would prevail when we got to Lo Monthang. We'd rescue Jack and get him home, where he belonged.

I glanced over at Wirek, but he'd almost fallen asleep by the looks of it. I chuckled. The trip must have been taking a lot out of him.

"We'd better get him in the tent," I said to Saano.

With his help, I managed to roll Wirek inside and into his sleeping bag. Soon enough, horrendous roars of snoring streamed from the tent. Usually, I need complete silence when I sleep. But I had a feeling Wirek's hefty chainsawing wouldn't affect me tonight.

Saano packed another pipe and nodded at me. "You get some sleep. I'll take first watch."

"Watch?"

Saano got a funny look on his face as he unsnapped his *kukri.* "Of course. This can be a dangerous part of the country; you always keep a watch at night. I'll wake you at two."

I crawled into the tent and got my sleeping bag rolled out

next to Wirek. He was out completely. I tucked myself in, and within seconds, my eyes felt glued shut.

Sleep came soon after.

I don't know what actually penetrated my subconscious and prodded me awake a few hours later. Wirek's snoring continued to fill the tent and probably much of the area outside.

At first, I thought it might be a small animal rummaging around outside the tent, but Wirek's snoring would probably have kept anything smaller than a blue whale at bay.

And then I realized the noise was coming from inside the tent. Something or someone was inside with Wirek and me. My mind raced. How had they gotten past Saano? Maybe he was already dead.

Maneuvering for a look would be a problem.

I'd zipped my bag up pretty far, since I like to sleep like a mummy. I had my *tanto* inside the bag with me, but getting it unzipped and out would be difficult to do fast.

I heard a zipper being pulled down behind me. I realized I'd have to do the move, anyway.

I took a long, deep inhale and then jerked my entire body around. I planned to rip my hands out, with my *tanto* at the ready, in what I hoped was a fairly fluid movement.

In the darkness, I could just make it out.

Saano sat astride Wirek's chest.

The image didn't make sense to me at first.

But as the sleep faded from my eyes and I focused, I could see Saano had been examining the base of Wirek's neck. Now Saano was peering at me with some sort of vaguely amused curiosity on his face.

I realized I had the knife upside down.

"So," he said, "I guess this explains it."

I flipped the knife over and freed myself from the sleeping bag. "Explains what? What the hell are you doing to Wirek?"

Saano smiled and slid off him. "Confirming what I suspected a few hours ago."

Uh-oh. "Yeah? What's that?"

Saano prodded Wirek, who grumbled and started to wake up. "That this guy and you, most likely, are vampires."

I tried to laugh. "What? Don't be ridiculous. Vampires don't exist."

"The hell," said Saano. "Remember when I told you I'd been around the block quite a number of times? Well, Mr. Lawson, I've seen plenty of things that defy description and I've met plenty of strange people. And"—he smiled—"I happen to know all about your birthmarks."

"Anyone can have a birthmark."

Wirek was awake by then. "What's going on?"

I nodded at Saano. "Thinks we're vampires."

Wirek's ample eyebrows jumped a bit. "Yeah?"

"Yes. You have the mark."

Wirek chuckled. "That old thing? Used to be a tattoo. That's all."

Saano wasn't buying our act. "Really? If that's the case, then maybe Mr. Lawson there will lift up his shirt and show me he does not have the same mark."

Unfortunately, that wasn't going to happen, and Saano knew it. The birthmark of the vampire race is like a stigmata for some and a badge of honor for others. Every one of us has it at the base of our neck, near our clavicle on our upper chest. It can't be erased. It can't be covered.

After another thirty seconds of silence, Saano smiled. "So, you see, that answers my question."

I looked at Wirek, who seemed upset. "Now what?"

Saano shrugged. "Now I get some sleep while Mr. Lawson takes the next watch."

"What about the whole vampire thing? You don't seem fazed by it."

Saano shrugged. "Why should I be?"

The looks on our faces must have amused him because he started chuckling. "You think I would stop guiding you simply because you're vampires? Please, gentlemen, don't mistake me for some sort of dreary racist. I have nothing against vampires."

Wirek perked up. "No?"

"Of course not," said Saano, unrolling his sleeping bag. He slid out of his jacket. "I'm what you might call a very tolerant guy."

"That's good to hear," said Wirek.

But then Saano unbuttoned his shirt and took that off as well. It was only then, when he turned to us, that we understood. For there, emblazoned on his chest, in exactly the same position as our own marks, we saw his.

Saano was a vampire, too.

Chapter Twenty-five

The rest of that night passed uneventfully.

I didn't get much more sleep. And I spent my time on guard duty thinking about Saano. He sure was something of an oddity, especially considering the fact that he was a vampire.

Maybe I should have guessed as much. Maybe Wirek should have guessed it, too. He looked a little ashamed the next morning when he emerged from the tent.

We had another quick meal. Saano brewed up some bitter tea and we had a bit more yak and bread. Again, another bit of energy seeped into my system and I felt a lot more awake.

Saano saddled up our mounts and we headed off down the trail just as the first rays of sun bled over the hills. Saano took a hefty lead this time, I think because he wanted to give Wirek and me some time to talk.

"Sorry" was what what Wirek said first.

"About what?"

He pointed. "Him."

"What—we should have known? C'mon, you know how tough that can be. We've had hundreds of years to practice our skills at blending into the local population. All Saano's done is prove how effective that camouflage can really be."

"I guess," said Wirek. "But I still can't help feeling like I should have caught it sooner than when you woke up and found him checking out my mark."

"Be glad it was him and not one of Arvella's henchmen. I'd have been hard-pressed to get my weapon out in time to save you."

Wirek nodded. "We'll deal with her soon enough."

"Yeah. I've got some questions for our guide, though." I kicked my horse forward a length or two and caught up with Saano.

"Got a second?"

He laughed. "Am I going somewhere?"

"When did you make us?"

He shrugged. "Not really until yesterday afternoon along the trail. Although your wooden sword there should have been something of a giveaway."

"I might just have been one of those fanatical martial artists that comes over hoping to discover they're the next reincarnated Tulku warrior god or something."

"Yes, you could have been—and heaven knows I've seen plenty of those fools—but your bearing was different."

"How so?"

He shrugged. "Call it a soldier's intuition. I had a feeling about you. Wirek was tougher to place. He's not a warrior, per se. But you—" He stopped and stared at me. "We're two of a kind, you and I."

"Oh, yeah?"

"Yes. You've seen combat, haven't you?"

What was the use? "Yeah. I have."

"And you know the frailty of life. Most of our kind do not. I recognized it on your face. More than that, your spirit, your presence, emanates it. You've seen some hard times and that"—he pointed to the *bokken*—"has saved your life. Probably on more than one occasion."

He was certainly right about that. "I have respect for this sword. It's much more than just a piece of wood," I said.

"More so, since it could just as easily kill you as another of our kind." He leaned in close. "Who are you planning to kill with that?"

"We're not here to kill anyone, if we can avoid it."

" 'If you can avoid it.' Hmph. More warrior-speak. I think you know you'll have to use that again."

"I'm hoping not to."

"No? So why come here?"

"To rescue a young boy."

"One of our kind?"

"Yes."

"Rescue him from what?"

"From a traitor."

Saano's eyes narrowed. "Who has him?"

"Her name is Arvella," Wirek said, riding up to us. "Have you heard of her?"

"No," said Saano. "Should I have?"

"Probably not. Probably better that you don't know about her. Or what she can do."

Saano patted his *kukri.* "I have yet to meet anyone who cannot be felled with a few slashes from my trusty knife here."

"What about vampires?" I asked. "Your *kukri* wouldn't necessarily kill them, would it?"

"I could take their heads off and then find a branch

to stake them with,'' said Saano. ''I did it that way once before.''

''Here?''

''Hong Kong,'' said Saano. ''I'd been with the Gurkha regiment less than a year and we had a leave in the colony. It was late one night and I ran into one of our kind out hunting. But he did not obey the laws of our society. He had killed a human. I saw the crime happen. And I took matters into my own hands. A quick slash with my knife, his head came off. A nearby piece of wood sufficed to stake his heart with.''

''What'd you do with the body?''

''Weighted down and dumped in Kowloon Bay. There are many sharks that come in close to the ports at night to feed. I am sure they never tasted anything quite so interesting as what I fed them that moonless evening.''

Remarkable. Saano had done the work of a Fixer and not even known it. ''How'd you get involved with being a Gurkha? Not many of our kind work in the armies of humans.''

He shrugged. ''We don't usually have the same meetings with the Council that you all have in the civilized world. We're left to our own devices for the most part. The communities of Tibet and Nepal are small. And since we enjoy some degree of respect from the monks in the mountains, we're left alone by the Council for the most part. Every so often, a magistrate or governor journeys up here to check on us, see how we're doing, but that's about it.''

''So you decided to join the Gurkhas?''

He nodded. ''Sure. Why not? Everyone else I knew was doing it. For me to not join up would have provoked more suspicion.''

"But what about the obvious question of food?"

Saano chuckled. "There are few places where blood is in greater abundance than on the battlefields of humans. I made sure to volunteer for the most dangerous assignments. I never had much of a problem. I also doubled my duties as a medic, so bloody bandages were easy enough to come by."

"Speaking of which," said Wirek, "I haven't seen you drink anything since we've been on the trail. How are you keeping your energy up? Where's your stash?"

"You had some of it last night," said Saano. "Surely, you noticed how good the bread made you feel?"

The bread. I knew there was something about it. "You baked the blood into the bread?"

He nodded. "Like I said, it's an old family recipe. My mother taught me how to make it. Virtually undetectable and somewhat more potent than drinking it straight down. The cooking process is slow and laborious, but the end product is something spectacular. And it keeps for a long time; so if you make a batch of the stuff, you're in good shape for a year or so."

"You'll have to give me that recipe," said Wirek. "That was some fantastic food."

"I'll tell my mother," said Saano. "She'll be pleased to hear it."

"How old is your mother?"

Saano shrugged. "Let's see, I'm two hundred forty. She must be about four seventy-five by now." He sighed. "As time goes by, I find I have a hard time remembering the dates and ages of my family."

"How many of our kind live up here?"

"We're scattered," said Saano. "Long ago, they decided we'd be better off if we didn't congregate as a community and instead spread ourselves out. This way, we can keep an eye on things all over this region and let the others know. We have a fairly nice network set up, so communication is not difficult."

He smiled. "In fact, it was one of our kind who first passed word down of the trouble up north."

"They live up there?"

"No," said Saano. "You remember the story of the trekker I told you about? He was one of us."

"Incredible," said Wirek.

"What it is," said Saano, "is troubling. What exactly are we going to find up there? If you don't mind me asking, now that we are all on equal footing."

"Have you heard of the Invokers?"

Saano frowned. "Only in the old legends. I thought they were just simple superstitions."

"They exist," said Wirek. "And they used to have a school right here in Nepal."

"A school? Here?" Saano shook his head. "They did a good job keeping it a secret."

"Considering what they teach there, it's better off that they did," said Wirek. "Anyway, they haven't used the school for years now. But recently someone reopened it."

"This woman you call Arvella?"

"Yes."

Saano looked at me. "Where does the boy fit in?"

I sighed. "He's got the power of Invocation. Arvella kidnapped him and is holding him hostage. Most likely, she intends to use him in a special ceremony during the New Millennium celebration in a few days."

"How did you find this out?"

"The boy's father made me promise to protect him before he died."

Saano nodded. "How did the father die? This Arvella woman—did she kill him?"

"No." I cleared my throat. "I did."

Saano's eyebrows jumped as he almost jerked the reins back on his horse. "What on earth for?"

Wirek stepped in, thankfully. "Saano, have you heard of the Fixers?"

"Of course I've heard of them," said Saano. "But again, we're so far removed from the mainstream of our society up here, I always thought they were another legend."

"Well, then," Wirek said, smiling, you've got yourself a legend riding next to you."

Saano looked at me again. "You're a Fixer?"

"Yes. The boy's father was supposedly committing crimes. I got the order to execute him. We found out later that it came from Arvella, who wanted the father out of the picture."

"So she could get to the boy?"

"Yeah. Needless to say, I can't let the boy down. I can't fail in carrying out his father's dying request. I have to find him and get him back. He's too important to leave behind."

Saano whistled. "That's some karmic debt you've gathered for yourself there, Mr. Lawson. I guess we'd better get you both up to Lo Monthang on time to stop this Arvella woman."

"Thank you, Saano," said Wirek.

"Answer me this, though," said Saano. "What will you do with Arvella when you get up there?"

"Hopefully, we'll reason with her," I said. "Bring her back to the States and have her face the Council for her crimes."

"Think she'll go along with that plan?"

"I don't know."

"I doubt she will," said Saano. "So, what if she refuses to go?"

I nodded at my back. "Then we'll just have to resort to other measures."

Saano's jaw hardened. "Mr. Lawson, I think you and I are going to get along just fine."

Chapter Twenty-six

We were climbing in altitude.

According to Saano and Wirek, by the time we reached the Mustang region, we'd be traveling at heights of 3,488 meters. That's pretty damned high. And seeing Everest in the far-off distance scraping the sky at a level most commercial jets fly really made an impact on me.

The horses seemed unaffected by the altitude changes. As we trotted along, carving away the miles between us and our inevitable showdown, the horses just kept snorting and plodding along.

Saano estimated one more night on the trail would put us within a day of Mustang. A few more hours the next day and we'd reach the outskirts of Lo Monthang.

Wirek and I strategized that we'd optimally need a day to set up an observation post. From there, we could figure out our approach. Whether we'd have the luxury of that day or not remained to be seen.

The lush green fields that bordered every trail surprised me. According to Saano, the Nepali people had long ago mastered irrigation, which brought the nurturing waters into every available acre of land. They grew an assortment of crops, harvested what they could, feeding some of it to the animals and their families, and then marketed the rest.

Between Wirek and Saano, I had a running commentary of the land we passed. Saano's monologue seemed more recent. Wirek gave me a lot of history about the region, which included tales of brave monks who sought to establish Buddhist monasteries in what had once been a predominantly Hindu land.

Around six o'clock, stopped for the day. The sun dipped lower in the sky, staining the white clouds pink and orange. I took a second to appreciate the beauty of the sunsets in this part of the world.

I hopped off my horse and rubbed my ass. After so much riding on hard leather saddles, the entire region felt numb.

"Got an itch?" asked Wirek with a smile.

"I can't feel a thing back there. I think it's totally numb."

Saano came over and took the reins of our horses. "Just imagine how they feel, carting us around all day." He led the mounts to another grassy spot and got them set up with feed.

Wirek and I got the tent back up. Then Wirek went off looking for a concealed rock he could go to the bathroom behind.

By six-thirty, we'd built another roaring fire that spread warmth in the shallow cul-de-sac we sat in. The cool winds felt stronger up here than the previous night. My breathing, meanwhile, seemed less labored. I guessed my lungs were acclimating to the altitude changes.

Saano got out more packages for dinner.

"More yak meat?" I asked.

He nodded. "And the bread."

"Ah, the blood bread," said Wirek. "I could use some of that."

Saano looked pained. "'Blood bread'?"

"Well, does it have a name?"

"As a matter of fact, it's called *rotti.*"

"What's that mean?" I asked.

"It means 'bread,' " said Wirek. He looked at Saano. "Doesn't it have a more descriptive name than that?"

Saano shrugged. "Why should it? I know what I am referring to when I ask for it. So does my mother. Before you and Mr. Lawson here, no one else really ever knew about it. So it doesn't need a special name."

I took a bite of the yak. "How about this?"

"That's called *chamri,*" said Saano. "It means 'yak.' "

After dinner, Wirek pulled out his hip flask and passed it around. We each had a few pulls from it.

Saano smiled. "This is good blood. Did you bring it from the States?"

Wirek looked a little uncomfortable. "Uh . . . not exactly."

I looked at him. "What's that supposed to mean?"

"Well, we used up most of what I brought on the plane trip over, remember?"

"Yeahhhh . . ."

Wirek shrugged. "I had to go get more."

Saano started chuckling.

I sighed. "You mean—"

Wirek nodded. "That night in Kathmandu when you went back to the hotel, I said I had some things to do—"

"Who'd you get to give up this much?"

"Parts of Kathmandu are kind of rough. Not really safe for tourists and stuff. I simply walked around until I found a stabbing victim."

"Stabbing victim?"

"Knives are a popular choice over here."

"Great."

Wirek sighed. "Listen to me, Lawson. I know that city like the back of my hand. I knew where to go to find what we needed. Aren't you glad I did? After all, we might be in hard shape right now if I hadn't."

I frowned. "Yeah, sure. I'm just not crazy about anyone possibly being able to deduce our presence from a stabbing victim missing more blood than his wound would have suggested."

"Come on, who the hell would even know what to look for? Saano said himself the number of vampires in this region are scattered." He looked at Saano. "How many you think live in the city?"

Saano shrugged. "Only a few that I know of."

"Any chance you don't know 'em all?" I asked.

"Of course, there is always that possibility," he said. "But I strongly doubt it. As I said, our network functions quite well around here."

I nodded. "Yeah, you did." I looked at Wirek. He looked upset. "Don't sweat it, Wirek. I'm sure it'll be okay. I just wish you would have told me. Let me know what you're up to. Remember, I'm the one who deals with the subterfuge and conspiracies, okay?"

He grinned. "Yeah, okay. Sorry about that."

"It's just that we don't even know if this blood is safe or not."

Saano laughed out loud. "Wow, you're concerned about blood diseases? That's funny."

"Aren't you?"

He shook his head. "Not really. I think we can extract life force from anything. And the tests with AIDS on us haven't proven much yet."

"It affects a small percentage of us," I said.

"Too small a percentage to worry about," said Saano. "I'd be more concerned about tetanus from the knife blade. Not too many people in Nepal have AIDS, anyway."

"Still a risk," I said.

Saano nodded. "Well, risk sure seems something we can't escape, eh?"

I smirked. "Good point."

Saano dug out his pipe and passed it around. We each had a few drags and settled back into the grass, letting the stress of the day's travel melt away.

Overhead, the stars came back out to play. Saano watched the sky for minutes and frowned most of the time. Wirek noticed him doing so and cleared his throat.

"See something troubling, Saano?"

Saano nodded. "You remember the story I told you last night?"

"About the warrior chasing his enemies? Yes."

Saano pointed skyward. "Look there. You see how much closer that constellation is to those stars to the left? It's as if they've moved closer than they were last night."

I looked up, trying to see what he was looking at. From my perspective, they seemed about the same. But then again, I have never made much of a point of studying the night sky. I'm usually searching the gutters for slimeballs.

Wirek seemed to notice, though. "You're right. I see what you mean."

I spoke up. "Listen, guys, you sure the movements of the stars just don't have anything to do with how the seasons come and go? I know as this planet spins through space our position changes in relation to the constellations and planets and stuff. You sure this isn't just one of those instances?"

Saano shook his head. "I've lived here my entire life when I wasn't off serving in the army. I know how the sky changes throughout the year. I'm telling you, this is different. It is not natural."

I glanced at Wirek, who was still peering at the heavens. "Think it's connected to the New Millennium?"

His eyes never left the sky. "I'm not sure. I wish I'd brought some of my books along, but there wasn't time to do so. I also wish we knew exactly what Arvella had planned. It might explain some of this."

"No ideas?"

He shrugged. "Only what I said before. Remember, I'm not an Invoker and my experience with them is very limited. The only thing I think might be a possibility is that she's trying to pool her powers with the boy's. Together they'd be able to summon some very powerful spirit forces." He nodded at the sky. "But I don't know if it's enough to alter the course of the heavens."

Saano took another long drag on his pipe. In the darkness, the fire danced and spun around us, leaving fading dots before my eyes. The fatigue of traveling seemed to catch up with all of us at the same time. Wirek suddenly dropped off to sleep, leaning against the log he'd claimed earlier as his dinner roost. Saano's eyes drooped, and I felt like a lethargic blanket had covered my body.

Wirek and Saano beat me to the tent, so I volunteered to take first watch. Saano and I rolled Wirek into his bag, and then Saano zipped up the tent flap, leaving me alone with the fire and the night sky.

Far off in the distance, I thought I could see another fire burning somewhere. Possibly there were other trekkers out here. But Saano had assured us they stuck to the more frequently traveled paths. Camping on those trails was rare, due to what the Nepalese called "teahouses." They were small huts set up to shelter travelers as they trekked to and fro. Some were run by local villagers as an extra way to make some cash, while others were freestanding units that were simply shelters with a fireplace.

The air around me still had the residual smell from Saano's tobacco. It made the night feel a little bit more homey. I took over Wirek's log and leaned back into it.

I kept the *bokken* close by and pulled the *tanto* out of its sheath, looking at the light from the fire bounce off the finely honed steel blade.

As a rule, I try not to interfere with humans and their lives. My role in vampire society has always been to preserve the Balance, that delicate conspiracy that keeps our existence as a people concealed from humans.

But there are times when I do allow myself to get drawn into human affairs. Japan in 1973 was one such instance.

I'd been over on an assignment to help support a Fixer operation, which eventually got canceled. With a few extra days to myself, I wanted to grab some classes at the Kodokan Judo school in Tokyo. Riding the subway one night back to my hotel after some extra training, I'd witnessed what looked like three young thugs giving an elderly man a hard time.

I would have let the matter pass.

But for the knife that suddenly appeared.

The matter apparently escalated beyond a simple harassment.

Maybe it was the fact that I'd just come from a good vigorous workout at the school. Maybe it was because of the canceled operation. It could have been any number of things, but what it boiled down to was that I wanted some action.

I intervened.

The knife-wielding thug tried to stab me—coming at me with a straight stab. The knife was a long, thin blade perfect for punching through vital organs.

I pivoted, using his momentum and sending him sprawling. The knife clattered away. They abandoned it, which told me they were either very stupid or very professional.

I didn't have much chance to consider it. All three of them rushed me at once, intent on punching my brains out.

Multiple attackers are a lot easier to handle if you can use your environment to your advantage. In that case, I positioned myself by the door, forcing them to come at me from one direction.

It didn't take much to tangle them up in each other. By the time we rolled into the next station, I sent them all out the door, sprawling to the platform floor.

It was only as I did so that I saw the intricate tattoo winding its way up one of the thug's arms.

The old man leaped from his seat, discarding Japanese etiquette, and pumped my hand profusely, thanking me for helping him out. At the next station, he insisted on taking me out for dinner.

Outside in the Tokyo night air, he dragged me down alleyway after alleyway, until I was completely lost. Tokyo, at best, is a difficult town to find your way around in. But once you start ducking down side streets and cul-de-sacs, any navigation skill goes out the window.

We stopped at what looked like a decrepit, old wooden house with broken eaves and dangling gutters. The old man smiled when he saw my reaction, but he kept tugging me toward the shoji screen doors.

Inside was a different story.

A cleverly concealed restaurant awaited our patronage. Soft ambient lighting bounced off small tables, tatami mats, and ornate scrolls.

I glanced around at the clientele and instantly knew I was probably the first gaijin ever to walk in there. The old man wasted no time explaining what had happened on the subway. We were soon seated at what must have been the best table, sipping warm sake and awaiting our food.

The culmination of the meal came in the form of a delicately prepared dish called fugu. The old man took great pains to explain how difficult it was to find such a fish prepared properly. The poison of the blowfish acts as a neurotoxin, shutting down the neurological system, followed then by the respiratory and the cardiovascular. You're basically paralyzed while you die.

Of course, the risk of being poisoned while you eat the fish is what makes the dish so attractive. The danger acts as its own adrenalizer. The old man chuckled when he told me that despite a number of deaths resulting from improperly prepared fugu each year, so far none of them had occurred at the restaurant we were in.

My first bite set my taste buds whirling.

As a rule, I'm not a big fan of seafood. I can't stand shellfish, for example. But this fish tasted unlike anything I'd eaten before. It literally seemed to melt in my mouth, helped along with each sip of sake.

Before long, my host and I were swapping war stories. He told me about his travels throughout Russia and Manchuria as a young man working for the Japanese government. I entertained him with some of my more daring exploits in Europe, edited for content and exaggerated just enough to keep him enthralled.

The dishes soon dwindled. The crowds died down. But the sake continued to flow. The lighting seemed to darken as well. The old man leaned across the table and locked eyes with me.

"You are what we call a *henna* gaijin. Do you know what that means?"

"It translates as 'strange foreigner,' doesn't it?"

He smiled. "Perhaps that is its literal meaning, but we

use it to denote a foreigner who seems to have an innate grasp of our culture.'' He leaned back and took some more sake. I refilled his cup, per the demands of etiquette.

He nodded. ''We see the ones every day who come over here pretending to know everything about us. Some of them actually believe they will be accepted by our society one day. That we would actually think of *them* as Japanese. They've never learned that to a Japanese, an outsider is always an outsider—no matter how well they speak the language. No matter how many kanji or Buddhist scriptures they know, they will never be Japanese.'' He shrugged. ''Perhaps fate has dealt them a cruel hand denying them Japanese heritage. Perhaps they are just insecure, unable to feel comfortable in their own skin.''

He leaned forward again. ''But there are those rare foreigners who come over here and understand that. They never try to be Japanese, per se. They simply accept our culture and traditions for what they are, while still remaining true to their inherent nature. They remain foreigners but have the respect for what we are about. Do you understand?''

''I think so.''

He nodded. ''You are one of these men.''

''If you say so.''

His eyes crinkled. ''On top of this fact, you are also a warrior.''

There didn't seem to be much point in denying it. I'd foolishly spoken of my various jobs. I cursed the sake inwardly. Damned stuff was potent.

He went on. ''For a warrior, there can be no doubt in his actions. Reaction and response become inseparable. Your sense of *nagare*—'flow'—intertwines with the harmony of the universe. You become one with everything around you. Tonight you demonstrated that when you defended me from those Yakuza.''

Shit. Now the tattoo on the thug made sense. I gulped. "They were Yakuza?"

He nodded. "Young guns. What we call *teppo,* 'bullets.' They like to roust old guys like me."

"With knives?"

"Mostly for show, I think."

"Has that happened to you before?"

"No." He smiled. "Thanks to you, I'm sure it will be the last."

Getting involved with the Japanese Mafia was not one of the things on my must-do-while-in-Japan list. He must have sensed my apprehension because he chuckled.

"Do not worry about it. I'm sure they'd never say anything. If word got out they were beaten up by a gaijin, it would cause them too much loss of face. They'd be chastised by their *oyabun* in front of everyone in the gang."

I breathed easier.

"I am indebted to you for your intervention. I owe you a debt—what we call *giri*—that I don't think I can ever repay."

"It's not necessary to repay me."

He cocked an eyebrow. "But you understand what I'm saying."

I nodded. I could tell him a million times that he didn't owe me a thing for saving his life and it wouldn't matter. According to Japanese culture, he owed me his life. And he would probably spend the rest of his life attempting to repay that debt.

Unsuccessfully.

He went on. "As you no doubt ascertained, I am rather well known in this restaurant."

"I assumed you were a regular here."

"I am. True, their chef is a master and his delicacies

would draw anyone. But am known here, not for my constant patronage, but because of my work."

"Your work?"

He leaned back and the flush of alcohol faded. Instead, a veritable cloak of honor seemed to drape his body. "I am a swordsmith."

I exhaled in a rush. The Japanese revered their swords as if they were part of their very souls. And the men who crafted the blades usually occupied a post of great prestige. I tried to maintain my composure, hoping about what might come next.

"My swords are very famous. I come from a long line of such artisans. My family has practiced and perfected its technique dating back almost six hundred years. Nowadays the wait for one of my blades is so long, I fear I will never be able to complete them all before my death." He smiled. "Although, thanks to you, there will be a few more completed now before that happens."

He called for more sake. The owner of the restaurant, despite the late hour, appeared and refilled both our cups. My host took a long sip, then smiled. "I will make you a sword, *henna* gaijin. A very special sword. There will be no other like it in the world. And when it is done, you will know that I have poured much of my life and soul into its creation. As you did for me tonight, so, too, will I do for you."

I breathed again. "I cannot thank you enough for such a generous offer. I am honored that you would consider me worthy of one of your blades."

He bowed. "The honor is mine."

I shifted. He looked at me and cocked an eyebrow. "You want to ask me something? Please do so."

I hesitated. "Please don't misinterpret me, but would it

be possible to have you make me a wooden sword instead of a steelblade?''

''A *bokken?*'' He tilted his head. ''That is an unusual request. What would you do with such a sword? Practice?''

''I would have more need of a wooden sword than a live blade. And I would be honored to carry one of your creations into combat.''

He smiled. ''Miyamoto Musashi, one of our most famous swordsmen, is said to have killed many of his opponents with a *bokken,* do you know that?''

I wondered if old Musashi ever battled vampires. The thought brought a smile to my face. Probably not. I simply nodded. He smiled again.

''Very well. You will have the finest *bokken* in Japan. But I insist on also making you a real blade. If not a *katana* or a *wakizashi,* then a *tanto.* You may find this piece useful for your work as well.''

Knowing the effectiveness of a good blade in decapitation, I agreed.

We parted ways that night. He with my address and I without ever knowing the name of the great swordsmith who had taken me to dinner.

Three months later, I received a package at my house in Boston. Inside, in delicately wrapped silk and oiled paper, sat my two weapons. The *bokken* had been carved from the hardest wood known to man, lignum vitae, but it looked as flexible as a spring willow branch. It felt light but supple, as if it had a spirit of its own embedded in it.

Power flowed from it, and after a few test swings, I knew I would treasure the wooden sword forever.

The *tanto* blade glistened from the thin layer of oil still coating it.

Truly, they were exquisite weapons.

As far as I was concerned, the swordsmith had certainly

repaid me for my actions that night on the subway train. No amount of thanks from me would ever release him from his debt, however, because he would always feel that he had not done enough.

Still, I used the return address on the package to send him a proper thank-you note. A letter appeared within two weeks.

In tentative English letters, his senior student wrote and told me the old man was dead. He was ninety-five years old that night on the train. He didn't look a day over seventy. When he told me that he would put his life and soul into the weapons, I didn't pay much attention to it. But looking back, I often wondered if perhaps he used up the rest of his own vitality making those weapons.

Maybe someday I'd be able to ask him.

I hefted the *bokken* again in the Nepali night. It still felt good to hold. Power seemed to ripple up my arms every time I held it. I stood and did a few quick cuts with it in the air, watching the glint of the fire bounce off its oiled length.

I sighed.

Then stopped—abruptly.

Because close by, somewhere beyond the range of the fire, something moved in the cold darkness of that night.

Chapter Twenty-seven

I breathed.

Slowly.

Beyond the fire, I could sense movement.

But whatever moved in the darkness knew the lay of the land because it made no noise at all. If not for the sudden change in the air, I might not have even noticed it.

Given the amount of loose rocks that would go skittering and clattering if you stepped on them wrong, whoever or whatever moved beyond the firelight was a pro.

No doubt.

And that made me very nervous.

The fire crackled and popped as another piece of dried wood split and fell farther into the flames. Shadows danced around me as I casually reached for my *tanto*. The *bokken* sat ready in my right hand.

I wondered if my weapons would work on the yeti that

Saano told us about yesterday. I took another breath. I didn't smell anything.

Being by the campfire put me at a definite disadvantage. Whoever was out there could use the fire to see exactly what I was doing. On the other hand, I had no night vision whatsoever, since I'd been staring into the fire for most of the night.

I couldn't see beyond a few feet of darkness.

I edged closer to the tent. Wirek's snores cut through the night air and I prayed at any second Saano would emerge, completely disgusted with the sleeping conditions, and offer to relieve me. That would be good.

Very good.

And of course, it didn't happen.

I felt somewhat ridiculous standing there with a knife in one hand and the *bokken* in the other. I thought I must have looked like some bad samurai to whatever was out there.

I hoped again it wasn't yeti.

I remembered reading reports that they sometimes came down into the valleys and harassed villagers and campers. And the last thing I wanted on my hands was a dead abominable snowman.

Something moved to my left.

I turned.

Something moved on my right side.

I turned again.

Double shit.

Now there appeared to be more than one.

After a long day of riding, the last thing I wanted to do was face multiple attackers in the Nepali countryside without a gun.

My options weren't really options at all.

I could yell for help and try to wake up Saano. But I doubted they'd be able to mobilize all that fast. I could charge into the darkness and try to figure out who was stalking us.

Most likely, I'd die.

Or I could wait.

Possibly all night.

My so-called choices evaporated when a maroon-robed bald man suddenly materialized by the fire eight feet from me.

Well, materialized is a weird word. He had walked into the circle of light from the fire, but he'd done it so smoothly and quietly that I hardly even noticed.

He stood there looking at me.

He looked like a monk.

Then he looked at the weapons I held. He seemed almost amused by the *bokken.*

He kept his hands folded in front of his groin, with his feet shoulder-width apart. Something about the way he stood reminded me of some old martial arts stance I'd seen ages ago. But I couldn't place it.

He stood there waiting.

Just waiting.

Only eight feet separated us. Easy striking range for the *bokken* and the *tanto.* Still, something about the way this old man stood, something about the energy emanating from him, told me I'd be a fool to attack him.

We watched each other for five minutes.

I tried to relax.

My arms grew stiff.

He seemed to smile then.

I wondered what the hell amused him, but in that *saano* fraction of time when my mind relaxed, something came up behind me and clocked me.

And even as I fell to the ground, strong arms caught me,

cushioning my fall. Other arms grabbed the *bokken* and *tanto.* I sensed scurrying feet rushing into the campsite.

But still no noise.

Then everything went black.

Black as the damned night.

"Well, well, well, look who finally decided to join the world again."

My tolerance for sarcasm is usually low when I've been snookered. The expression on my face must have conveyed a distinct lack of fondness and admiration for Wirek, who was leaning over me when I opened my eyes.

He pulled back. "Oops, I guess Lawson's not in too bright a mood."

"I wonder why."

That remark came from Saano. I looked and saw he was sitting on what might have been hay. Motion rumbled up from below me. I blinked and saw that we were in some kind of wagon with bars on it.

"What the hell happened?"

Wirek frowned. "You tell us. We woke up like this a few hours ago."

"There was a monk, I think," I said. "Last night, by the fire. I sensed movement on the periphery of the camp. Then this little old guy appeared in the camp. We had a staring contest. The next thing I know, someone clocked me from behind."

"I thought Fixers were incredible fighters," said Saano.

"Who told you that?"

"Everyone believes it." He frowned. "Staring contest? Hmph. Some fighter."

"Yeah, well, they got us, too," said Wirek. "And without a fight."

"What about our stuff?"

"Probably along for the ride. I don't think these guys would leave it behind."

"Who the hell are they?"

We looked at Saano, who frowned. "Don't ask me. I haven't got a bloody clue."

"I thought you knew this country backward and forward."

He shifted. "Well, obviously, I have not heard of any bands of monks traveling around and kidnapping trekkers; otherwise, I probably would have said something."

Wirek whistled. "Guess Lawson isn't the only one feeling chipper today."

I examined the bars. They were made from what looked like high-quality steel. I rattled them. They didn't budge.

"Don't bother," said Wirek. "Saano and me had a go at 'em earlier. They're solid."

I slumped back. "Any idea where we're headed?"

"Hopefully up to Mustang," said Wirek. "But I can't be sure."

"We are still headed northeast," said Saano.

"How's that?"

He pointed at the cloth covering the wagon we rode in. "See the way the sun hits the canvas? That shows our direction. I've been plotting it since I woke up." He sighed. "We are still headed for Mustang. And Lo Monthang, most likely."

I looked at Wirek. "You said there were temples up there, right? Two of them."

He nodded. "Yeah, old ones. Hundreds of years old, but I never heard of those monasteries having monks like this. What's your estimation of their skill?"

"Well, they sure put one over on me. And they grabbed you two without waking you up? That's got to count for something."

"I thought you studied martial arts," said Saano, glancing over. "Didn't you even put up a fight?"

I sighed. "Yeah, I study. I've studied for years. But that doesn't mean there won't always be someone out there who's a helluva lot better than I am."

He frowned again. "Maybe *I* should have kept watch last night."

Wirek shook his head. "You can't blame Lawson. He did his best, believe me, I know him. If he says he was taken out by professionals, that's exactly what happened."

I rubbed my neck. "Good solid hit, too. They knew just where to strike me."

Wirek looked. "Nice bruise. Who do you think these guys are?"

I shrugged. "I don't know much about Nepali martial arts. Or monks who practice, for that matter."

"I'll bet these aren't Nepali monks," said Saano. "I've never heard of Nepali monks that would do this. And since we're still headed to Mustang, then they are most likely Tibetan monks. Possibly they are former Khampa."

I looked at Wirek again. "Those guerrillas you told me about."

"Freedom fighters," said Saano. "There is a difference."

"What if they're not Khampa?" asked Wirek.

"Then they are possibly warrior monks," said Saano finally. He looked at me. "If what you say is true, then they may be from a secret sect I have heard of only in whispers."

"What kind of secret sect?"

"They have many names, none of them are usually correct. I have heard them called *dop dop* fighters, the Lion's Roar sect, and so on. But most of the few people that have ever run across them have only called them one thing: deadly."

"Great." I lay back down in the hay. "That's just fucking

great." I didn't have time to be dicking around with a sect of warrior monks. Not with Jack's life dangling by a thread. Not with Arvella planning something decidedly nasty for a night or two from now. The timing couldn't have sucked worse.

Saano scooted over. "Sorry. I shouldn't have said some of those things a few moments ago."

"Forget it. I'm just as upset."

He looked at me and grinned. "Wirek's right about one thing."

"Yeah? What's that?"

Saano pointed. "It is a real nice bruise."

Under us, the wagon wheels continued to bump and roll along. We were setting a good pace, though, and elsewhere I heard the footfalls of more horses.

I asked Saano, "Are we in some kind of caravan?"

He nodded. "I make perhaps a dozen horses in total. If we are setting the same pace we set the past few days, we should be in the Mustang Province by now. And we may well reach Lo Monthang by this evening."

"What time is it, anyway?"

Saano showed his wrists. Wirek grinned. "They took our watches. And anything else that might be conceivably used against them, I gather."

"So, why kidnap us? Why go to the bother of having to herd us like this?"

Wirek shrugged. "Your guess is as good as mine, Lawson. Maybe we violated some kind of cultural taboo."

"Don't be ridiculous," said Saano. "We violated nothing. After all, I would know if we had done something the locals might find offensive. We have been most respectful." He scratched his armpit. "No, this was a simple snatch. What we used to call in the army a 'cosh and carry.' "

"Sounds Brit all right," I said.

Saano nodded. ''I participated in several of them. Steal into the enemy lines, grab one of their top people, and get back to the good guys before the bad guys even know we were there. Very effective.''

''I guess that just leaves us with more questions, then,'' I said. ''But most important is why we've been snatched.''

Wirek lay down in the hay. ''We're not going to figure it out in this wagon, that's for sure. Might as well rest up in case we have to take action when we do stop. An old guy like me needs his rest.''

Saano looked at me. ''You know what that means.''

''Yeah. It means you and I are going to be lulled to sleep by the horrendous noise he makes when he snores.''

Wirek flipped his middle finger up at me. ''Go to hell.''

''I'm sure I'll be there soon enough, Mr. Chain Saw.''

But despite the fact that Wirek immediately fell asleep and began snoring, the rhythm of our bumpy ride soon lulled Saano and I asleep as well.

I hoped when we woke up that things looked better than they did just then.

Chapter Twenty-eight

When the wagon finally stopped, darkness seemed to be seeping back into the sky. The interior of the wagon was darker than outside.

In the dim light, I could see both Wirek and Saano sitting up, alert. We were ready for action.

The canvas tarp that covered the wagon was yanked off.

Only then did we finally see who our hosts were.

The first face I saw belonged to the old monk who had stepped into the firelight back at our camp. He peered close to the bars, scrutinizing us each in turn, then smiled at me. He turned to a younger monk and nodded.

The younger monk unlocked the back of the cage and gestured for us to get out. I went first, followed closely by Saano and then Wirek. After being cooped up all day long, my legs buckled at first as blood rushed back into them.

I finally stood and it felt good to do so.

The old monk smiled again and then cleared his throat. ''Welcome to Vajra.''

His English sounded perfect. I looked around. The temple or monastery we were in looked as if it had been made from mud brick hundreds of years ago. Saano and Wirek scanned the courtyard. High brick walls enclosed the inner courtyard on all sides.

Saano spoke first. ''Are we in Lo Monthang?''

The monk nodded.

Saano frowned. ''I know of only two temples up here, Jamba and Thubchen. Where is this one located?''

''Close by to the other two, although you would never notice it. It is better that way, we think. After all, if word got out of our existence, there would be repercussions.''

''What sort of repercussions?'' I asked.

The monk smiled. ''Some of our . . . friends to the north might decide to suddenly come south and visit us. That would be bad.''

''Friends to the north? You mean the Tibetans?''

''No, we are Tibetan. I mean the Chinese.''

Wirek rubbed his shoulder. ''Why are we here?''

The old monk smiled again. ''I think you know why you are here. Otherwise, you would not have trekked so far already, no?''

''I mean, why did you kidnap us?''

''We didn't kidnap you. We protected you,'' said the old monk. ''Believe me. You would never have reached your goal if not for us.''

Circumspect speech has a way of annoying me pretty fast. Especially after riding on the back of an animal all day long. ''What are you talking about?''

''You must be tired,'' said the old monk. ''Let me show you to your quarters. We can talk later.''

Saano started forward. ''We should talk now—'' He

reached forward, trying to grab the old monk's arm. But as he did, the monk simply turned so slightly, it barely looked like he moved at all.

But Saano moved.

He found himself flying through the air and landing in a crumpled heap a few yards away. The old monk shook his head.

"Please refrain from trying that in the future." He turned back to Wirek and me. "This way, please."

Saano got to his feet and brushed himself off, muttering a string of what must have been obscenities in Nepali.

The old monk led us up a winding staircase that seemed to dissolve into the wall itself. A small doorway led inside.

Cool darkness enveloped us.

We stopped for a moment.

On all sides, giant statues of Buddha and various other Tibetan deities seemed to converge. One of them, with a particularly fearsome scowl on his face, sat directly in front of us. He held a strange-looking sword in his right hand, while the other hand clasped a coiled rope. The old monk paused to bow before it and then continued leading us along the giant passageway.

The scent of what smelled like myrrh filled the air and our footfalls hardly registered in the cavernous temple. Around us, in the deep shadows, we could see other monks tending to their duties. The temple appeared to have been carved right out of the very mountain itself.

Wirek came up next to me. "Man, this is weird."

I nodded. "Doesn't seem like they mean to harm us, though."

Saano harrumphed at that and rubbed his hip where he'd fallen. "You didn't get thrown through the air. Did you see what he did? The monk never even touched me."

"He just turned at the right moment," I said. "I've seen

techniques like that before, but he must be very advanced at his age. I wouldn't screw around with him again."

"Yeah. One time is enough to convince me," said Saano.

Ahead of us, the old monk turned and gestured to a wooden door. I opened it. Inside the room, there were three beds. Our gear was in there as well. I was surprised and happy to see my weapons. Saano nearly began sobbing when he saw his beloved *kukri*.

I turned to the old monk. "You must have a name. What should we call you?"

He smiled. "Lama Siben is fine. Or simply Siben, if you prefer."

"Siben," I said. "Is that a title?"

He smiled. "Of sorts. It means 'chili,' as in the pepper. A leftover name from my younger years. I think you Americans call it a nickname."

"You know we're American?"

Siben shrugged. "I know all about you, Lawson, Wirek, and Saano. We went through your wallets last night."

I nodded. "When can we talk?"

"Freshen up first. We will serve dinner in an hour. Afterward, we can talk." He turned and glided back down the corridor, until he vanished around a corner.

I turned back into the room and saw Wirek checking over his stuff. "Everything's here," he said. "Nothing's been taken."

I looked at Saano. "What do you think the old man meant when he said we would never have gotten here on our own?"

Saano shrugged. "I don't know. Perhaps there was an ambush."

"Ambush?"

"It's possible. If someone got word you and Wirek were in Nepal, they would have had plenty of time to set one up."

"Even on the route we took?"

Saano grinned. "Only so many ways to get up here. Even for a guide like me, there's only a few routes. Other people know them."

Damn. This might complicate our rescue attempt. Well, we'd deal with that shortly.

I glanced around. "I suppose running water is out of the question, eh?"

"Not quite," said Wirek, pointing to another room in the back. "There's a cold waterfall in there. You can use that." He grinned. "Probably shrink your balls up real fast, though."

"Such a comedian," I said. "Guess I'll see how cold it is."

Cold turned out to be an understatement. Wirek wasn't kidding. Stepping out from under the frigid waterfall, someone might have thought my throat was swollen, but it was just my nuts.

Wirek and Saano took turns getting washed up.

When we were finished dressing, a soft knock sounded on the door. I could see Saano debating about trying to conceal the *kukri* on himself.

"Put it away," I said. "If they even thought it was a threat, you wouldn't have it now."

He frowned but saw the logic. Reluctantly, he slid the *kukri* back into his pack.

I opened the door and Siben stood there. He smiled at us. "You all look refreshed."

"Thanks to the freezing cold shower you've got installed back there," said Wirek.

"You mean the water from the mountains."

I blinked. "That's Himalayan melted snow we just bathed in?"

"Of course. In case you didn't know, we don't have many

free-flowing rivers up here. The mountains provide the vast majority of our water."

"Does it flow in all of the rooms?" asked Wirek.

"No," said Siben. "We routed some off our meditation chamber to our guest room here a few years back."

"Meditation chamber? You mean you meditate in the cold water?"

"Certainly. But we also meditate under the waterfall itself. It's quite exhilarating." He gestured to the hall. "Your meal is this way."

We tagged along after him, but he always seemed just ahead of us. His flowing robes covered his feet, so he almost seemed to levitate down the hardwood floors that had been built on top of the hard interior mountain rock underneath.

At last, we came to a room where a long, rough-hewn wooden table sat with several dishes on it. I sat down and saw some meat dishes, rice, and vegetables. I frowned and looked at Siben.

"I thought most monks were vegetarians."

"Most are." He smiled. "We are not."

Wirek was busy gnawing on what looked like a beef rib. Saano was still examining his food. Siben produced a small flask from his pocket.

"You may also require this for your sustenance, I think."

Wirek's eyes lit up when he saw his flask. "I'll take that, thank you."

Siben handed it to him and then stepped back. "Am I right in assuming its contents are blood?"

For an old monk, he didn't miss a trick. Wirek looked at me, but the hesitation may as well have been a giant affirmative. Nevertheless, Wirek nodded.

"Yes."

Siben smiled. "Thank you for being honest with me. I appreciate that." He sat down, seemingly satisfied. He turned to me. "I wondered when we would see the arrival of your team."

"Team?" I stopped eating some of the rice. Wirek handed me the flask and I took a sip. "What do you mean?"

Siben's perpetual grin wavered only slightly. "Ever since the occurrences began. We have waited for the one who would set the scales right again. You," he said, pointing at me, "are that individual."

"What occurrences exactly?" asked Wirek.

"The evil *yidam* that now hunt the local villages, of course. They are your kind, but evil." He raised an eyebrow. "We have known of your existence for hundreds of years. But we have respected your secrecy in much the same way we would want others to respect our privacy." He sighed. "But now this evil group has taken up residence here. They must be stopped. That is why you're here, isn't it?"

"Part of the reason, yes." I ate some of the beef.

Siben nodded. "Then allow me to explain why it became necessary to 'kidnap' you, as you called it." He looked up and suddenly a young monk entered the room bearing a steaming cup of what must have been tea. Siben took a small sip and thanked the monk, who withdrew; then he turned back to us.

"Your enemies have been aware of your movements and have followed you since you left Kathmandu."

"How?"

Siben shook his head. "We do not know exactly."

I shot Wirek a look. There was a good chance his borrowing of juice from that stabbing victim back in Kathmandu had raised the alarm.

Siben shook his head as if reading my mind. "I do not think it was due to any action you took in the city. If this group is as capable as they seem to be, they must surely have anticipated your arrival and set up watchers." He took another sip of tea. "Regardless, they knew you were heading this way. And they were prepared for you."

"An ambush?" asked Saano.

Siben nodded. "You would not have gotten five miles farther along the trail before you were trapped and killed. We realized what was happening and took the necessary steps to ensure your survival."

"How so?"

"By kidnapping you last night and secreting you in the midst of our caravan, we were able to get past the ambush without arousing suspicion. Furthermore, a group of three volunteers from this *gompa,* this monastery, selflessly volunteered to pretend to be your party and trek off to the west of here in an attempt to throw off your ambushers."

"They're posing as us?" asked Wirek.

"Yes, but they will not hold up to scrutiny if the ambushers decide to get close and investigate. But hopefully by then, your mission will be done and over with, so the point is moot."

"What about the three monks posing as us?" I asked.

"If things go well, they will return here."

"And if not?"

Siben shrugged. "They are quite skilled. And they have been instructed about the techniques necessary to kill your kind. Perhaps they will escape unharmed." He took a sip of tea. "Perhaps they will die."

That seemed rather callous to me and I said so.

Siben smiled. "We believe in reincarnation. Death is merely a temporary stop as the wheel goes around. And perhaps some of them will escape the wheel this time around. One never knows."

"But they're sacrificing themselves for us—they don't even know us."

"That is true, but they are prepared to sacrifice themselves for the cause. And in this case, the group that is inhabiting the old school your kind used to run up here must be destroyed. They are upsetting the harmony of this sacred region." He looked at me. "You must succeed in your task."

"You know about the school here as well?"

Siben smiled. "We know much of what goes on in this region. Our survival depends on it."

Wirek cleared his throat. "Excuse me, Siben, but would you mind telling us about your sect here? I traveled this way many years ago and never heard of you."

Siben nodded. "I would be disappointed if you had. We have endeavored to remain undetected for as long as possible." He leaned back and took another sip of his tea. "We are guardians of sorts, a sect that strives to protect the old ways of our ancient traditions. We are unlike many of our comrades in the more orthodox temples. We believe in physical perfection as much as mental and spiritual perfection. To that end, we have sometimes been called warrior monks. When the Bodhisattva first visited this region thousands of years ago, he brought with him certain physical exercises, what you would call martial arts. We still practice those ancient ways. Every day. Every one of us practices. Until we die."

"Amazing," said Wirek. He looked at Saano. "So the rumors are true."

Saano nodded. "Apparently so."

"And you knew that we would be coming here?" I asked.

"Not in the concrete way you are thinking. But the universe does not unleash such an evil group as this without also releasing a counterbalance. We looked to the night sky and saw that you would be coming."

"You've been in Nepal a long time?" asked Saano.

"We established this monastery many years ago. Some

time later, we moved north to Tibet. When the Communists took over and began their systematic annihilation of our culture, we escaped, came back here, and resumed our way of life."

"Do you fight the Chinese?"

Siben smiled again. He seemed to do that a lot. "We do not struggle against the flow of a harmonious universe. We endeavor to help the flow of cosmic justice."

Saano looked at me. "Well, that tells me absolutely nothing."

I waved him off. Human politics didn't exactly concern me at that point. "What can you tell us about the group?"

"They are led by a woman," said Siben. "And for one of your kind, she is remarkably powerful. She is able to call the spirits from their homes on other planes and bring them onto this plane with ease."

Wirek frowned. "You know a lot."

"We see a lot," said Siben. "And we have seen the fear of the villagers. Yet we have been powerless to stop them. We tried. Several of our brethren lost their lives in the attempt." He finished his tea. "We are glad that you are all here."

I leaned forward. "Have you seen a boy with this group?"

"A boy?" Siben frowned. "I have not heard anything about it. But I will check. We try to keep their activities under close watch without letting them know we are around. Tonight I will hear what our scouts have to say and see if they have seen this boy you speak of."

"He's not evil," I said. "We're here to rescue him as well."

Siben nodded. "I understand." He stood. "Please. Finish your meal and then rest. Tomorrow we can discuss your options. And hopefully, within a day we will be rid of this evil presence. Good night."

He disappeared out of the room, leaving the three of us with the rest of our dinner. But I don't think anyone felt much like eating.

I know I sure didn't.

Chapter Twenty-nine

We awoke to a fresh covering of snow blanketing every nook and cranny of the mud brick. Cool breezes stole through the *gompa* and tried to invade our room. But somehow the fire roaring in the hearth kept them at bay. I suspected monks had come into our room throughout the night to keep fresh wood on the fire.

Again I'd heard nothing.

We bathed quickly. Quicker because the freezing water made you want to jump out of your skin as soon as it touched you. I longed for a long, steamy shower back home in Boston. Just that thought alone reminded me of how truly far away from home Wirek and I were.

Siben waited for us outside the room and seemed happier today than yesterday. I chalked that up to his unease at getting acquainted with a bunch of vigilante vampires. Even if he and the rest of the monks here knew about our kind, they might not necessarily be inclined to trust us.

But evil has a way of clotting unlikely allies. We might even form a tough scab. And hopefully, Arvella wouldn't be able to pick us off before we could get to her and her cronies.

Personally, I wanted a little face time with Petrov. I had some evening up to do with that bastard.

"Did you sleep well?"

Actually, we all had. There seemed to be something about the monastery that made sleeping nice and easy, the way it should be.

Saano stretched himself out some and yawned again. "What's for breakfast?"

Siben demurred. "We don't have much. Breakfast for us is usually just some fruit and a porridge. You're welcome to some, if you'd like."

We ate in the same room we had dinner in the night before, which gave me the distinct feeling that as much as Siben was welcoming us here, he was also making sure we interacted as little as possible with the rest of the monastery's inhabitants.

Not that I could blame him.

After all, we represented a serious threat to the sanctity of life here. Even though these were not your average monks, they were all still here for the common reason of seeking enlightenment, or some semblance thereof.

Add to that the fact that we were vampires, and I'm sure it was all Siben could do just to keep us entertained and out of everyone else's way.

After breakfast, we followed him out to a larger room where roughly twenty monks were engaged in a vigorous practice of martial arts. I stopped, enthralled by what I was seeing. Having been involved with various styles for years, I was a bit of a junkie when it came to researching and watching styles from days gone by.

Siben noticed my interest and stopped so I could watch for a few minutes. I heard Wirek sigh behind me and start explaining to Saano what a freak I was for "this stuff."

I looked at Siben. "How old is the style?"

He frowned. "There are varying reports as to its age. Some say it came with the Bodhisattva himself almost two and a half millennia ago. Others say it is more recent, perhaps only as old as the fourteenth century."

"Six hundred and some odd years is still a long time."

Siben nodded. "Indeed. There are many similarities between this and some of our older cousins to the north in China."

"It's fascinating." I pointed to two of the students. "How long have they been training?"

Siben smiled. "Those two. They are brothers. We found them twelve years ago out in the mountains. We think they were with their parents crossing over from Tibet when they were attacked by brigands. The parents were killed; they were left for dead. We adopted them. They've been here ever since. And trained ever since."

"They look fantastic."

"They're coming along," said Siben. He gestured down a long corridor. "We need to go there. Please."

We followed the corridor for almost five minutes before it suddenly opened out onto a vast vista of snow-covered mountains. Siben pointed to the east.

"That is Annapurna. She is magnificent."

Magnificent barely did it justice. The mountain zigged and zagged, angling up toward the heavens. Snow and ice broke off like jagged knives thrusting brutally into the horizon.

My appreciation for the mountains ended when Saano whistled. "What the hell is going on over there?"

I looked to where he pointed at a snowfield closer to the

monastery. A single monk sat in the middle of the snow, naked, except for what looked like wet sheets draped about his body.

Siben smiled. "You are looking at an example of what we call *tumo.*"

"*Tumo?*"

Siben nodded. "The initiate sits without his clothes under a blanket of wet, cold cotton cloths. Using only his mind, he increases his body temperature to the point where he can literally dry the sheets."

Wirek's eyebrows jumped. "Amazing."

Saano remained unconvinced. "You've got to be kidding me."

"I assure you, it is not a joke," said Siben. "Watch carefully."

And as we did, steam began rising from the sheets covering the monk. After twenty minutes of this, he stood and walked calmly back toward the monastery and past us. As he did so, I felt the sheets and found them dry, almost warm to the touch.

Saano looked shocked. "Incredible."

I grinned. "You've lived here all your life and never seen this?"

Saano frowned. "I'm a soldier. I'm not used to this stuff."

Siben smiled again. "Shall we go and have a look at your target?"

"Please."

We followed him along a carefully concealed walkway overlooking much of the valley below. What had been green fields yesterday were now snow-covered sheets of white canvas.

"We control most of this mountain here," said Siben. "Over the years, we've carefully constructed walkways and tunnels such that it is impossible to see them unless you know precisely where to go. And if you happen to stumble onto them, or are a potential threat, we also employ a number of what you would call 'countermeasures.' "

A cold wind snapped up a fresh burst of snow into our faces. Wirek sighed and wiped his eyes. "I miss the warm weather back home."

I looked at him. "What warm weather? It's February and it sucks back in Boston."

"Yeah, but spring is coming and that's good enough for me right now."

Saano cleared his throat. "Guys."

We stopped.

Siben pointed across the valley. "There. Across the valley is where the old school for your kind was." He looked at Wirek. "Was it also a monastery?"

"Of sorts," said Wirek. "Of sorts."

Siben nodded. "From what I heard last night, the woman you are after has a number of followers with her. Most are from the local region, it would seem. But my scouts also tell me there are some who look as you do. Westerners." He looked at me. "And my scouts say there is also a small boy with them."

I breathed a sigh of relief. That was good news. If Jack hadn't been with Arvella, there was no use in going on as far as I was concerned. But his being here meant our assumptions back in Boston had been correct. I wasn't sure if that realization comforted me much.

"How many are with her in there?"

"Almost twenty." Siben regarded me for a minute. "Tall odds, wouldn't you say? There are but three of you."

I nodded. "Yeah, but we don't have any choice. Odds aren't something I've ever really tried to get on the good side of. I just accept them and do my job regardless."

"But even you must admit that there are times when help is something you would not reject."

"Absolutely. Which is why I'm lucky on this trip."

"Lucky?"

I nodded. "I've got these two jokers along to keep me company."

"Three against twenty?" Siben chuckled. "And you call that lucky. You have an interesting perspective, Lawson. I appreciate your view of things."

"Are you driving at something, Siben?"

He shrugged. "An offer of help if you want it. Some of us would go with you."

I shook my head. "You don't know what you'd be facing in there. We do. It's better if we handle it alone."

"We know of your kind. We know how to kill them."

"I'd like to do this without your help, if possible. They've already killed a fair number of humans in this valley. I would not want any more to join those numbers."

"You're sure?"

Part of me wanted to say no. Part of me wanted to say, *Cool, come along and help me kill some badass vampires who have kidnapped a small kid.* But these guys weren't even supposed to know we existed. And they definitely weren't supposed to be helping us kill our own kind. So, while part of me dearly wished I could say yes, a bigger part of me knew the answer would always be no.

"Thanks, anyway. We'll handle it alone."

"As you wish. I insist on at least having one of us show the way inside. Otherwise, you'll be spotted as soon as you enter the valley and your entire trip will have been for nothing."

"All right. We'll take a guide. But only on the condition that as soon as we reach the temple, he comes back here. I don't want any stragglers. Once we get close, anyone is a potential enemy."

Siben nodded. "Agreed."

I looked across the valley at what looked like just another mountain. But looking real close, I could see the detailed carvings that made it stand out. I doubted if you were up close that you'd notice the peculiar lines, but being here I could see it plainly. I looked at Wirek.

"How old did you say the school was?"

"Ages. They started teaching Invokers there over a thousand years ago."

"And they closed it down when?"

"Maybe twenty years back. When Arvella first came to the Council. They'd been wanting to change locations for years, but she'd insisted on remaining in the Himalayas. Part of me used to think she got promoted to the Council just because they wanted to move the school."

"Maybe you're right."

He shrugged. "Maybe. Doesn't matter much now. We're still here, after all."

Siben pointed. "Look there. By that snowdrift. Do you see?"

I scanned left to right, finally coming on to the larger bank of snow. A patch of what looked like brown stood out.

"What is it?"

"One of your kind, I would think," said Siben. "Or it could be a human with a strong tolerance for sitting in cold snow for hours. Either way, it is a sentry like the ones I told you about. There are several scattered about the valley. I fear our ruse to mislead them may not have worked."

"Can your guide get us past them without confrontation?"

"Yes."

I nodded. "Good. Then we'll go tonight. We don't have much time left."

Chapter Thirty

According to Wirek, darkness slid over the top of Annapurna like a bad hangover following a night of slamming back tequila. I guessed he had enough personal experience to know.

Saano, Wirek, our guide, and I waited for the darkness to ooze down to the valley floor before we moved out.

Siben had graciously given us a change of clothes that were darker than what we'd brought along. They seemed warmer as well.

"Where you're going," he'd said, "you'll need every piece of concealment you can get."

Our guide, Chudao, a wiry twig of a guy who looked no older than twenty, took point. He guided us out of the mountain temple's relative safety and down the rocky pathways. Snow crunched underfoot, grinding our footfalls against loose rocks and slippery lichen as we made our way to the valley below.

My *bokken* sat strapped across my back for ease of movement, while my *tanto* lay ready in its sheath. I followed behind Chudao and behind me came Saano. Wirek brought up the rear.

Chudao moved slowly.

But he guided us past piles of loose shale hidden under refreezing snow and ice. The time we spent moving quietly was worth it. If anyone heard us coming, we'd be dead before we got anywhere near rescuing Jack.

Sweat covered all of us by the time we reached the valley, despite the falling temperatures. A flash of a breeze washed over us, making goose bumps spring to life on my skin. The steady seep of adrenaline dripping into my bloodstream, like an IV, increased as my pounding heart ticked up a notch.

Chudao bent, examining the ground. Snow that had melted during the day's sunlight was now freezing up again. We'd have to speed our process or risk slipping on new ice during the ascent. And we couldn't afford any injuries.

Chudao sensed the urgency in my eyes. We moved faster.

We were approaching the position of the sentry that Siben had pointed out earlier. Chudao didn't slow down. What if the sentry saw us? What if he raised an alarm?

Still, Chudao refused to slow down.

Worry got the best of me and I finally tugged on his sleeve.

He turned and looked at me. I frowned and mouthed, "What the hell?"

He just smiled.

And kept moving.

And then I saw him.

The sentry?

No.

A big, bald head and brilliant smile appeared.

Siben.

He waved. I looked behind him. The body of the sentry lay askew in the snow. Was he unconscious or had Siben killed him? I looked at Siben, but he merely bowed.

Chudao gestured for us to keep moving.

As we walked, I marveled at Siben's skill. In the short span of time between when he gave us the change of clothes and when we began the trek, Siben had come down here and taken out the sentry. Pretty damned impressive for an old guy.

The trail now wound its way back uphill, off the level valley floor. The walking became tricky again. My foot slipped off some loose pebbles concealed under some of the snow and sent them skipping off larger boulders, spilling back down toward Wirek.

I looked back.

Wirek frowned at me and put a finger to his lips.

Well, let him come up and try being quiet. I turned and kept moving.

Chudao's hand shot into the air a second later.

We stopped—and shrank off the trail into the side of the mountain, using the shadows to conceal us.

Chudao turned and told me to wait while he went ahead.

I'm not much for entrusting my fate to someone I only met about twenty minutes ago. But since I'd only recently demonstrated my inability to move quietly, I'd shut up and sit tight while Chudao checked out the trail ahead.

We watched him slip up the trail. He rounded a corner.

And disappeared.

The sound of abrupt movement filled the night air, but the wind drowned out any detail. Then a few small rocks came tumbling down the trail toward us. We ducked farther into the shadows, holding our breath.

Chudao appeared a moment later and waved us on.

We rounded the bend.

Another sentry lay off to the side of the trail. I wondered if he was knocked out or dead. But then a flash of lightning lit the area up.

A stake jutted out of the sentry's heart.

Dead.

Chudao was quickly earning my respect. Most humans aren't much of a match for vampires. We're tough to kill, stronger than humans, and able to withstand all sorts of damage.

But Chudao had only taken a moment to kill this guy.

The relative ease with which Siben and his sect killed was shaking up my previous perspective on Buddhist monks. I thought they were all sworn against taking any life. Somehow, Siben and his sect were different. If we had time, I'm sure it would have made for interesting conversation.

The trail leveled off some, but it kept winding around, bend after bend. Each twist made me more nervous than the last, and I knew we'd be getting closer to the entrance of Arvella's fortress.

Chudao increased the distance between us. I assumed he wanted to be able to take out any threat quickly. But no other sentries stood watch along the trail.

We stopped in a small cul-de-sac for a three-mmute break. We needed to catch our wind. Wirek passed up his flask and I took a quick hit before passing it on to Saano. I'd need a lot of energy before this night was over. Thankfully, wirek had remembered to bring his stash.

Saano wiped his mouth on his sleeve and glanced skyward. And frowned. I looked up. The constellations were closer together. Hell, they were almost touching.

The hunter and the prey.

Closer than ever before.

And the new vampire millennium was about to dawn.

Chudao gestured our break was over. Saano passed the

flask back to Wirek and we kept walking. Over the howl of staccato wind gusts, I thought I heard something far off in the distance.

It sounded like a cry.

Like a wounded animal.

Chudao stopped, seemed to listen, and then continued on.

I wanted to stop him and ask what the hell had made that noise. Memories of Saano's abominable snowman tales filled my head again. Being ambushed by yeti before we got to rescue Jack would really suck.

Another sound permeated the night air. This time, I could make out a type of chanting. But it wasn't the same chanting that we'd heard back at Siben's *gomba.*

This was the old language.

Taluk.

The tongue of the vampire.

Older then most of the oldest languages on earth, it was impossibly tainted by eons of dialect changes, variations of script, and even grammar structure. Each generation until recently put their own spin on it, making it more difficult to pass down to the next.

Nowadays, not many of my kind even bothered to learn it beyond what we were taught in school. Even then, it wasn't much good by the time we graduated.

The volume of chanting grew as wc drew nearer to another bend. Chudao called a halt and explained that he was going on ahead again. I shook my head—motioned that I wanted to go with him. He thought about it for a minute and then nodded.

Smart guy.

Underfoot, the trail changed from loose rocks and ice to hard-packed dirt, bits of lichen, tufts of yellow grass, and more snow. Chudao moved with his hands held out in front of him, almost as if he were walking a tightrope. I kept myself hunched low, with my weight over my feet. My knees stayed deeply bent as I rocked forward in a rolling motion. I tried to remember some of the lessons in stealth movement I'd learned over the years.

Chudao slowed as we crested the bend.

And then I saw it.

A giant stone door, which looked as though it had been carved from a massive slab of the mountain itself, barred our way. Above the door, ancient Taluk script haloed the frame, ringing it like some Christmas garland.

But now was not the time to be jolly.

Not unless I was able to count Arvella's and Petrov's deaths as a present from the gods.

I nodded to Chudao. He disappeared back down the trail to get Saano and Wirek. I leaned against the mountain, my ear pressed into the cold, hard rock. Muffled chanting filled my ears, emanating from deep inside the ancient school.

Who knew how many vampires over the years had learned to call forth the spirits? Who knew what kind of untold power sat ready to be unleashed upon the world?

Saano and Wirek rolled up. Wirek studied the door.

I whispered in his ear, "Can you make it out?"

He nodded. "It's an old saying: *'Karchat mag dalho dyub jugan mag anhar.'* "

I sighed. "Would you mind translating that for me?"

He frowned. "Still studying?"

"Well, gee, yeah, you know—when I have free time and all."

Wirek shook his head. " 'Only those who master self master others.' It's the motto of the Invoker school."

"Does it say anything about how to get in?"

"No."

Nifty. I looked at Chudao. He held up his hands. He'd

done his part getting us this far. I almost felt sorry to have to say good-bye to him here.

But we were going to have to go ahead alone. I didn't want humans involved in the coming bloodshed. Chudao would be safer back at Siben's temple, anyway.

He bowed to each of us and then simply seemed to disappear in the darkness of the mountain.

Saano came up, unsheathing his *kukri.* "Are we ready to do this, or what?"

"I hope so." I looked at Wirek, who suddenly seemed to come to life.

"Of course," he said.

I leaned forward. "What?"

"It's been years since I visited here. My old memory is going, I think—"

"Wirek—"

"Never mind, it's not important," he said. "I know what to do."

"Know what to—"

He nodded. "Yeah, I remember how to get inside."

Chapter Thirty-one

''You'll both have to stand back.''

Saano and I gave Wirek some room to work. He stepped closer to the giant stone door and ran his hands over the coarse rock, skimming the cool, moist surface. He placed his ear close to it. Finally satisfied, he stood back and moved to the right of the door, again peering closely at the structure.

I saw his mouth move but heard only what sounded like a murmur come out.

Saano and I waited.

Wirek waited.

Nothing happened.

Wirek frowned. ''Shit.''

I stepped forward. ''Is there a problem?''

''Yeah.'' Wirek sighed. ''Looks like the old coot must have changed the damned password.''

''Makes sense, doesn't it?'' asked Saano. ''I mean, if she

knows anything about Wirek's background, him having been here before and all. Of course, she'd change the password."

"Yeah," I said, "but where the hell does this leave us? We're still outside and we need to get in there." Over the constant breezes, I could still hear the muffled chanting. "Sounds like they're getting the ceremony started in there. We don't have time to play guessing games out here while Jack's in there."

Wirek had turned his attention back to the door. He seemed to be muttering under his breath. I gave him a minute and then cleared my throat.

"What do you think?"

"What I think, Lawson, is that we are fucked. This old door had the same password for hundreds of years. And now she's gone and changed it on us. Damned inconsiderate of her."

"Welcome to my world," I said. "Problems always come with the territory."

"This is an awfully big problem, Lawson."

"Yeah. I know. You got any ideas?"

"I'm thinking, I'm thinking." Wirek leaned against the door while Saano stood watch. "Arvella was one of the longest-serving headmistresses the Invoker school ever had. Makes sense she'd know how to change anything about this place. But what would she change it to? Would it be something related to the ceremony she's going to perform? Could be. Might also be something connected with this guy Petrov you keep mentioning. Hell, it could really be anything at all."

"We're running out of time," I said. "If you can't figure something out soon, we'll have to find another way inside the mountain."

"Another way?" Wirek poked a finger at the stone door. "Lawson, this is the only way."

"No fire exits?"

"Not unless you happen to be inside the mountain. Then there are a few other routes to get outside, but you have to be inside to use them. Trying to get inside using one of them would be suicide."

"Why's that?"

"They're booby-trapped."

"Booby traps can be disarmed, Wirek."

"Not these, my friend. They're magical."

I shook my head. "Wirek, there's gotta be another way inside. I can't imagine this place being built with only one entrance."

"Well, if there is another, I don't know about it. As far as I'm concerned, it's this door only."

"What about those sentries we passed—did they use this door as well?"

"Sure. Why wouldn't they?"

"Just that their positioning on the mountain seemed a bit removed from here. It's a long way to walk if they came out this door."

Wirek nodded. "It's possible there are other entrances. I was only here a few times and I never did go to this school. But we don't have time to go searching in the dark looking for what are sure to be carefully concealed entrances."

He had a point. As much as I didn't want to admit it, we were on a big mountain and there were probably a huge number of crevices and nooks and crannies that would take us weeks, if not months, to explore properly. And we didn't have a map of the place, so we'd have to go by pure luck.

And I don't happen to like entrusting my future to luck.

The chanting suddenly grew louder. I turned toward the door at the same time Saano and Wirek did.

"Shit," said Wirek. "It's opening."

And it was.

The massive rock door groaned, slowly creaking open on unseen hinges. Light spilled forth from the growing fissure, illuminating the surrounding area as it opened like a yawning maw.

Saano tugged my shoulder and pointed.

A shadow broke the stream of light.

Someone was coming out of the mountain.

I glanced at Wirek. He was already pressing himself into the side of the trail close to the door. I knew he'd try to get in behind the shadow. That way, he'd be inside and could open the door if Saano and I got occupied killing this person.

Saano quietly shrank into the shadows of the mountain. I scrunched down behind a large boulder.

The chanting grew louder now.

I heard a rough hacking cough.

Then a hefty spit.

And then someone started speaking.

"Fucking miserable-ass duty."

His footsteps ground snow, ice, and small pebbles underfoot as he came closer to the boulder.

I readied myself.

I could see his shadow cast by the light inside the mountain looming large.

Adrenaline flooded my system.

My heartbeat tripled.

Then I heard a swift clunking sound, followed by Saano's voice. "The sword, Lawson—do it now!"

I stood up and saw Saano had neatly decapitated the man, but his body was still standing upright. I yanked the *bokken* off my back and plunged it into his sternum, penetrating the chest cavity and the man's heart.

Instantly, a surge of blood erupted, spraying out of his neck, coating the nearby rocks. I pulled the *bokken* back out and wiped it on a patch of scraggy lichen.

I'd clean it properly later. I had the distinct feeling it was going to get a lot dirtier before the night was through.

Wirek waved at us from the opening, his voice a harsh whisper. "Move your asses! The door's starting to close!"

I stood and sprinted for the opening. Saano made the door just in time.

He looked at me. "Sorry, I had to dump the head."

"What'd you do with it?"

"Tossed it over the side of the trail."

"What about the body?" asked Wirek.

"No time to hide it," I said. "We'll just have to take our chances. If someone notices it, we'll already be inside, anyway. Most likely, we'll be neck deep in bodies."

Wirek looked nervous, so I said, "Don't worry. There shouldn't be anyone coming in from the mountain, anyway, not since Siben and Chudao disposed of the other sentries."

"They got the sentries on this side of the mountain," said Wirek. "What about the other side?"

"Like I said. We'll just have to take our chances."

He nodded. The situation wasn't perfect, but we weren't dealing with an optimal scenario here.

"At least," said Saano, "we are inside."

We looked at the cave. The ceiling here loomed overhead, roughly carved out of solid stone. Condensation from melting snow dripped down on us. A series of torches spilled dancing light and shadows all over the walls.

I looked at Wirek. "You know where to go from here?"

"I'm thinking. Trying to remember is hard after a few hundred years."

"Well, you'd better hurry; the chanting's getting louder again." I looked at Saano. "What time you got?"

"Almost twenty-three hundred."

Eleven o'clock. Damn, we'd wasted a couple of hours just getting here.

By midnight, I wanted Jack safe. And I wanted Arvella and Petrov out of commission. Dead if need be. At this point, it didn't much matter.

If we didn't get this done by midnight, before Arvella got a chance to make her dreams come true, we were screwed.

The path ahead of us branched right and left. Wirek stood at the fork, looking both ways. Smooth stone walls covered with old Taluk script beckoned in either direction.

"You remember?" I asked him.

"I remember walking in here and down one of these damned corridors." He looked at me. "Christ, Lawson, I'm sorry to be such a forgetful bastard here. I think this trip has made me really start realizing what a crusty old fool I've become."

"Don't get misty-eyed on me now, Wirek. You know where you're going. Just trust yourself and I'm sure it'll all come back."

Saano wiped his bloody *kukri* blade on his pants and nodded. "Please choose a direction. I'm having fun and wish to have some more."

Wirek glanced at him. "Saano, you're a violent prick, you know that?"

"Humph," said Saano. "I'm an old bastard just like you, Wirek. But I'll be damned if I'm going to stand here and moan about my age slowing me down. I haven't had this much fun in years." He pointed at the fork. "Now, if you would, please choose a path for us and let's get bloody well going."

Wirek grinned and looked at me. "Trust me?"

"You haven't let me down yet, pal. Just keep your wits about you and lead on."

Wirek nodded. "All right, then. I'll take that as a vote of confidence."

He closed his eyes, took a deep breath, and then opened them again. "This way." He pointed left.

"You sure?"

He shrugged. "Makes sense that it would be. After all, the mountain itself gets larger in this direction. It tapers off to the right, if I remember correctly how it looked from outside."

"If that's your best guess, then it'll have to do."

"We going here or what?" asked Saano. "My *kukri* is hungry for more bodies and so am I."

Wirek eyed me. "Real fun guy you found us there."

"Hey, as I recall, you picked him up in Jomsom, not me."

"Oh, yeah, I forgot. You ready?"

"Lead on."

Wirek nodded and started down the left pathway.

Saano and I followed.

Chapter Thirty-two

Dank.

As we moved down the left corridor, that was the only word that crawled into my mind. More melting ice dripped from the stone ceilings and fell with boring predictability to the floor below, creating grimy puddles that we avoided as much as possible.

At varying intervals, torches crackled overhead, illuminating another patch of the hallway. And despite the warmth emanating from somewhere ahead of us, the air remained raw. Chills worked their way up my spine as we walked on.

The chanting had died down.

It seemed to be intermixed with periods of silence. We had no idea what Arvella might be doing, but we all knew it wouldn't be good. Whatever it was.

Saano chimed in with a time hack.

Minutes dropped away from us with appalling rapidity.

We had to find our way into the bowels of the old school and confront Arvella. Soon.

Wirek paused by another fork. He closed his eyes again and then quickly chose another left turn.

The air changed almost instantly.

Waves of heat flooded the corridor. The hairs on my arms stood up. It felt like we were walking on some kind of static-elctricity generator.

Wirek called a halt and motioned us together. "Feel it?"

Saano nodded. "Yeah, what's the deal?"

"Spirits," said Wirek. He looked at me. "She must be starting the ceremony already."

"She wouldn't use Jack yet, would she?"

"I don't know." Wirek checked his watch. "Probably not yet. But soon. Let's hustle."

"How much farther?"

"We should be close." He turned back, and Saano and I fell in behind him, although we stayed closer.

Saano had already drawn his *kukri* and I gripped the *bokken* a little tighter than I had been. I hoped we wouldn't be facing spirits. Arvella, Petrov, and their supporters would be difficult enough to handle.

Wirek paused again and wiped his brow.

His hand came away soaking wet with sweat.

The heat grew overpowering.

I had to keep reminding myself that Wirek probably couldn't put up with as much as Saano and I. But he pressed on, regardless of his discomfort. I admired that.

The air suddenly exploded with chanting again.

We were close.

The hallway ended up ahead.

Wirek huddled us up again.

"Around this bend," he said, wipping his face. "Damn, it's hot."

"She must have a fire blazing in there," said Saano.

"Something like that," said Wirek. He looked at me. "How do you want to hit them?"

I looked at Saano. "Got any ideas?"

"You're the leader."

"Yeah, well, this is a meritocracy, so chime in all you want."

Saano nodded and looked at Wirek. "What's the layout of the room?"

Wirek wiped his forehead again. "Been a while since I was here last. But if I remember correctly, it's big. Almost an auditorium. It's got a stage at one end. The way we're going in, it'll be like walking into a concert hall, I'd expect."

"So we'll be working to get to the stage," said Saano. "Place'll be thick with her followers."

"Don't forget the spirits she'll have in there," said Wirek. "We might have to deal with them, too."

"And these will be the spirits of vampires?" asked Saano.

Wirek nodded. "Spirits of humans make the room feel cold."

Saano frowned and looked down at his *kukri.* He was probably wondering if his beloved knife would be much good against the spirit world. "How do we handle them?"

"Hopefully, we won't have to," I said. "The goal is to get to Arvella as fast as possible. She'll be protected by another Fixer named Petrov and probably a few trusted supporters. We take them out, then take her out. That should do it."

"You make it sound easy," said Saano. "The last time something sounded that easy, half my old unit got killed."

"We can't spare half a unit," I said. "Just get in there. I'll take the right side; you can go left. Wirek, you look for Jack."

Wirek nodded. From out of nowhere, he suddenly produced a three-foot staff. "Got it."

I blinked. "Where'd you get that?"

He smiled. "Haven't I shown this to you before?"

"No."

"Hmm, well, even us Elders have occasion to need to use force every now and again."

"You're good with that?" asked Saano.

Wirek smiled. "I'd offer a demonstration, but time is short."

I patted him on the shoulder. "If things go the way we expect, you'll be demo-ing your skills in no time, buddy." I eased up the corridor and peeked around the bend.

Ahead, there was a single archway twelve feet high and bordered by more Taluk script. Beyond and into the room, I could make out perhaps a dozen black-robed figures with hoods. The chanting grew even louder.

I ducked back and gave Wirek and Saano the final game plan. Wirek might have had the toughest job, what with having to find Jack and battle any of Arvella's people who got in his way. But Saano and I had just as much work ahead of us. Storming Arvella and dealing with Petrov would keep us deep in dead bodies, no doubt.

Hopefully, not our own.

The adrenaline surged in my blood.

We moved up to the archway.

The heat became thick—the air stifling. Breathing took a lot of effort. Each step forward seemed like we were bathing in a skillet of fire.

I looked at Saano, wondering if he'd be all right. I'd known far too many supposed soldiers who said they were good at killing only to have them go yellow at the worst possible moment.

Saano's expression, however, told me that he would be

perfectly fine. His eyes had assumed the stonelike expression necessary for when you're going into combat. He held himself low over his feet, wiith the *kukri* ready in his right hand. I could see beads of sweat glistening on his forehead, running down the side of his swarthy face.

I glanced at Wirek.

He seemed okay. His breathing looked labored, though. Between the heat and fatigue, he was suffering. Hell, we all were.

Still, the staff he held didn't waver.

And the firm set to his jaw emanated reluctant confidence. He'd do well.

And as for me, as many times as I'd been in the shit, my stomach still lurched like I'd eaten a bad burrito every time I got ready to go into action.

But butterflies are normal.

Seasoned combat vets will tell you they still get nervous.

But they don't freeze up.

Time to go.

We all knew what we had to do. Even if being as far away from this place was what we wanted most.

Shadowy figures shifted in the room ahead of us. We hugged the walls and watched. They moved toward the stage. Away from us.

We edged closer.

Wirek pointed; I looked.

Onstage stood Arvella.

She was draped in deep purple cloaks with her arms out to the sides. Around her swirled pink energies that must have been spirits. She seemed to bend and fold them with just a flicker of her fingers. Her resonant voice filled the hallway, lifting the temperature even more.

And now the cloaked figures of her cronies joined the chanting, lifting their arms and moving in time to her sways.

Then the chanting abruptly stopped.

And Arvella spoke.

"The time, at last, is at hand," she said. "We have waited for so many years. For the point in our glorious history where our destiny is at last possible. Where others have failed before us, we will not. Where others have sought only the superficial, we will seek the powers beyond time and space. And where others have been ignorant of the true calling of our vampire kindred, we comprehend our divine role as saviors of the very cosmos itself."

I glanced at Wirek. He was watching and listening closely.

Arvella continued. "We have the opportunity tonight to open the very portal into the spirit world. Ordinarily, this feat would be impossible due to the powerful forces that must be controlled. But tonight we have the ability to unleash the minions of the dead and bend them to our will. They will bring us the power and conquest we desire. The power and treasures we deserve."

She turned to an attendant flanking her on the right. "Bring him to me."

Quicker than I would have expected, the attendant nudged a small boy forward.

Jack.

He looked scared.

Cancel that, he looked absolutely terrified. And if I'd been scared about taking this place down a few seconds ago, that fear was immediately replaced with a burning rage and a need to get Jack the hell out of here.

I might have killed his father by mistake, but I wasn't about to let Arvella exploit this poor kid.

I felt Wirek and Saano looking at me.

I nodded my head.

It was time to hit them with everything we had.

I just prayed it would be enough.

Chapter Thirty-three

The heat hit us like an eighteen-wheeler slamming into a mosquito.

Waves of it washed over us as we literally melted through the archway and into the room itself. The elongated hall culminated in a stage at one end. Along the walls, tapestries depicting ancient scenes of Invokers controlling spirits hung heavy but ruffled slightly in the spiritual wind. Light filled the room courtesy of wrought-iron candelabras that twisted down on chains from the ceiling high overhead.

I eased right, feeling the stone wall at my back.

Saano broke left.

Wirek held back, searching the room and using one of the cloaked goons for cover as he did so.

Surprise was the one thing we had going for us.

But it didn't look like it was going to do much.

Especially when Arvella suddenly stopped chanting.

"We have guests."

Her voice floated out across the room, causing the three of us to stop in midstride as her cloaked followers suddenly turned in one motion.

I heard Wirek say, ''Shit.''

From her position on the platform, Arvella smiled and opened her arms like some wacky hostess at a Tupperware party. ''Come in, come in. You must be tired after your long journey.''

She turned to one side of the platform and grinned. ''I thought you said they'd never make it past your sentries, Alexander.''

I could just see him standing there. Arms folded. Leather jacket. A thin, tight smile creasing his sallow face.

Petrov.

He didn't look too pleased to see us. He cleared his throat. ''Clearly, I overestimated the skill of your followers, Arvella.''

Arvella smiled. Her thick black tresses flowed down behind her back, interspersed with veins of pure white. Even from this distance, I could tell her eyebrows were painted on. Thick lashes made her look like some televangelist's wife.

At first, I couldn't believe I hadn't met her before. But then I figured my mind—God bless it—had mercifully purged itself of the horrifying memories of her face.

''Are you sure you overestimated my people, Alexander? Perhaps you simply underestimated your opponents.''

He shrugged. He didn't seem to care much. ''Maybe.''

She turned back to look at us as her cronies edged a bit closer en masse. ''No matter. They're here now and that's what counts.''

I gripped the *bokken* a little tighter, eyeing the crowd closest to me. My positioning was bad. I spoke up, not taking my eyes off the crowd. "We're just here for the boy. Give him to us and we'll leave."

I could feel Wirek's eyes on me. He must have been saying, "What the hell" to himself, but it didn't matter. I was just hoping to buy us some time. If we could keep Arvella amused enough, Wirek might be able to get close to Jack.

At least that was the plan.

Arvella just laughed. "As if I would actually permit you to take him back." She squinted. "You are the one they call Lawson, aren't you?"

"I am."

She smiled again. "Alexander here tells me you caused him quite a lot of trouble back in Boston. And all for the sake of this boy. Why would you do such a thing?"

"I don't imagine honoring the pledge you make to a dying man is something you could ever understand," I said.

I could see Jack's eyes glistening. He looked close to tears.

Arvella pursed her lips. "Ah, yes, I'd almost forgotten about dear Henry Watterson. He was rather an unwitting obstacle in this whole dreary affair." Her eyes twinkled. "Too bad you killed him, Lawson."

Jack's eyes almost rolled white.

So much for my plan to tell the kid when the time was right. I felt a wave of heat knock me back a step and then saw Arvella's hand go to Jack's shoulder.

"Not yet, dear. Give him a few more minutes of life."

I took a breath. Breathing became more difficult. I forced myself to look up. "The order to kill Jack's father came from you, Arvella. You lied about his crimes. He was an innocent man only trying to protect his son. You had him killed to get at Jack."

"I don't give orders to kill innocent men, Lawson." She snickered. "You're lying to try to save your own skin."

"If I was lying, why would I have flown halfway across the world to save his son? Why would I care about some kid? I'd be back in Boston relaxing."

She waved me off. "I wouldn't presume to fathom your reasoning. You are, after all, merely a Fixer."

"Of course you wouldn't," I said. "Because you know it's the truth. Henry Watterson knew he'd been set up by someone on the Council, someone who wanted to possess his son. He made me promise to protect Jack because he knew only a Fixer would stand a chance against you, Arvella." I brought the *bokken* up slightly, keeping at bay one of the goons who'd inched closer. "That's why I'm here. To honor the promise I made."

"Yes, I was told you valued honor above everything else." Arvella sighed. "Very well, if that is your intention, I can see our continued talking is pointless." She nodded to Petrov. "Kill them all and then let us finish what we have started here."

I missed the signal from Petrov.

But instantly, the crowd surged toward us.

From across the room, I heard the telltale clang of Saano's *kukri* blade biting into necks. Wirek stepped forward with his staff held at an odd position—it reminded me vaguely of an obscure fighting system I'd heard of once.

Five goons closed in on me from odd angles.

I stepped back and raised the *bokken* so it jutted out about midway up my body.

And then it was on.

I faked a stab at the closest goon's heart—he and the goons closest to him on my right ducked back. I pivoted, then sank on my knees and drove the point of the *bokken* into the sternum of a goon on my left.

He sagged on buckling knees as a shower of blood vomited from his chest. I yanked the wooden sword and immediately pivoted right, sidestepping the attack of a goon who'd lunged with a wooden stake. I knocked his arm down with the back edge of the *bokken,* bringing his body forward, then drove the *bokken* into his neck under his voice box.

He went down even quicker.

I kept moving, trying to maintain the distance between my attackers and myself, always keeping the *bokken* in between us.

I feinted again.

Then brought the *bokken* down low against the knee of a third goon. A sharp crack sounded over the din of battle. I jerked the *bokken* back up, stabbing into his stomach.

I wheeled and barely missed a flying tackle that would have brought me to the ground. He flew past me, trying to recover his momentum.

Too late. I reversed the *bokken* and plunged it behind me, through the back of the fourth goon. He screamed as the hard wood broke through spinal cord and ribs, penetrating his heart.

Again I withdrew the *bokken.*

Another goon held back some.

In his hands, he held a staff similar to the one Wirek was using. He'd adopted a stance with the staff held horizontally in front of him. I noticed both ends were sharpened. One poke from either side and I was a goner.

I backpedaled and drew the *bokken* up into the middle position again. The goon kept his distance, aware of what I could do with the wooden sword. I needed to goad him into attacking me. Already I could feel the heat increasing.

I stepped back and brought the sword down by my rear leg, leaning in and exposing my left shoulder. If I positioned myself properly, he'd jump at the exposed side of my body.

At least that was the plan. The move was a classic Japanese kenjutsu sword technique I practiced back in Boston. Now I wished I'd practiced them more.

The goon's eyes lit up.

He stepped in, going for a straight thrust to the left side of my chest.

I sidestepped and swung the blade up, almost windmilling it down onto the staff. The jarring effect knocked him forward. I snapped the *bokken* back up into his throat.

He sagged, coughing blood, and slumped to the floor.

We'd have to decapitate the bastards later. Right now, time was wasting. I could see Wirek and Saano moving through the throngs with ease.

Wirek surprised me. According to him, he hadn't had much experience with close combat. But from the way he handled that staff, I'd never have known. He emanated confidence and control, quickly dispatching another two of Arvella's supporters as I watched him.

Saano's *kukri* sang like a metal harp as he hacked his way through two more goons. There was little time to count how many we'd brought down, but it seemed like there were more than twenty.

More remained between us and the stage.

And they were really pissed.

I glanced at Wirek. "Get Jack." I jumped in front of him and took out another goon, who had rushed headlong onto the tip of the *bokken*.

Saano closed his distance between the left side and the stage, prompting Petrov to direct more goons to take him on. I kept Wirek behind me as long as possible, until we suddenly saw an opening. He rushed ahead while I tackled another goon in front of me.

The ground underneath us grew slick with blood.

The smell of copper hung heavy in the hot air.

My own breath seemed cool by comparison, and beads of sweat cascaded down my body causing the clothes Siben had graciously provided us to stick like tape to my body.

I hacked another goon across the chest, pivoted, then drove the point home again and again as another two fell.

I could hear Saano shouting what sounded like Nepali curses as he ground his way through more of Arvella's followers. His *kukri* clanged once more.

And then silence.

We stood before the podium, surrounded by the bodies of two dozen goons, the floor thick with coagulating blood.

Wirek climbed the stairs on the right side of the stage.

He eased closer to Jack.

Arvella casually glanced around. I was amazed she'd stayed there during the attack rather than fleeing with Jack. Strange, but she seemed unfazed by her impending doom.

That concerned me. It always seemed like the bad guys I encountered never sensed when things were going south for them. Either that or they had another deck of cards up their sleeves.

I hoped Arvella didn't know how to deal.

"You're as good as the reputation that precedes you, Lawson," she said, directing her attention to me. "Alexander, indeed, has underestimated your skill and perseverance." She nodded toward Saano. "And the skill of your comrades as well. I must say I am duly impressed."

"Save the flattery, Arvella. It's over."

"Is it?" She smiled. "You might think so, but I assure you it is not." She gestured to the bodies of her followers. "You think they matter one bit to me? They were never all that important. I don't need them to unleash my plan." She shifted. "You've no doubt noticed the temperature in here. Rather stifling, isn't it?"

"You could do with an air conditioner, yeah."

"Humor too. Quite a specimen, Lawson." She spread her arms and began chanting in Taluk. Instantly, the pink swirls I'd seen earlier materialized again and began swirling around her. Her voice grew somber. "Now you will feel the true measure of those born with the power to Invoke."

Her arms gestured once and streams of spirit energy shot at me like cannon blasts. I toppled back over as they slammed into me. The *bokken* clattered away, but I wasn't concerned about losing it. I didn't know how to stab a dead vampire spirit, anyway.

I tried to get to my feet.

Another volley of spirit energy slammed me again and again, tossing me back through puddles of grime and blood.

Across the room, I heard Saano screaming and clutching at his eyes.

We had to do something.

Arvella's voice rose above the screeching of the spirits as they zoomed around the room. "Join me, son of Watterson! Join me as the rightful heir to the Invocation sect. Join me and kill the men before you. Take your place as a true Invoker of the New Millennium."

Another wave of energy burst into the room, slamming us over again and again. I felt like like a speck of dust, coated and basted in the copper blood of my enemies. The energy sent me sprawling all over the room.

I tried to clear my eyes.

Where was Wirek?

Another blast threw me across room. I heard a sharp crunch in my side—felt a wave of intense pain double me over—at least one of my ribs was fractured.

It hurt like hell to take a breath.

And still the spirits kept coming. I felt certain they must have been toying with us, awaiting Arvella's final command to kill us once and for all. We'd made a pain of ourselves and she seemed determined to punish us before finally releasing us into blessed, merciful death.

Saano howled somewhere to my right now; I'd been tossed around so much I had no idea where in the room I was. Another crack in my side made me retch and cough up some blood.

And another wave of pink energy washed over us.

Then, just as suddenly, it stopped.

And I heard a small voice say quietly . . .

"No."

The temperature dropped a few degrees.

I lay on my side, gasping for breath. Saano's screams waned to moans. I tried to get to my feet, but the pain was intense. I could barely make out Jack standing on the stage.

And the look of disbelief on Arvella's face.

"What do you mean, 'No'? He killed your father! You must kill him!"

"I won't," said Jack. "You tricked him. He didn't mean to do it."

Arvella's eyes blazed with a white-hot fury.

Her voice drew down to a harsh whisper. But I think each of us heard it somehow.

"You are not the only one, boy. There are others like you. Others with the same gift as you. I am offering you a chance to have power beyond your wildest dreams. You would be the most powerful vampire in the world. Think of it!"

Jack shook his head slowly. "I just want to go home."

Arvella sighed. "Then . . . you leave me no choice."

Chapter Thirty-four

I tried to shout "No!"

But the sudden roars that filled the room drowned it out. My ears almost popped—I clamped my hands over them, squinting at the scene unfolding on the stage.

Wirek.

He'd edged up onto the stage. He held his staff low and was just a few feet from Arvella.

If he could just get close enough . . .

Arvella turned . . . and flicked her wrist. A stream of spirit energy shot into his chest, knocking him back. He sprawled across the stage, his staff clattering off into the shadows.

Arvella turned her attention back to Jack, who stood there as if frozen to the floor.

I wanted to shout at him to save himself—to run for it—to get out of that place. Be anywhere but there at that moment. But he'd never hear my words over the roars filling the room.

All around us, the air came alive with the dead souls of vampires long since deceased. They shrieked and howled, their pain echoing off the walls of the chamber. It felt like an audio orgy of terror. All I wanted to do was curl up in a fetal position and wish the whole damned mess away.

But I couldn't.

Not with Jack still in danger.

I started crawling through the puddles of blood toward the stage. Toward Arvella. Slowly, inch by inch, I extended my hands toward the steps, trying to draw down the distance between Jack and myself.

I had to reach him.

Had to protect him.

Had to.

But Arvella noticed me.

In the next instant, I was being hurled back where I'd come from. She wanted no one interfering when she set her sights on Jack.

Which is exactly what she did.

Her mouth began moving again, chanting the strange sound of Taluk. Calling forth the spirits to help her wrest power and wield it as she saw fit. And right now she wanted the spirits to destroy the young boy standing before her.

The young boy who'd had the courage to stand up to her.

Suddenly, the spirits that had been zooming around the room seemed to collect up near the ceiling in one amorphous blob. They hovered there, swirling, transmuting—flowing into one another.

Then they shot down—straight down—into Arvella's open mouth.

For a second, everything was quiet again.

Arvella shook violently.

An aura of frothy pink energy engulfed her entire body. Her eyes turned almost the same color. I might have guessed she'd been possessed, if I knew better. But Arvella would never allow something to control her body.

Instead, she'd chosen to have the spirits enter her—lend their energy to hers—thus making her more powerful.

I saw in that instant how truly demented she was. How far she was willing to go to gain the power she so desperately craved.

She had to die.

But how?

None of us could get close to the stage.

None of us could reach Jack.

He continued to stand his ground, despite the look of abject terror in his eyes. His legs wouldn't move, even though every fiber in the little guy's body must have been screaming at him to run with all his might to the nearest exit.

The kid was amazing.

And then something happened.

Jack's eyes closed. A wave of invisible confidence washed over him. Suddenly, he didn't seem very afraid.

Then his mouth began moving.

And he started chanting as well.

His body took on a different glow. A bluish tinge seemed to radiate from his body, expanding slowly outward.

Arvella's eyes widened.

She shot a bolt of pink energy at him.

Jack didn't move.

The energy bolt slammed into the blue aura surrounding Jack and bounced off, dissipating into the air around him.

Arvella tried again.

I could tell by the glowing red color of the bolt that she'd increased the voltage.

And again, it simply bounced off Jack.

His eyes were locked shut in concentration, his mouth

still mumbling the ancient Taluk that brought him his own spirits.

Arvella rushed him from across the stage and they clashed, bright explosions of spirit energy crackling like live wires as they made contact. Jack's eyes stayed closed the entire time, but each time Arvella tried to strike him, his hands and feet simply blocked all of her strikes.

Finally, she retreated.

I sat there, gasping for breath—the room felt like it would explode in flames from the overpowering heat.

Arvella seemed to draw down into herself. She inhaled deeply, and at once a huge column of red flame shot out of her and engulfed Jack.

The flames licked all around his body.

But he never wavered. And still the aura of blue spirit energy surrounding him continued to protect him.

Arvella screamed with fury. Her attacks were completely ineffective. Jack was immune to the energy with which she sought to destroy him.

That was when he opened his eyes.

And spoke.

But the voice did not belong to Jack. The rough, deep, gritty tones belonged to someone older than him. It seemed vaguely familiar to me as I listened.

"Your quest is over, Arvella. What you seek remains forever out of your reach. You are defeated."

No!" she shrieked, drawing herself up to full height. Her hair flashed out at odd angles. "I will never surrender. I deserve the power. It is mine alone to control. Give me what I seek!"

The voice coming from Jack spoke again. "Very well. You will have what you seek."

Arvella almost smiled.

But it vanished quickly. Jack's whole body began to

vibrate and the blue glow intensified. At once, his whole body blurred and a column of blue flame shot out, engulfing Arvella.

She screamed.

My God, how she screamed.

The blue flames danced over her skin and melted it down to sheer white bone, which then charred quickly in the hot flames as it devoured her. Her cries faded to sobbing moans as the room filled with the stench of her flesh being burned to a crisp.

At last, her cries faded. As they did, so did the blue flames. Then there was a sudden rush of more blue energy, an explosion on the stage where she'd been standing—and then when the smoke cleared at last . . .

Arvella was gone.

Jack's head slumped low on his chest. The chamber fell silent and the room instantly began to cool as the spirit energy finally waned.

Again I made my way toward him, but this time there was nothing keeping me back.

He looked up as I crested the stairs. I walked toward him, wincing from the pain, and finally dropped to one knee.

"You okay?"

He almost grinned. "Yeah." Briefly, his face clouded. "I know what happened, Lawson. I know you were lied to."

I said nothing.

"My father . . . he came back. He explained it to me."

I nodded. The blue energy must have been Henry Watterson back for his revenge. "Yeah."

"I don't blame you, Lawson. My father told me. He told me you'd honor your word. That you'd protect me."

"I always will, Jack. I promise."

He glanced over his shoulder. A single singed slice of black char marked the ground where Arvella stood only a minute earlier. "She's gone now. She finally got what she wanted, after all. Just not how she figured it."

I held my side. Broken ribs are a real bitch. "Most people never figure that their deepest wish can turn out to be something so unexpected."

A single tear found its way out of Jack's right eye and meandered down his cheek. "Lawson?"

"Yeah?"

"Did my dad . . . Did he suffer?"

I swallowed, feeling the knot in my throat grow a bit bigger. "No. He died honorably. His only concern was always for the safety of his son. For you, Jack."

He nodded. "I'm . . . glad."

I put an arm around him. "You ready to go home now?"

"Yeah."

We walked to the edge of the stage and found Wirek coming back to consciousness. His arm looked broken, judging by the odd angle at which it hung. "This is gonna hurt like hell tomorrow morning." He glanced around. "Where's Saano?"

I whirled, looking for him. No one moved among the dead bodies.

"Saano!"

And then Jack pointed to a feebly raised hand. "There!"

We hustled over.

As we drew closer, I could see the unfortunate truth.

Saano was dying.

Blood streamed out of the poor guy, his *kukri* lay by his side.

Saano looked up at us slowly and coughed once. "Damned

. . . wooden knife. Cut me just below my armpit. I got some of the . . . splinters . . . not many . . . but . . . enough."

Wirek checked him over, but the glance he shot me confirmed what I suspected. In addition to the wood killing him slowly, he'd suffered a cut across his neck.

I laid a hand on his shoulder. "You fought honorably, Saano. We can't begin to thank you enough for everything."

He coughed again. "You can thank me . . . by making sure I get home. Bury me in the mountains . . . where my home is. . . ."

Wirek bowed his head.

Jack stooped by Saano and hugged him. "Thank you, sir. You saved my life."

Saano grabbed Jack's hand and held it for a long moment, searching his eyes in silence. Then his grip faded and his hand slumped back to his lap. He coughed once more and muttered, "Lawson."

I leaned closer. "I'm here."

His words were a whisper. "Thank you."

"For what?"

He coughed. Frothy pink bubbles popped on his lips. "For letting . . . me . . . live . . . again. . . ."

Then he sighed once more—

And he died.

For a long time, we all stayed with him in that now cold, desolate chamber. Drips of water echoed as they hit the blood puddles covering the stone floor.

None of us wanted to say good-bye.

Chapter Thirty-five

It took us a long time to behead all of Arvella's followers. Wood is enough to kill a vampire, but beheading helps make sure they stay dead.

Between Wirek, operating with only one good arm, and me, hurting like hell, we were exhausted by the time it was all done.

Jack remained quiet throughout most of the process. We'd tried to keep the gore of decapitation from his eyes, but he'd seen quite a bit already and didn't seem as shocked as I thought he would have.

It was Wirek who brought Petrov up.

"He's vanished, Lawson."

In the confusion of battling Arvella and her spirits, Petrov had disappeared. I don't like loose ends. Petrov was a big one.

"You think he's still around?"

Wirek shook his head. "He's outnumbered now. He's no

fool. Between you and Jack's now apparent invocation skills, he'd be a fool to try anything."

"What about later?"

He shrugged. "If he's smart, he's gone to ground. Probably crawled back under whatever rock he crawled out from. He's safer there."

"I hope you're right."

"I wouldn't worry about it."

By the time we finally left the school and began the hard task of carrying Saano's body down the mountain, my arms felt like lead weights.

At the valley floor, Siben met us with a band of his monks, who fanned out as we came down, as if they expected trouble.

Siben looked first at Saano. "I would not have expected this one to die. He must have fought well."

"He did."

"We can take him from you, if you wish."

I shook my head. "That's okay."

"You're injured."

The pain must have been etched on my face. Truth was, I hurt like hell. "I made him a promise up there on the mountain. I've got to see it through."

Siben smiled a little. "You are a man of many promises, aren't you, Lawson?"

"Sure seems so lately." I sighed. "It's not intentional."

"True honor never is," said Siben. He turned his attention to Jack. "I see you achieved your goal, nevertheless."

I nudged Jack forward. "This is Jack."

Siben bowed. "I am honored to meet you, young sir."

Jack grinned. "Hi."

Siben looked at Wirek. "He has much power about him, this one."

"More than you can know," said Wirek. "Almost got

him killed, too. He needs training to learn how to control it.''

''I take it you have a place for such training?''

Wirek nodded. ''A school not entirely unlike the one we just left. But better. And run by someone who will not fill his heart with evil.''

Siben's eyes twinkled in the predawn gray. ''I think that evil will never have a home in this one. There is too much good within his soul.''

I smiled. Thank God someone still represented the goodness in the world. I'd seen so much evil, sometimes it made me wonder who the hell was left that believed in the light. And if that was Jack alone, it was enough for me.

Siben touched my arm. ''The woman . . . the evil one . . . is dead?''

''Consumed by her own desire for power,'' I said. ''But there was another with her. A second-in-command, so to speak.''

''Yes?''

I frowned. ''He escaped.''

Siben nodded. ''No one has come down the mountain since you went up. Perhaps he is still up there. Are you sure he did not take refuge within the mountain?''

''We searched. We didn't find him. Wirek believes he's running. Trying to get away from here as fast as he can. He knows we'll hunt him down. He's got to be punished for his crimes.''

''It is possible,'' said Siben, ''that he has been punished already.''

''What are you saying?''

''Just that his failure to achieve what he sought may be punishment enough. Sometimes the universe works in mysterious ways where justice is concerned.''

I glanced at Saano's body lying on the litter. In the moonlight, he looked peaceful. "That might work for your monastery." I looked back at Siben. "It doesn't work for me. We lost a good man . . . a friend up there. Petrov is responsible for his death. He's got to pay."

Siben nodded slowly. "You carry a lot of weight on your shoulders, Lawson."

I took a deep breath of the cool predawn air. "I don't have any other choice."

We made better time heading back to Jomsom, thanks to a wagon and horses Siben provided for us. We found our way back to Saano's bar and asked around, finally finding out where he lived.

His home lay two miles farther east, shrouded by the mountainside and green mosses that covered the slopes before trailing away into rich green fields.

Bright sunlight spilled over Saano's mud-brick house with its thatched roof and tufts of grass poking out the sides. A few chickens scattered, clucking and flapping their wings as we rode up.

We dismounted and walked to the door.

It opened as we came up to it.

I found myself staring into the face of an old woman who looked truly ancient. Her eyes were moist, but she smiled through her evident sadness.

Wirek spoke to her softly in Nepali, explaining how Saano had died valiantly. She nodded and said something back to him that caused his eyebrows to jump up a bit.

I looked at him. "What is it?"

"She knew he was dead. Said he came to her in a dream. Explained the whole thing. She's been waiting here for us to show up."

I didn't have much to say. Truth was, I didn't feel like it.

"She's got a burial site behind the house ready." Wirek sighed. "Let's do this properly."

We carried Saano's body behind the house. His mother laid out a plain white sheet of soft cotton. We folded his arms across his chest and prepared to wrap him, when I remembered something.

"Hang on a minute."

I ran back to the horse and fished out Saano's *kukri*. The dark bloodstains on the blade had crusted over during our journey back. I considered washing it first, but thought better of it. The blood was evidence of his heroism.

I gripped the handle tightly, feeling his strength one last time before heading back around the back of the house.

Wirek nodded when he saw the *kukri*. "Proper."

I placed the bloody blade in Saano's right hand, the same way he'd carried it when he'd been alive. Finally, we wrapped him in the sheet and set him down in the grave.

Saano's mother scooped up handfuls of dirt and tossed them onto her son. Fresh tears streamed down her face, but she smiled at us again and spoke to Wirek, who then turned to me.

"She says we have honored her son's final request. She's very thankful."

"Tell her we are forever in his debt. We never would have made it if it hadn't been for his help."

Wirek spoke to her again, and she smiled weakly, speaking again.

"She says if he died in battle, he died happy, and that's all she could ever ask for."

We took turns scooping more dirt into the grave, filling it quicker than I expected. Finally, dirty and sweat stained, we finished.

Saano's mother placed a single rose on top of the grave. Where she'd found a rose I didn't know, but it made the pile of dirt look a lot more respectful.

Wirek bowed his head and was silent for a while.

I did the same.

I'm not always sure who it is I pray to. I'm a pretty spiritual guy, but organized religion doesn't have a home with me. I know of thousands of deities, all of whom I pay respect to. Mostly, it comes out in the form of gratitude for getting through scrapes in one piece.

This time, I simply prayed for Saano to enjoy his afterlife.

Jack stood close to me. We waited for Saano's mother to pray for a few minutes. She finished, wiped her tears, then stood up.

She ushered us inside for a long meal and told us stories about Saano's army exploits.

I guess it was her way of working through the pain. She didn't have any other children. Over blood bread and yak meat, she told Wirek that the greatest shame in life is for a parent to outlive her kids.

I happened to agree.

We stayed with her that night while cool breezes caressed the *Saano* house on the mountainside. A couple of times, I thought I sensed a presence there with us. Jack only nodded when I asked him if Saano was looking out for his mother.

We set out the next morning back to Jomsom and the rinky-dink airport for the flight back to Kathmandu. We left the wagon and horses with Saano's mother. Over the next week, a bunch of Siben's warrior monks would swing by to pick them up.

Saano's mother waved at us as we headed back down the mountain toward Jomsom. We watched her wave until her house and Saano's final resting place slid out of sight.

Jack tugged on my arm.

I looked at him. "Yeah?"

"That man . . . Saano . . . did he know about me?"

"He knew you were in trouble."

"And he came to help . . . just because of that?"

"Yes." I watched his face shrivel up in concentration for a moment. I stopped walking and looked at him. "One of the most important things you can do in your life is be of service to someone else. There are very few in our world who act without regard for themselves, without hope of any reward. True virtue, courage, and honor come from helping others. That's what Saano did for you."

"It's what you did for me, too, Lawson."

I sighed. "Maybe." I knelt down on the damp grass. "I wish I could bring your father back for you, Jack. I wish more than anything I could." I looked away. "But I can't."

"I know it."

Neither of us said anything for a minute; finally, I stood back up. "We'd better catch up to Wirek. I don't think he's noticed that we've stopped walking yet."

Jack grinned. "Think he'd keep walking if we didn't say anything?"

I smiled. "Definitely. He'd probably keep walking straight to Kathmandu."

"He looks pretty tired," said Jack. "We'd better stop him."

"Yeah."

We ran after Wirek, skidding down the loose gravel trail toward him. He turned around as we came up.

"You guys ready to go home?"

Jack nodded. "Yeah."

Wirek smiled. "I don't know about you, but if I don't get a real decent hamburger soon, I'm gonna go out of my mind."

"What's the matter, Wirek? You don't like yak meat?"

Wirek sighed. "You know, sometimes you aren't nearly as funny as you think you are."

I clapped him on the shoulder. "Yeah, but it sure is fun trying to be."

Jack ran ahead, sunbeams bouncing off him in the green meadows. And for the first time since I'd met him, he actually looked happy again.

Chapter Thirty-six

We caught the same bumpy-butt twin-prop plane out of Jomsom and then settled in for the twenty-four-hour blisteringly boring trip back to the States. Still, after living for the last week in the rough, there was some obvious comfort about catching up on sleep in the cramped confines of a jumbo jet.

But only just.

Jack's spirits continued to rise.

He was much more talkative, asked more about my work, Wirek's background and past, and then questions about his own future.

"You need schooling," said Wirek when the showing of the latest teen comedy finished on the overhead screen. "To properly develop your skills."

"But I'm already in school," said Jack. "In Boston."

Wirek nodded. "True enough, but that school won't help you understand the full aspects of what you can do. You need depth of training. Despite what Arvella claimed, there are not many like you at all.''

''Did she ever tell the truth?'' asked Jack with a grin.

I smiled. ''She didn't lie when she told you how important you were. She made that clear by dragging you across the globe to some remote stretch of earth. That should be proof enough, huh?''

''I guess.'' He looked at Wirek. ''What would I learn at the school?''

''The usual things we all learn. You'll get a standard education, but you'd also get special training on things you can do. Stuff you can use your skill for. You've got the potential to be a great help to others in our society. It's not something you can just sort of let happen on its own. Not now. You're growing into a young man and need to meet others of your kind.''

''Of my kind? But I thought you said there weren't many more like me.''

''There aren't,'' said Wirek. ''But there are some. And more than enough to fill a small school full of new friends waiting to meet a cool fellow like yourself.'' Wirek grinned. ''After all, you've just returned from a fairly amazing adventure.''

Jack nodded. ''Where's the school? In Boston?'' He sounded hopeful.

Wirek looked away. ''It's not in Boston.''

Jack looked at me suddenly worried. ''Not in Boston?'' He looked at Wirek. ''Where is it?''

''In the mountains of Canada. The Canadian Rockies. Obviously, it's got to be remote, so humans won't find out about it. But it's still a lot closer than Nepal.''

''But . . .'' Jack sighed. ''I was looking forward to going home again. I've got stuff to do. My friends—''

I patted his shoulder. ''Listen, slick, going to school is

the best place for you right now. I know it doesn't seem like that at all. Probably the last thing you want to do is go off and have to make new friends. But it's for the best. And it's also not really our decision to make. The Council will decide what's best, now that your folks have both passed on."

He nodded but looked close to tears again.

"For what it's worth," I continued, "you're welcome to visit me anytime you want. Holidays, vacations, even a quick weekend here and there. Anytime you need to get away from the grind or just want to hang out, you give me a call, okay?"

"You really mean that?"

I grinned. "You bet. I can use a good friend in my life, believe me. After all"—I pointed at Wirek—"this dude's getting too old to stay up very late."

Jack giggled. Wirek frowned at me. "You're an ungrateful"—he caught himself—"jerk."

I laughed. "That is probably true."

"It's definitely true," said Wirek with a grumble. He looked at Jack. "You can hang out with me, too, if you want."

I leaned close to Jack. "Bet you never thought you'd be so popular, huh?"

"No," he said, smiling. "But I think I can get to like it."

We dropped our bags back in Boston and then headed for the Council. Wirek frowned as we drove up.

"Never did like this place. Bunch of stodgy old fools."

I slid the Volvo into a rare parking spot a few doors down on Beacon Street and stepped out into the early spring sunlight. It seemed like all of Boston had thawed while we were chasing Arvella. A warm breeze blew over us.

It felt good to be home again.

Arthur met us at the door, looking very relieved to see Jack. He scooped him up and gave him a hug.

"Master Jack, I'm very pleased t'see ya in one piece!"

Jack gave him a quick hug. Arthur put him down and turned to us. "They're waitin' on ya."

I nodded. "No sense putting it off then."

Arthur led us all down to the Council chamber, knocked once and opened the doors for us to enter. Six high-backed leather chairs sat in a half-moon circle facing us. Only five of them were occupied.

The same faces that greeted me a few months back when I visited after killing Cosgrove looked at me again. Vague amusement registered on all of them, as if they were beholden to some great secret.

I didn't let it irk me so much this time.

The oldest man in the Council, a pompous bastard named Belarus, cleared his throat and spoke.

"Welcome back."

I nodded. "It's good to be back."

He peered closer at Jack. "This is the boy?"

"His name is Jack," I said.

Belarus nodded and scrutinized Jack for another minute before turning his attention back to me. "You left us in quite a lurch here, Lawson. Deserting your post without so much as even a note explaining your whereabouts. What were you thinking?"

"One of you betrayed us. I couldn't risk leaving a note and possibly informing her of my intentions. It would have been suicide."

Belarus put up his hand. "Stop right there, Lawson." He

frowned. "We know all about Arvella's actions. But your refusal to inform us of your travel plans implies that you didn't trust the rest of us with that information—that perhaps even one of us might have been in league with Arvella?"

"Try to see it from my standpoint," I said. "I'd been given a bogus sanction, my movements had obviously been tracked from the start, my very survival was in question. What would you have done?"

"We're not here to speculate idly on what might have been." Belarus looked at the other members of the group and then back to me. "At the very least, you should be fired, Lawson."

I sighed. "Arvella was planning something very big. She needed the help of Jack here—"

"Why?"

"He's an Invoker," said Wirek, suddenly speaking up. "And, apparently, a very special one. He obviously needs to go to the right school so they can teach him how to develop it."

Belarus squinted at Wirek. "Do I know you?"

"I'm a retired Elder."

"Retired?" Belarus grunted, then sighed. "Lawson, why does it always seem like we're discussing your inability to keep your superiors informed of your whereabouts?"

"This wouldn't have happened if you got me a replacement Control—"

"You killed your last Control."

"Only because he was a traitor." I looked around the room. "This was one of those times when I couldn't take the chance. The boy had to be rescued. He came first."

"What was so urgent about the nature of this that you couldn't have filled us in first?"

Wirek cleared his throat. "We concluded that Arvella's aim had something to do with the New Millennium. What it was, we're not sure exactly, but we had a feeling it had something to do with the calling up of powerful spirits to help her take over the vampire community.''

''Rubbish,'' said Belarus. ''That would never have succeeded.''

''Why not?'' I asked. ''Who among you is powerful enough to fight spirits?''

Several of the Council members looked away. Belarus bristled. ''Are you insinuating something, Lawson?''

''No need to insinuate. I'm just asking a question.''

''Arvella's plan would not have succeeded.''

I looked at Wirek. ''This, as usual, is a waste of time.''

''What did you say?''

I looked at Belarus. ''You heard me. Why do you refuse to accept the word of a loyal Fixer?''

''Well, honestly, Lawson, you are a bit of a conspiracy freak. What with the whole Cosgrove affair just a few months bacn and now this.''

''This is ridiculous.'' I shook my head. ''Seems to me the Council has always had a problem accepting the role of Fixers in society. I don't know if this is a personal grudge or what, but no matter how apparent the danger is, you always react the same way. Disbelief combined with stupidity.''

The color rose in Belarus's pasty face. ''I'll remind you, Lawson, that you are addressing the Council.''

''Don't I know it.'' I looked at Wirek and Jack. ''Why don't you two wait outside for a minute?''

Wirek raised an eyebrow. ''You sure?''

''I'll join you in a second.''

''All right.'' Wirek led Jack outside. I waited until the door shut and then walked over and plopped down in Arvella's old chair. If I was going to piss them off, I might as well go balls to the wall. "Let's get a few things in order, shall we?"

I leaned forward. "First, the boy goes to the Invoker school. He needs to be there, and since he has no father—courtesy of me and a bad seed among your ranks—it only makes sense.

"Second, get off my back. I do my job well, and despite that, you all seem to think it's open season on me. That stops here and now, or else."

"Or else what?"

"Or else I walk."

"What makes you think we won't simply find a replacement?" asked Belarus.

"Because I know who you have to choose from. And you know as well as I do it's damned hard to find talent like me out there among the untrained newbies coming out of the Academy."

Belarus smiled. "I never took you to be so self-assured, Lawson."

"Nothing wrong with knowing you're good at something." I glanced around the chairs and continued. "Third, you have a vacancy on the Council. You need a replacement."

Belarus's eyes narrowed. "Yes?"

"I think Wirek would make a fine addition to the Council."

"Him? The old Elder? You can't be serious!" Other Council members began murmuring to themselves. I grinned.

"I'm absolutely serious. His love for our society knows no bounds and he's used to dealing with Fixers. Hell, you could hand off all Fixer liaison work to him and wash your hands of it entirely. You'd like that, wouldn't you?"

Belarus said nothing.

"Wirek's got a great service record and you'd be fools to discount it so quickly."

Belarus coughed once. "Yes, well, we'll certainly take these things into consideration, Lawson."

I stood up. "You do that."

"By the way, what happened to Arvella's body?"

"Destroyed. No trace of it left."

"Indeed?"

I thought I saw him smile. "Yeah, she got wasted by another spirit. Turns out she wasn't as powerful as she thought."

"And the conspiracy ends with her, does it?"

"Not exactly. She had help from an old Fixer. You might know him. Alexander Petrov."

Mentioning his name produced a series of gasps, which I thoroughly enjoyed. "Yeah, turns out he wasn't so thrilled about being the fall guy for one of your dirty little secrets. So he sided with Arvella."

"You—you killed him, too, right?" Belarus suddenly seemed a little less sure of himself.

I shook my head. "Y'know, funny thing about that. The guy sneaked away during the fight. Must be all that good Fixer training coming back to him." I grinned. "Mind you, I wouldn't want to be on the guy's shit list when he comes calling. I spoke to him once and he seemed pretty steamed about the whole affair. Said something about 'getting all those Council bastards,' or something like that."

I turned to leave, then stopped and turned back around. "When do I get a new Control?"

Belarus recovered himself somewhat. "Within two weeks. He's finishing up some work in Saudi Arabia right now."

"Good."

"Lawson?"

"Yeah?"

"Where are you going now?"

I thumbed over my shoulder. "Got to take the boy to school. Then I need to get some sleep."

Chapter Thirty-seven

Jack and I spent the next two days gathering up his belongings and packing away most of his home. He decided he wanted to keep the house so he'd have his own place whenever he came to Boston.

"That way, I don't have to inconvenience anyone," he said.

"You're not inconveniencing me if you ever want to stay over."

He nodded. "Yeah, I know. But I should have the house, anyway. I had a lot of good memories there."

"Your dad would be proud of you." I hoped it didn't sound too corny.

He smiled again. "I think he already is."

We flew out of Logan the next afternoon, west-bound. At Denver's new airport, a mile up, we caught a private plane bound for a small Canadian town with a nothing name, in a nothing place.

Jack got a real thrill out of the plane, which the Council had loaned to us.

"They really said we could use it?"

"Yeah. Believe it or not, they're actually a decent set of people sometimes." I didn't tell him one of the reasons they'd been so gracious was because despite a worldwide Fixer sweep for Petrov, the sneaky bastard hadn't been found yet. The Council wanted to stay on my good side in case he came calling.

The pilot came on over the intercom and told us we'd be taxiing shortly. I strapped Jack into the seat and watched the excited look on his face.

"Is the pilot one of us?"

I shook my head. "They're Loyalists."

"What's that?"

"Humans who agree to help us."

He looked shocked. I grinned. "I felt the same way. I only found out about it a few months back."

"Are there many of them?"

"I was told there weren't. But I think there are more than a few."

He considered this and then peered out of his window. "They said we'd buzz the mountains on the way up. Isn't that cool?"

I smiled. He'd matured a lot in the short span of time I'd known him, but he was still a kid. I hoped that however much he grew up, he'd still keep some of the child within him. Too many adults shirk that childish behavior.

Me? Well, lately, I'd been thinking it's kind of healthy to keep some around. Especially since sometimes I considered myself a great big excuse for a kid as well.

"The coolest," I said. "Maybe we can convince him to do a barrel roll, too."

Jack's eyes widened. "Oh, man—you think they would?"

I explained what I knew about barrel rolls while we continued to taxi on the runway. Finally, the engines gunned and we raced down the tarmac; then there was that single moment when the wheels left the ground and the ride suddenly got a lot smoother.

"I love takeoffs," said Jack.

"I hate landings," I said.

We looked at each other and grinned.

Ten minutes into the flight, the pilot announced we'd reached our temporary cruising altitude. Jack spent the time craning his head around the double-paned window, spotting craggy mountaintops and puffy clouds.

I leaned back into my seat and wondered about whether the Council would actually choose Wirek to be a new Council member. Probably not. That would be too smart a move for them.

That was the problem with bureaucracies, any bureaucracy. The more entrenched those in power became, the harder they were to dethrone. And the harder it was for them to see trends and dangers that should be taken care of. This was twice now in the past six months they'd annoyed the crap out of me.

If it kept up, I just might have to think about retiring.

I grinned to myself. I was still far too young to think about that. And besides, I was the only Fixer who seemed to be able to spot trouble.

They needed me, whether they liked me or not.

I sighed again, relaxing back into the brushed velvet of the spacious seats, and stretched my legs. I seriously considered taking a nap.

"Excuse me, sir, would you like a drink?"

I'd forgotten about the flight attendant. A drink might actually taste good. I cracked one eye and looked up.

"Or maybe you'd just like a bullet in your fucking heart, instead."

Petrov.

He stood a few seats away, pointing a gun at us.

I sighed. "You really have piss-poor timing, Petrov."

"Go to hell, Lawson. You don't even know how much trouble you've caused me in the past few weeks."

"I can guess. That worldwide manhunt must have made things tough for you, eh?"

"You could say that."

"And killing Arvella must have pissed you off. Robbed you of some silly power grab, did I?"

He shook his head. "You don't even know the half of it, Lawson. You think I really gave a damn about Arvella? You think I cared about some old washed-up hag like that?"

"Sure seemed that way." I pointed to my legs. "Mind if I bend 'em back? They're getting stiff." Beside me, Jack clutched the armrests tightly—not saying a thing.

Petrov frowned. "Go ahead, but do it slow. The rounds here are subsonic Fixer bullets. They won't go through your body and rip into the plane. I can comfortably kill you anytime I want without a fear of losing cabin pressure."

"Glad to hear you worked that all out, Petrov." I bent my legs into a figure-four position with my left on top of my right. "Ah, that's better."

He regarded me for a moment. "You shouldn't have followed the boy to the Himalayas, Lawson."

"Yeah, well, I've got this bad habit of sticking to my word. There's nothing I can do about it; I'm just like that, I guess."

"I've got a solution," said Petrov, waving the gun slightly.

"I can see that." I glanced at Jack. "So, what's the whole

story, then? We aren't going anywhere for a while. You might as well tell me."

"I started to tell you back at Arvella's estate. Weren't you listening?"

"As I recall, you were busy pumping voltage into me. I think I can be forgiven for my lack of mental acuity at that time. Electrocution has a way of making me a little forgetful."

"The Council sold me out. I took the fall for their stupidity."

"Nothing new there. The Council's well known for their inability to keep things running correctly."

"You still work for them, though. What does that say about you?"

"Probably that I'm just a big fool." I shrugged. "But, see, I've got all these skills that don't really lend themselves too well to the general business world. Being able to double tap someone from ten meters doesn't exactly qualify me to be CEO or something." I smiled. "Besides, I like being a thorn in their side."

"They'll turn on you someday, Lawson. Mark my words. You'll find yourself in exactly the same position I found myself in. I went from being their pride and joy to being an outcast." He frowned. "And now a hunted criminal."

"Maybe so," I said. "But I won't ever sell them out."

"You still cling to that foolish naïveté that what we do makes the world a better place."

"Yeah, I do. But that's my problem, not yours. What the hell do you care—it's my life. I can do what I want with it."

"I didn't care before. I do now, though, especially since you may not have much of a life left to live."

I redirected him. "So go on and tell me all about you and Arvella."

"I seduced her—"

"Hey, c'mon—" I gestured to Jack—"be mindful of the boy, would you?"

Petrov cracked a thin smile. "Still with the humor. All right, have it your way. Arvella and I became lovers."

I grimaced. "Didn't you just call her an old hag?"

He nodded. "I obviously didn't do it for the enjoyment."

"You don't say."

"I became her lover in order to get back at the Council for what it did to me. Using her, I was able to find out about her own secret agenda. She told me about the boy. She told me about what she could do if she pooled her power and the boy's power together. What she could do to the power structure of our society."

"So you went along with it."

"Absolutely. I had contacts, resources that could be used to keep her in the dark. I went after the boy, first approaching his father. He wanted no part of the deal." He smiled. "Killing him would have been easy but not prudent."

Beside me, I could feel anger rising in Jack. It came off him in waves of heat. I looked at Petrov. "So you had Arvella concoct some bullshit story and then set me on him, is that it?"

"Yes. You were the perfect choice because you had no Control. A Control would have seen through the story immediately."

"You didn't know my last Control. I doubt he would have suspected it."

"Anyway," said Petrov, "you got the file and did your work perfectly. You should be complimented."

"I'd rather not be."

He ignored me. "Once the father was dead and gone, we felt free to move ahead with the plan. I dispatched a team to the house to grab the boy and bring him back to me."

He frowned. "You, however, saw fit to interfere at that stage. You and your damned sense of honor."

I shrugged. "Told you it was a bad habit of mine."

"You caused a lot of sleepless nights for me, Lawson. Do you have any idea how gruesome it was to watch a wrinkled old woman like Arvella stomp and shout at my inability to kidnap a simple boy?"

"No, and I don't think I ever want to."

"Well, it's pretty disgusting," said Petrov. "And then you tracked down one of the team members. Fortunately, I'd rolled him up shortly before you got there. But you still managed to track down my cell phone."

"You seemed surprised when I called you, though."

Petrov nodded. "I was surprised. Although not at it being you, just that you'd managed to get that far. Realizing you were hunting me changed things dramatically. I couldn't take the chance that you'd eventually discover the connection to the Council."

"That's when you paid me the visit."

"I thought we'd be able to wrap things up then, too. We'd torture you and get you to reveal the whereabouts of the boy. I knew he couldn't be far away. But then you pulled that stunt and escaped." He sighed. "And I had to listen to yet another night of her caterwauling."

Part of me actually felt sorry he'd gone through that. It must have been pretty horrendous.

"Fortunately," he continued, "every cloud has a silver lining—isn't that the expression they use over here?"

"One of 'em."

"Arvella was able to track the boy using her own Invocation powers. We tracked him down to that shabby apartment, stormed it, and finally grabbed him."

"How come you just didn't do that from the start?"

"Arvella had been trying to do that, but it wasn't until

the boy began practicing his skills that she could fix on his position. I don't quite understand it myself, but she was successful."

"But you didn't kill us," I said. "Whose dumb idea was that?"

"That was me giving you a bit of respect. And a second chance. I thought you might back off if you knew how close to death you'd come. I thought you'd leave us alone."

I smiled. "Petrov, I've been closer to death more times than you know about. That's a bullshit explanation. Tell me the truth."

"All right. He smiled. "I hoped you'd do exactly what you did."

"What—go to Nepal?"

"Exactly. That you'd track us down and kill Arvella. Then I'd be free to pursue my real agenda."

"Which is?"

"I take the boy when we land."

"Where?"

"I've got a buyer lined up for him. Arvella wasn't the only Invoker of any degree of skill in our world, you know. A simple selling pitch by me and this particular Invoker saw the possibilities immediately."

"What's so special about Jack, though? Why not just grab any student out of the school?"

"According to Arvella, he's one of the few whose got more raw power than others. He's rare."

"You know I can't let him go without a fight."

Petrov nodded. "Unfortunately, it won't be much of a fight." He thumbed the hammer back on the gun.

"Good-bye, Lawson."

Chapter Thirty-eight

Thank God for turbulence.

As Petrov's finger tightened around the trigger, the small plane jumped. We had hit a pocket of disturbance. Petrov stumbled forward a step and immediately I lashed out with my left leg, straight into his groin.

He buckled, grunting as the full impact from my heel jarred his scrotum.

I moved into him from the seat, trying to gain control as quickly as possible.

I needed to keep Petrov away from Jack, knowing that in the closed confines of the plane, his gun could go off. Even if he didn't want to kill Jack, accidents do happen.

I rushed him back.

We tumbled over a row of seats. His gun slid across the thin carpeting on the floor and under a chair a few feet away.

"Damn it, Lawson—" His words came in spurts.

Petrov sank his elbow into my sternum. That hurt a lot.

I gasped for breath. Petrov continued his assault, slapping both my ears and following up with a hook to my jaw.

I braced up and tucked in at the last second; the punch only connected slightly.

It still hurt like a bitch.

"I've had enough of you messing up my plans."

He backed off and lashed out with a straight kick to my stomach, catching me full on while I tried to recover from the ringing in my ears. I doubled over as the kick impacted, folding and catching Petrov's foot.

I pivoted inside his leg and got my elbow on his kneecap. I straightened his leg and sank down so he'd fall back on his butt. But he'd grabbed my sleeve in the midst of my counter and pulled me down on top of him.

I landed with my knees hitting the inside of his thigh. He shouted in pain and tried to squirrel out from under me.

I wasn't having it.

I moved up his body with my elbows and knees, trying to pin him and then go for a choke or neck break. As I came up, I nailed him in his lower ribs and then his throat.

He gagged. I thought he might puke on me, but he head-butted me over the eye, instead. My vision blurred and tears shot out of my eyes.

He scrambled away and lashed out with another kick to my temple. I wondered if he knew savate.

I brought my hands up too late, catching the top of his foot across my wrist. I heard a snap and knew I'd just lost a bone.

Pain surged up my arm, but I ignored it long enough to duck and roll forward, closing the distance again. If I could get him on the floor, I might have a chance.

He grunted as I came out of the roll and shot both my heels into his stomach and sternum. He twisted and tried to go for a leg lock on me. I moved in and bent my knees as he did so, nullifying the attack.

Instantly, he abandoned the leg lock and scrambled away again. I had to remind myself that as long as he was able to keep the distance, he could use those devastating kicks to his advantage.

I tried another roll, but he was expecting that and brought his elbows crashing down on my back. I grunted and tried to twist and absorb the impact. I reversed myself and brought another knee up into his groin.

As he doubled over again, I reached up and caught his shirt. Continuing my backward rolling action, I tossed him over me and onto his back.

I came out of the roll astride his chest and went immediately into a double-lapel choke. I rammed my right forearm across his windpipe and used my left to add pressure.

His eyes widened.

He sputtered, realizing what I was after.

His arms flailed, but I kept my head tucked in tight to his collarbone, giving him an occasional head butt to soften him up.

It was working.

I felt his strength begin to ebb as his arm movements became more erratic. A couple of times, he tried to punch my ribs, but I ignored the impacts and tightened my choke.

"Lawson! He's got the gun!"

I looked up in time to see Petrov's arm coming up. He'd managed to recover the piece while we grappled on the cabin floor.

I missed it somehow.

I had to abandon the choke and go for a disarm. As his arm came up, I smothered it and went for a technique called *ura onikudaki,* which looks something like a chicken-wing type of armlock. I wrenched his arm back, keeping the pistol aimed toward the front of the plane.

Petrov brought his right knee up, trying to dislodge me from being on top of him. I slammed his arm back, trying to torque it beyond its breaking point, but the floor of the plane wouldn't let me wrench it back too far.

For now, I'd have to keep it there while I finished him another way.

The plane jumped again, bucking us both as we hit more turbulence. We must have dropped a few thousand feet, judging by the sudden rush in my throat and stomach. I felt a rise of bile, but I pushed it back down and kept the pressure on Petrov.

We leveled out again.

Somewhere ahead of us, I heard the door to the pilots' cabin click open and a voice say, "Sorry about tha—what the?"

Petrov chose that moment to squeeze off a round.

The explosion made me wince. My ears rang.

The bullet slammed into the center of the copilot's chest. Blood exploded as the round impacted, sending him ass over teakettle into the cockpit.

I heard another shout from the pilot, but at that point, Petrov succeeded in freeing his other leg. He upset my balance.

We rolled over, with him getting the upper hand now. I still had his arm wrenched back, but he immediately slammed his head down over my bruised eye.

Another crack told me that my orbital bone wouldn't be up for any beauty awards any time soon. My vision blurred again and I could feel the swelling rise.

The pilot stumbled out of the cabin and over the dead body of his copilot. "What the fuck is going on here?"

Petrov shot the gun again, this time killing the pilot.

My ears hurt. The smell of gunpowder hung in the air.

But the report of the gun caused Petrov to wince, too.

I took advantage to wrench his arm back farther. Without the floor impeding it anymore, it popped. I heard another grunt from Petrov.

He dropped the gun and his arm hung by his side, the shoulder popped oot of its socket. I used my hips to buck him off and then drove my elbows hard into his rib cage, again and again, until I heard another series of cracks.

He cried out and rolled off me, grasping to find the pistol.

I got to my feet, a bit unsteady—I only had vision out of one eye.

Petrov flailed across the carpet, scrambling with his good arm to reach the pistol. I dived for it as well, skipping off his back.

I reached the gun first.

I turned around.

Petrov had gotten to his feet—he was rushing at me like a marionette with one good limb and one broken string.

I drew the gun down, lining up the front sight.

The rear sight.

Center mass.

And squeezed.

Once.

Twice.

Three times

The bullets popped out of the gun in rapid succession.

And thudded into Petrov's chest as if someone were pounding on it with their closed fist.

He stumbled, shocked.

Then looked down as his shirt exploded crimson.

Blood soaked through fast. He took another step backward, closer to the cockpit.

He lifted his head, looked at me, still disbelieving. His

mouth moved—starting to say something—but then turned around and fell face forward into the cockpit.

Instantly, the plane lurched.

"Lawson!"

Jack's voice careened off the interior of the plane over the roar of the engines and the sudden whine of an alarm from somewhere in the cockpit.

I got to my feet again, tried to right myself, and stumbled forward, tripping over the bodies of the copilot and the pilot.

Petrov lay sprawled across the instrument panel in the cockpit. I yanked his body off the controls and saw immediately that his last effort had been to disengage the autopilot setting.

Jack came running up behind me.

"Are you okay?"

I nodded, trying to clear my head of the thousands of angry mosquitoes that were buzzing around inside of my battered skull. My wrist throbbed and my stomach felt like shit.

"Lawson!"

Jack's shouts brought me back, but only just. The plane gave another angry lurch and the dials ahead of me began spinning wildly.

"Shit."

Jack pressed his face into the cockpit. "What's going on?"

I pointed at Petrov's corpse. "Help me drag him out of here!"

Jack grabbed his feet while I got his shoulders. We pushed and pulled him out of the way, until he was sprawled next to the other two bodies.

The plane tilted forward then, tossing us forward and back into the cockpit. I slammed my bad wrist against the paneling and grunted.

"Goddamn it!"

Jack managed to get to his feet. "What's happening? What's going on?"

I pointed to the copilot's seat. "Get yourself strapped in there, good and tight. Do it now!"

He didn't argue.

I slid into the pilot's seat and strapped in. The altimeter was spinning wildly out of control. A quick check told me we were only a few miles up and losing altitude fast.

I glanced at Jack. His face looked white as a winter blizzard.

I looked back at the controls and tried to remember anything I'd ever heard about flying a plane.

And anything didn't equal very much in this case.

We were going down.

Chapter Thirty-nine

I've often said that a life without adventure is not a life worth living. It's funny how so many things we say always seem to come back and haunt us at the most inopportune times.

This was one instance when adventure could go on vacation, for all I cared.

I slid the headset on and tried radioing a Mayday. The damned radio didn't seem to be working. And since our altitude was falling quickly, dicking around with the radio could wait as far as I was concerned.

I grabbed the yoke and tried pulling us out of the dive.

The yoke didn't want to give.

I pushed the throttle forward, increasing our airspeed, trying to speed up and gain us some altitude.

That didn't do much.

But gradually, I was able to pull the plane back somewhat

from the deep dive. Now we were only descending at a partially critical angle.

That didn't make sense.

We should have been climbing, given that I'd pulled the yoke back as far as it would go. Our altitude was still decreasing, and worse, our airspeed was falling dangerously close to stall speed.

"What's happening, Lawson?"

I glanced at Jack. The kid was gonna need years of therapy if he had to endure much more bad luck.

"We'll be okay." I wished I meant it. I did another visual check of all the controls. Everything said we were still going down, and I couldn't figure out why.

Then I saw it.

The fuel gauge was spinning like mad.

We were dumping fuel.

"Goddamn Petrov." He must have punched the button when he hit the instrument panel.

The only good news was that I'd finally determined why we were about to crash. The bad news was . . . Well, hell, it was pretty obvious.

"Jack, head toward the back of the plane and see if you can't find an emergency cabinet with parachutes, all right?"

He didn't question me, which was good. He simply unstrapped himself and headed back, using the seats like handholds. Kid was a trouper, no doubt.

I had no knowledge of where we were, and since the radio was out, there seemed little point in trying to land anywhere. Plus, we were flying over some of the rockiest and most inhospitable land known to planes.

Jumping seemed a good option.

Our airspeed was closing in on seventy knots and we'd probably stall in a few minutes. I took off my belt and wrapped it around the yoke, then attached it to the seat belt to keep it pulled all the way back. I needed to keep the plane level for just a few more minutes until we could jump.

If not, well . . .

"Lawson! I found the chutes!"

I floundered toward the back of the plane and found Jack already heaving two of them out. I checked them over as fast as I could. There was no way to tell if they'd open or not, but our choices were pretty limited.

I helped Jack into his chute and then strapped mine on. It had been a while since I'd jumped. The key for us right now was not to jump until we'd descended below thirteen thousand feet. Any higher and we'd need oxygen to survive the fall.

I maneuvered my way back to the cockpit and checked the altimeter. We'd just passed fifteen thousand and were falling about a thousand feet every thirty seconds.

I checked my watch and headed back to Jack.

"You okay?"

He nodded, but his chattering teeth showed his fear. I put a hand on his shoulder.

"We'll be fine. Just do exactly what I say and you won't have any problems, okay?"

He nodded again.

"When we leave the plane, you're going to make a starfish in the air with your arms and legs out. That will stop you from spinning, okay? I want you to count to twenty and then pull this cord here." I showed him.

" 'Kay."

"Once the chute opens, look for me and use two steering ropes to direct your flight. It's just like a video game, okay? It'll take you a few seconds to get used to the controls and then you'll be fine."

"I can do it."

"Right before you land, yank down hard on the control ropes and you'll land as soft as cotton, okay?"

"I'll be fine."

I smiled. "I know you will, slick." I checked my watch. Time to go. "You ready?"

Jack smiled and gave me a thumbs-up.

I headed to the cabin door and rotated the T-bar, sliding the door open and in. A huge gust of wind smacked me in the face—roar filled my ears—and I had to fight to stay standing. Too much cloud cover prevented me from seeing anything.

I motioned for Jack to come up to the door, and just as he started to, the plane went into a dive.

Jack tumbled forward, hitting a row of seats.

"Lawson!"

"Fuck." I went after him and found him tangled between two rows. My belt must have snapped off the yoke.

There was precious little time. I heaved Jack over my shoulder and got us back to the doorway.

"You go first!"

His eyes bloomed white when he looked at the open air. I shook him once. "You can do it! Ready?"

He nodded and I pushed him out, watching him fall.

No time left.

I vaulted out of the plane, too, feeling the slipstream smack me like a poor wet newspaper. I tumbled for about three seconds before I straightened myself out into the starfish pattern.

Below me, I could barely see Jack. He'd evened out, though; that was a good sign.

In my own mind, I'd begun ticking off the seconds until his chute should have opened. As soon as I reached zero, I saw the streamers billow out of his back, rushing back up toward me as the foils filled with air and braked his fall.

Thank God his chute opened.

I was coming in on his position fast and pulled my own rip cord. Instantly, my own cells filled with air and the straps bit deep into my groin, making my bowels ache.

But we'd done it.

I grabbed my risers and took a deep breath. I glanced back and saw the plane nose-diving toward the earth. The air seemed silent, aside from the slight whine of the plane's engines as they died somewhere below us.

Thirty seconds later, I heard a massive explosion.

Impact.

I hoped there were only mountains beneath us and no villages or towns with innocent people suddenly caught unaware by a falling plane.

Overhead, Jack waved once. He seemed okay now that he had his chute opened. He was drifting easily to earth.

I breathed easier.

Gradually, the lower-level clouds seemed to dissipate and I could see below us. Lots of trees and hillsides. We weren't all that high up in the mountains, which was a good thing.

The bad thing was that we were on a collision course with the fiery crater containing the wreckage of the plane.

I grabbed my risers and steered us left, praying my rate of descent wasn't too great that we'd stay locked toward the plane.

Overhead, I could see Jack following my lead. I pointed at a grassy knoll and hoped he wasn't having a problem steering.

Pines and evergreens came up at me faster than I would have liked. I yanked down again on the risers and braked somewhat. The ground looked like a mix of slush, snow, and tufts of yellowed grass.

Twenty feet and I began pumping the risers, hoping Jack was watching and would follow suit.

Ten feet.

Five.

Ground.

My feet touched down lightly and I immediately began ditching the chute. I turned and watched Jack come in.

"Pull your risers!"

He pulled and slowed down even more. In truth, the little guy didn't look too scared, and he wasn't coming in all that fast considering he didn't weigh as much as a normal full-grown adult.

I almost caught the guy.

I showed him how to shrug himself out of the chute and we paused to catch our breath. Jack looked in the direction of the crash about a half mile away. Smoke billowed up from the crash site, staining the sky black.

"Wow."

"Yep. That could have been us."

He looked back at me. "Where are we?"

I smiled. "Jack, old buddy, we are on the ground. And right now that is about the best place to be in the whole wide world."

The grin he gave me told me he felt exactly the same way.

All in all, we didn't do that bad.

We'd parachuted out of the plane only about twenty miles from the Invoker school. Once I took a bearing and compared it with the directions that we'd gotten from Wirek and the Council, we decided we'd just hike it and not concern ourselves with trying to get a ride somewhere.

For his part, Jack didn't want to cause any undue attention upon arrival.

"I don't want to make enemies before I have a chance to make some friends," he said.

The weather seemed to be cooperating as well. For the next two days, we hiked north along the timberline, catching fish in the cold mountain lakes, building fires, and sleeping out under the stars on warm beds of pine needles and loose branches. Jack had even brought a survival kit out of the plane with him before he jumped. Inside was a small supply of juice that would keep us going until we got to the school.

Helluva kid, this one.

Jack loved it. For someone who'd never been camping, he took to it with a natural ease that seemed to echo everything else in his life. Hell, he deserved it, given all the crap he'd come through in the past few weeks.

I diagnosed my wrist as having a hairline fracture, which wasn't too bad. I splinted it as best I could. Combined with my fractured ribs and all the other wounds I'd suffered on this jaunt, I figured I'd be a candidate for short-term disability.

Too bad the Council didn't recognize short-term disability.

Over a rainbow trout dinner, Jack seemed a little quiet, so I asked him what was wrong.

He shrugged. "We'll be there tomorrow, right?"

I nodded. "Yeah."

"What are you gonna do when you get home?"

"Me?" I smiled. "Lessee, get a cast on my wrist, tape up my ribs. Take a long nap, probably."

He was quiet for a minute. "I'm scared, Lawson."

"You've got nothing to be scared about, Jack. You're going to be among friends at the school. They'll help you take control of your abilities."

"Wish I didn't have this ability sometimes."

I knew the feeling. There were many nights when I wondered exactly what the hell I was doing as a Fixer and whether any of it ever made a lick of difference in this world.

"That's a pretty special gift you've got there, Jack. Like I said before, someday you might find out why you got that gift. You might be called on to help everyone. Not just vampires."

"You mean humans, too?"

I shrugged. "You never know. One thing I've learned in this life is that trying to guess what's coming down the road is about as big a waste of time as trying to scratch your back with your tongue."

He laughed. "You're kinda weird, Lawson."

I smiled. "True enough. But I think I'm getting some of it from you."

We sat looking at the flames jump about the fire for another few minutes. Overhead, somewhere off in the forest, an owl hooted for the first time that night. Smoke danced in front of our eyes and tickled our noses.

Jack sighed. "I miss them both."

I nodded. "It's okay to be sad, slick. Just remember that the ones we truly love never really leave us at all. Just because we can't see 'em doesn't mean they still aren't around. And it doesn't mean they stop loving us."

He was silent for a few minutes. Then he cleared his throat. "Did you mean what you said before?"

"What?"

"About me staying with you?"

"Absolutely. You've got my number. Call me anytime. You need to talk, hang out, let loose, whatever. I'm here for you. My promise doesn't end just because you're safe and sound now. It's for life—you understand?"

He nodded. "That woman, Arvella, she stole my family away from me, Lawson."

''Yeah. Yeah, she did.''

He looked up at me from beside where we sat on an old maple log. ''But you know what?''

''What?''

''She gave me the best friend in the whole world.''

Then he gave me a quick hug.

And damned if I didn't feel pretty special after all.

Please turn the page for an exciting sneak peek

at the next thrilling installment of the

Lawson Vampire series,

THE DESTRUCTOR,

coming in March 2003 from Pinnacle Books!

Chapter One

For most humans, coming to the North Shore in Hawaii means big waves. It means a chance to surf with some of the best, if that's your game. Or you can just hang out on the beach watching eye candy and supreme athletes mingle in the sand and sun. The scent of sex wax and tanning lotion wafts across the gently sloping beach, seducing you into a mellow state of mind.

For me, the North Shore meant a chance to finish up a case.

A bad case at that.

Details, a vitally important ingredient to any mission, were missing. I wasn't all that surprised. I'd been a Fixer for years, hunting down vampires who break the laws of our society, and I felt almost too used to sketchy second-hand intelligence.

I'd been humping jets for the past three weeks—skipping

time zones like a side-armed rock bouncing across a pond. I felt like shit.

Which again was par for the course.

My target was a woman. I had a grainy surveillance photo that looked like someone wearing Coke bottle glasses and suffering from acute glaucoma had taken it. I could make out very little.

Which meant I had to rely on informants.

Ask any intelligence operative or law enforcement professional about how great it feels to have to place absolute trust in the word of a sleazebag who turns over for a few bucks and you'll know why I was just so gosh-darned excited about being in Hawaii.

I would have rather been home with my cats.

At least I know what they look like.

A giant tube crashed out about fifty yards from shore taking a few surfers under the swell. I saw boards go flying and feet inverted. Seconds later they all surfaced intact.

Helluva way to score some thrills.

Maybe I should have swapped jobs.

I felt the crystalline sand grind between my toes. The sun's warmth beamed down on my skin. I was lucky enough to have inherited my father's skin. He tanned well. Whenever we'd gone to the beach, he used to brown nicely.

I'd rather be brown than burned red.

According to the low-grade heroin addict who knew something about my target, she'd begun frequenting this beach since a week back. That would have been right after she'd ditched Bangkok.

I'd been in Pnomh Penh skirting crazy moped drivers and tricycle taxis at the time, trying to find her trail.

A trail that had gone cold.

I turned up in the islands two days after she did. Directed

here by my Control back in the States who'd sent word someone had spotted her in Hawaii.

At Honolulu International Airport, the local Fixer met me. He gave me some more information and then turned me loose.

Two days later he was dead.

She'd killed him.

I'd started coming to the beach soon after getting word from the informant who'd worked with the now deceased Fixer. My first question to him had been to ask what she was doing hanging out on the North Shore.

He'd only smiled and walked away.

He was lucky I let him do that.

I spent every day on the beach. From just after sun up to just after sunset.

Waiting.

Waiting.

Waiting.

I kept my gun with me all the time, even though it was a little tough wearing a piece on the beach. I usually kept it in the cooler next to me. Or else when I slid the Hawaiian short on, it went behind my right hip, where I like to wear it normally.

I kept phoning in updates to my Control. No progress. No luck. Nothing.

He kept telling me to stay put.

So I did.

A day later I sat on the beach again watching more surfers carve half-pikes in the frothy ocean, wondering if there were any tiger sharks in the area.

"Excuse me."

My sunglasses did a good job of blocking out the sunlight so I didn't have to squint. Not that I wanted to anyway.

The woman in front of me stood about five feet six inches

and weighed maybe a buck ten. She had more curves than a corkscrew and they were barely contained by the triangles of fabric that made up her bikini.

I smiled. Cleared my throat. "Hi"

She smiled back. I love progress.

'I've seen you here for a few days now."

"Yeah?"

"Mm hmm. You never go swimming, though."

"I'm allergic to water."

"Really?"

"No. But the truth is a lot more boring than that."

"So you just sit here."

"I just sit here."

"Watching?"

"Some watching. Mostly waiting."

"What are you waiting for?"

"A friend."

She crinkled her eyes. "This friend of yours . . . is it a he?"

"A she, actually."

"Really." Her voice dipped.

"Not that kind of friend."

"Really." Her voice lifted.

I grinned. I thought about how funny it would be to tell her the truth. That I was there to put a few bullets into the body of some woman I'd never even seen a clear picture of. Then I realized how utterly stupid the truth sounded. Sometimes life's like that.

"Why don't you sit down?"

She sat. I looked her over. Her long dark hair framed her almond-shaped eyes and smooth creamy tanned skin. Her smile spilled white against the mocha background of her face.

"You're from Hawaii?"

She shook her head. "No. Back in New Jersey, actually."

"Filipina?"

"Yeah." She brightened. "Good eye."

"What's a Jersey girl doing out here?"

"You ever been to Jersey?

"Few times."

"You shouldn't have to ask then."

"Question withdrawn."

"I work here."

"What's work?"

"I'm something of a consultant."

"Self-employed."

"Don't say it like I'm some out-of-work wanna-be entrepreneur who hasn't got a dime in the bank. I'm very much employed. And I make a pretty damned good living."

"Fair enough."

"What about you?"

"Me?" I spread my arms. "I'm just waiting."

"We covered that."

"Yeah."

"Do you think I'm pretty?"

I smirked. "You're not much on subtlety, are you?"

"Life's short. Answer the question."

"I think you're the most beautiful woman on this beach." I glanced around for effect. "Nothing finer around here."

"You're sweet."

"Well, I was kinda put on the spot there."

"How much longer do you have to wait?"

I cleared my throat. "Until my friend shows up."

"And after that?"

"I don't have to wait anymore."

"Good." She turned and looked out toward the ocean. "You mind if I wait with you?"

"I was sorta hoping you'd say something like that."

We watched the waves roll in for another hour. We watched the sun trek west, spilling oranges and reds into the blue green of the Pacific. We sat close together as a breeze kicked up sand and bounced it off our skin.

And time ticked by.

People left the beach.

Until we were alone.

And she looked at me. "Are you through waiting?"

"I'd sure as hell like to be."

"Your friend didn't show up."

"Maybe tomorrow."

"Maybe you should just kiss me now."

I did. I kissed her full lips, tasted the sweet coconut oil, felt her moist tongue part my lips and search for my own. I felt her hands touch the back of my head, fingers roaming through my short bristly hair. Then they slid south. Down my back. Down past my hips. Down lower.

And lower.

She broke the kiss and smiled at me. Her eyes a mere inch from mine.

"I'm glad you asked me to wait with you."

"Why's that?"

She gave me another peck on the lips. Her hands tightened around my butt. "Because it's a lot easier killing somebody at night."

Her words barely had a chance to register before I felt her fingers turn into claws, digging into my butt, ripping, shredding their way north.

Toward my kidneys.

I cried out, twisted under her grasp, and tried to roll away. She tucked her body into mine and rolled with me. I could hear her laughing as we tumbled toward the waves.

"You won't get rid of me that easily, Lawson."

Oh crap.

It had to be her—the woman I'd been sent to kill.

As we rolled I brought my elbow up and smashed it into her face. My pistol was back at the cooler. If I could just get to it—

She grunted as I struck her nose. I heard a crunch and figured I'd broken it. I smelled blood a moment later and fought back the sudden rise of saliva in my mouth.

We broke free.

"Are we having fun yet?"

In the dark I could see her almost as well as during the daylight. Vampires can see pretty well at night. Waves crashed at our feet. We circled under the new moon, embraced by a million stars overhead.

She crouched low—between the cooler and me.

And my gun.

And then something else happened. She began to . . . change.

One minute she was the foxy Asian woman who'd sat down next to me. The next minute she was different. Her voice, her hair, her body structure.

All different.

What the hell was going on?

It struck me just as she lashed out with a roundhouse kick to my temple. I slid inside the arc of the kick and caught her leg, punching into the underside of her thigh.

She yelped.

Christ.

A lycanthrope.

I swore under my breath. What the hell had I been assigned to kill a lycanthrope for? I killed vampires for a living, not were-creatures.

She rolled away, yanking her leg out of my lock.

I ran for the cooler.

She tackled me halfway there, taking me down at the

knees in a way that would have a scout for the NFL drool with desire. I went face first into the sand and came up spitting beach.

She grabbed my head from behind and rammed me back into the sand. I bucked up with my hips and butt, trying to unseat her.

She laughed.

"I've played ride 'em Bronco before, Lawson. I'm very good at it."

Maybe. I rolled to the side and she fell off. I straddled her and went for a chokehold, slamming my forearm into her throat and shoving it down trying to cut off air and circulation.

She struggled, but the beach enveloped her, making it tough to get any purchase.

And then I felt her claws on my lower ribs. She grabbed a handful of skin and twisted it like a doorknob.

And she opened me up.

I gritted my teeth as I felt my body rise just a little bit. That's all it took. I felt the knee shot a second later.

It thundered into my groin and my bowels dropped south like a cinder block tossed off a building. I grunted and rolled off her, clutching my crotch.

She rolled away from me, gasping for breath and retching in time to my own.

Her voice hissed across the beach. *"Bastard!"*

The cooler lay twenty feet from me. I turned over on to my stomach. I had to get to it. I clawed at the sand, trying to find the strength to stand.

She was on all fours. She looked at me. "You're good."

I didn't say anything. I just had to reach the damned cooler.

She stood, massaging her throat. "Almost had me."

Ten feet from the cooler.

"I ought to kill you the way I did the other Fixer."

Eight feet.

"I ought to."

Six feet.

"But I won't."

Four feet. Almost within . . . reach.

"Good-bye, Lawson."

I felt the plastic under my hand and tore the lid off. I felt the gun a second later and tore it out, flipping over on the sand, searching for a target.

But she was gone.

She'd disappeared.

Right in front of me.

Almost like she didn't even exist at all.

And if it wasn't for my swollen and bruised scrotum, I might have almost believed she'd been a ghost.

A ghost that had almost killed me.

BOOK YOUR PLACE ON OUR WEBSITE AND MAKE THE READING CONNECTION!

We've created a customized website just for our very special readers, where you can get the inside scoop on everything that's going on with Zebra, Pinnacle and Kensington books.

When you come online, you'll have the exciting opportunity to:

- View covers of upcoming books
- Read sample chapters
- Learn about our future publishing schedule (listed by publication month *and author*)
- Find out when your favorite authors will be visiting a city near you
- Search for and order backlist books from our online catalog
- Check out author bios and background information
- Send e-mail to your favorite authors
- Meet the Kensington staff online
- Join us in weekly chats with authors, readers and other guests
- Get writing guidelines
- AND MUCH MORE!

Visit our website at
http://www.kensingtonbooks.com